Come Wild
Sexy
Stories
Collection

VOLUME 27

13 EROTIC SHORT STORIES

TRISTA JACO

Publisher's Note: This is a work of fiction. Names,
characters, places, and incidents are a product of
the author's imagination. Locales and public
names are sometimes used for atmospheric
purposes. Any resemblance to actual people, living
or dead, or to businesses, companies, events,
institutions, or locales is completely coincidental.

Come Wild/ Trista Jaco. -- 1st ed.
Xplicit Press, an imprint of TLM Media LLC

ISBN-13: 978-1-62327-558-7
ISBN-10: 1-62327-558-X
eISBN: 978-1-62327-608-9

Printed in the United States of America

CONTENTS

1 ANY WILL DO

Prologue

Bella doesn't take rejection very well. When Clan shuns her, she vows to herself that if he would not have her then she would have...everyone but him.

Clan had always been attracted to Bella. But she was his best friend's sister and he'd sworn to her brother he'd leave her alone. But when she starts trying to get it on with everyone in town, he decides to rein her in, the only way he knows how...

"You look lovely tonight, Bella."

The sound of Clan's deep, stirring voice in her ear made Bella swivel round, her heart thumping in sudden awareness. She could not help but notice how good-looking he was in a snug-fitting white dress shirt and dark pants and with his hair falling slightly across his broad, manly forehead. His eyes were twinkling in their narrowed depths, and she could hardly tear her eyes from him. As always, everything about him spelled sex god and Bella, as always, could find nothing sensible to say.

"I saw you from over there and just had to come over and tell you that dress is hot," he added, when she just stood there staring up at him. A quizzical smile crossed his lips for a second. "Bella?"

His saying her name in that concerned tone caused her to snap out of her daze. One would think that, at twenty-two, she'd have more control over her emotions, and not act like the love-struck teen she'd been those years ago when the sight of Clan got her weak at the knees. Well, she still went weak at the knees at the sight of him, but now, it seemed to have gotten even worse. She wondered how was it possible that just the sound of his voice could make her panties feel damp. There was no denying that Clan was the most gorgeous thing she had ever seen. All her friends in college seemed to think so. The fact that he was her brother's best friend and now business partner always managed to keep Bella in check because if her big brother Kirk ever found out what sort of nasty thoughts she was having about his best pal, he'd go ballistic and she knew it.

Not that it stopped her from dreaming. For several years, and even after two steady boyfriends down the drain, she still had those pussy-pulsing fantasies of Clan no matter who she was with. No matter which guy was fucking her, all she had to do was close her eyes and it was Clan. It was his warm, large hands cupping her breasts and squeezing roughly, whispering in her ear how fucking sexy she was. It was his cock shafting into her and making her cunt throb with every pistonlike thrust. It was the thought of him groaning out her name and pumping his hot, spurting semen into her that got her climaxing incredibly every time with her lover none the wiser.

And now she had at least two days to work out just how to get him. The engagement celebrations were to last the whole weekend; tonight's party was a start-off of the festivities. Most of the family and closest friends were staying here in Kirk and Bella's parent's family mansion.

Biting her lip, she shoved those stirring thoughts to the back of her mind and smiled up at Clan. "Sorry, I was just so surprised to see you. It's...been a while."

"I know," he grinned suddenly, and that flash of white got her heart throbbing again. His smile turned his gorgeous face into something it almost seemed to hurt to look at. It was official, Bella decided. She was never ever going to get over her crush for Clan. Not unless she did something about it and soon. The germ of an idea began to formulate in her head as she returned his smile.

He continued, "With you away in college and me being busy all the time, it's no wonder we never get to see each other. And I meant what I said earlier. You look stunning. I have to remind myself you're the girl I used to see in pigtails. You've grown into a lovely young woman."

Bella couldn't help squirming with pleasure. Okay, this was the fifth time or so, in the span of ten minutes, that Clan had told her she looked great. She couldn't help thinking that maybe, for the first time, he was actually going to look at her like more than a "kid sister" of his best friend.

"Thank you," she said with a smile she hoped was flirty without being creepy. "You don't look bad at all yourself."

He seemed pleased by her comment, even though he waved it aside. "Hey, it's Kirk's engagement party after all; had to spruce up for the occasion. They look happy together, don't they?" he asked, indicating the laughing couple dancing on the other side of the crowded room.

She turned her head to look at her brother and his fiancée, Melanie. They were clasped in each other's arms, with eyes for no one else but themselves as they moved to the music playing in the room. Bella couldn't help feeling a sentimental pang, seeing the cloud of love that seemed to surround those two. It had to feel great to be in love like that, to find someone who fitted perfectly into that mold of who you'd want to spend forever with.

Well, Bella knew she had found someone like that but he could never be hers. He was standing right next to her, but he probably had no idea how much she totally desired him and thought the world of him. Clan was incredibly good-looking, and he seemed to have a way with women. Not that he exactly set out to acquire their attentions, they simply just, well, literally fell into his lap. She'd seen a few come and go, and with every new, hot-looking babe she saw on his arm, her heart would lurch and she'd think this is the one. This was the girl that would take Clan away from her for good and after every breakup she would feel utter relief.

She knew for a fact that right now, he was single. And so was she. He'd never shown more than a friendly, almost brotherly interest in her, but Bella was woman enough to know that under all those layers of propriety he was attracted to her. She could sense it when he looked at her, and she thought that maybe it was time to take things to a different level if only to see if all those red-hot fantasies had even a ring of truth.

"Yes, they do," she replied at last, turning to face him again.

Their eyes met in a sudden flash of awareness. Bella's heart tripped over itself as she felt it again: that darkness in his eyes and in the very air around them. It made her shiver deep inside and the dampness in her crotch grew... Damn it! Bella swore in annoyance at herself; I'm practically panting for this man! If I don't keep my hormones in check, I may do something stupid, like ask him to fuck me.

She wondered what he'd say and what his reaction would be if she suddenly blurted out, "Clan – I want you to fuck me. Just throw me over your shoulder and take me to some dark abandoned closet, lift my dress, and just fuck my brains out."

"Want to go outside for some fresh air?" she asked suddenly, fanning her face. "It's starting to really feel hot and stuffy here."

"Sure," he said before placing his hand in the small of her back guiding her out of the ballroom through the French windows, and though it was a light, impersonal touch, it sent thrills up and down her spine.

Outside the air was mild, with just enough breeze to stir the leaves of the trees reaching over the balustrade. Bella gripped the edge with both hands, taking in deep, steadying breaths. Behind her, Clan asked for the second time that night, "Look, Bella, you're sure you're okay?"

She faced him again and her eyes were very bright, her lips parted slightly as her chest seemed to heave like she'd just run a mile. "Clan, do you want to go to bed with me?"

The words hung in the air for the next few seconds, and the second she blurted them out, she realized that she was glad she had. There was no point in beating about the bush, she wanted him now. All he had to do was say yes and she'd grab her purse, jump into his car with him, and they could drive off to some hotel.

His eyes widened in shock but he recovered quickly and a short laugh escaped him for a second. "What?"

Bella drew closer, till just an inch of air stood between them. She had to crane her neck to look straight up into his eyes, her hand resting on his chest. It felt like marble beneath her fingers; even through his short, she could sense the strong thump of his heartbeat beneath the firm muscle and flesh. The tip of her tongue went slowly over her suddenly parched lips, and she saw his gaze follow the movement fixedly. Strengthening her resolve, she finally closed the tiny space between them till their bodies fitted together like two pieces of a jigsaw puzzle. She heard his swift intake of breath and saw his nostrils flare as a blaze ignited in his eyes. She knew then that he felt it.

"Clan," she breathed, slipping her arms around his neck and lifting her lips to slide along the edge of his tantalizingly. "I need you tonight. Deep inside me, taking me hard and fast like nothing else matters. I know it might sound crazy, but it isn't. Not when it's something we both want. Make love to me."

Make love to me...

Hearing Bella say those words in that dreamy, spell-binding voice made Clan's cock harden all the more painfully. How the hell had she guessed? Had he in some way betrayed himself? He'd tried so, so hard for more than three years to hide exactly how much he wanted Bella. No one, not even her, was ever supposed to suspect.

And yet she was pressed up against him so tightly that he could feel every maddening, soft curve. His hands itched right then with the urge to shove his hands into her dress and grab her perfectly rounded tits. From the moment he'd set eyes on her that night, he'd had to curb a burgeoning erection. Her slim, shapely frame sheathed in that sinful black dress which was slashed deeply in front and at the back and her hair, long and artfully mussed, seemed to cry out to be mussed even further by his hands raking through the silky locks. He'd wanted her from the second she'd walked into the room and wanted to rip that floor-sweeping dress off her and just fuck her. It had taken a few glasses of wine for him to get his fevered thoughts into a semblance of normalcy.

But then he'd found himself walking up to her as if drawn by a magnet, and he'd wanted to kick himself for acting like a hormone-blasted teen. Bella was Kirk's sister, for goodness' sake! The last thing he should be thinking was how to get in bed with her.

So it was a shock to him to hear her actually ask him to, like it was the most normal thing in the world to do.

Her lips slid softly over his. Clan's hands fell on her waist and he gripped her tightly. Damn! Having her close felt so good, too good. Her mouth seemed made for kissing, and he longed so much to crush that mouth and kiss her till the earth spun the wrong way round.

"Bella, you don't know what you're saying," he gritted out, forcing every part of his body to ignore its own deepest needs. It was like cutting his own arm off, but he knew this was what he needed to do. "Just how much have you had to drink tonight?"

She giggled, nibbling teasingly on his chin.

She's trying to drive me crazy, Clan thought with an inner growl. His fingers bit deeper into her hips, and he was tempted, very tempted, to succumb to what his cock was screaming out for him to do.

"Not much," she told him with an enticing lick at his slightly parted lips. He could swear that his cock was about ready to rip out of his now too-tight slacks. "Hardly a celebratory sip or two, nothing to write home about. And I'm very much in my right mind, so don't think this is some prank, either. I'm not some tease, Clan. Well, maybe just a little one."

She smiled sensually and her teeth sank into his bottom lip. Clan groaned deep in his throat as he grabbed her round the waist and kissed her. He heard her moan as his lips ground against hers, their tongues clashing and meshing. With one hand he slipped past her bodice and beneath her tiny bra to cup her breast, squeezing hard till she moaned again. His thumb and forefinger twirled her pointed nub roughly, delighting in the way her skin and curves felt in his palm.

Do it, Clan, said the voice in his head. Just give in to what you've wanted for years. Just take her away somewhere and bury yourself inside her again and again, like you've dreamed so long of doing. Lose yourself deep within her till nothing else matters.

He wasn't sure where he found the strength, but, moments later, he was clamping his hands on her shoulders and putting her firmly from him. She looked up at him in clear surprise, and he had to close his mind to how sexy she looked, her lips swollen

9

from his hard kisses, her bodice somewhat awry from when he'd shoved his hand in.

"We can't do this, Bella," he said as calmly as he could. "Whatever it is you're asking me for, the answer is no."

"But you told me I was beautiful...I thought you wanted me."

"Bella, you are beautiful. Probably the most beautiful I've ever seen. You're certainly the most beautiful in the room tonight. But we could never have anything between us. It's just not going to happen. You're Kirk's little sister."

"I'm twenty-two, Clan, not twelve," she cut in sharply with her eyes flashing in annoyance. "I think I should be able to choose who I can sleep with by now."

"Yeah well, so can I," he told her with a shrug. "And Bella, I'm sorry but I choose not to sleep with you. Okay? So get that idea out of your head right now. It's Kirk's and Melanie's engagement party; let's just go back inside and forget this ever happened."

She looked really mad right then, but what could he do? He'd had to be a little cruel to get her to see reason. There was no way he was going to be fucking Kirk's sister, no matter how flipping hot and beddable she was. She had the body of a temptress, the face of an angel, and the heart that was too precious to be messed with. And Kirk had warned him a long time ago never to do a thing to hurt her and had made him promise. And Clan intended to keep that promise.

"Yes, let's," she said calmly, as she straightened her clothes and hair with dignity.

"I guess I should have known you'd be too worried about holding on to your 'halo' to give me what I want. Maybe I'd better find someone with fewer scruples and more guts, huh?"

She made to brush past him, but he gripped her arm and twisted her round to face him again. "And what the heck is that supposed to mean?"

She shrugged his hand off. "Like you said, it's Kirk's party and I intend to enjoy every second of it. I'm sure there'll be one – or two – guys in there willing to help me out with that." And before he could say more, she'd stalked off, leaving him standing there.

What the fuck? Clan shoved his hands through his hair as he tried to regain some semblance of self-control before returning to the party. He was still trying to figure out what in the world she was talking about. Find who to help her out with what? If she meant what he thought she did, things were going to go bad very fast.

He scowled deeply, remembering that it wasn't just him who'd been unable to take his eyes off her since the evening began. He could think of a few of their friends who'd been ogling her all night, guys who'd have no qualms about giving in to whatever she offered. Clan's teeth gritted as her words really started to sink in. He made his way back into the ballroom, thunderous scowl still in place.

Sure enough, he found her a few minutes later, giggling in the corner of the room with some guy Clan knew was a total player. His name was Ned, one of the guys they worked with. Clan glanced around to find that Kirk was too distracted with other guests as well as his fiancée to notice Bella's antics. Soon she took to the dance floor with Ned and began to dance suggestively with him. Clan ground his jaw every time she turned and bumped her ass into Ned's crotch in a decidedly raunchy move. The music playing was a salsa tune, and Ned was quick to match her step for step, his hands falling to her hips once or twice as they swayed to the hot beat.

Clan thought. He could ignore it; after all, all she was doing was dancing with some twerp, why should that bother him? Yet he found himself grabbing a glass of wine from the passing tray, gulping it down in one swallow. Damn you to hell, Bella! What sort of game are you playing?

It was hell looking at her and seeing her act so wantonly, flinging her arms around Ned and whispering something in his ear. Clan could have sworn he saw Ned's eyes gleam in comical glee, before he nodded and whispered something back in her ear. Clan could have given all he possessed to hear what they'd said to each other.

But that was only the beginning. Over the course of half an hour, he'd watched her dance with two other partners, and it was always to say something privately in his ear before the dance was over. Clan kept telling himself, ignore her. She's just doing this to get on his nerves, to get back at him for turning her down. Well, what had she expected him to do? Simply give in? Clan felt he had the sense to act with much more delicacy.

And yet, maybe it wasn't delicacy she

wanted...

It was almost an hour later when he saw her head for the exit. The party was far from over, where the devil was she off to? Clan had a mind to go over to Kirk and warn him about Bella's strange behavior, but he decided against it. This was Kirk's night and Clan wouldn't want to ruin it for him and his fiancée. It looked like he'd have to watch out for Bella himself. A particular task he'd always done in the past anyway and with the best intentions...

He caught her just as she was grabbing her coat in the hallway and heading out the door. "And where do you think you're going?"

She turned sharply at the sound of his voice, almost stumbling on her heels as she faced him. He took hold of her elbow to steady her. It was obvious she was tipsy, and her eyes were angry blue flames as she glared up at him. "I don't remember making it any of your business."

"You know it is. Kirk is far too distracted to wonder what you're up to, but I'm not. Just where the hell are you slinking off to?"

"Well, if you insist on knowing," she drawled carelessly, "I have a little ménage waiting for me."

"A what?" Clan exploded, eyes narrowing with reined in fury.

"I'm sure you know what that means, Clan," she told him mockingly. "I'd rather you didn't hold me up, you know. I've just got two hot guys willing to give me a good time tonight, well, three actually," she added with a humorous frown as she seemed to mentally take count. "Yeah, I remember I was able to convince one more randy devil to join in."

Clan gripped her arm so tight she had to let out a yelp as she tried to struggle out of his hold. "Are you meaning to tell me you're off to have sex with three different guys at the same time?"

"Correct," she clipped out, smiling cattily up at him. "Why so bothered? I thought you said you 'choose not to sleep with me.' Well that's a choice you're going to regret, buddy. I'm going to get thoroughly fucked tonight and it won't be by you! And don't think I'm going to stop there, oh no. I'm going to make sure I go through all Kirk's friends till I've had every one of them. What good will your halo be then, Mr. Good Guy, when you realize I'm going to let every guy but you have me?"

"I'll kill you first," Clan gritted, surprising himself by slipping his hands round her throat. "I'll break your neck before I let you do something so stupid."

But she was smiling deeply, enjoying the way he seemed to suffer at the idea of what she'd said, his face a mask of anger. "I'm not scared of you, Clan. And I'm sick of you being scared of what Kirk or anyone thinks. I thought you and I could have something really special. It didn't even have to be more than just sex if that was all you wanted. But you don't even want that, do you?"

"You don't know what the fuck I want," he growled, his eyes boring deep into hers. The urge to wring her pretty little neck had passed, almost, but a storm still raged within him just thinking about what she was threatening to do.

"And now I don't even care," she told him simply. "Let me go, Clan."

Before he could reply, someone popped his head round the door. It was Ned, and he was looking quizzically at Bella and Clan. "Hey, sorry to interrupt. Bella, the guys were wondering if you were ready to go."

"She's not going anywhere," Clan bit out, turning suddenly on the other guy, who couldn't seem to help jumping a little. "Not with you, not with anyone."

Ned's eyes seemed to dart from Clan to Bella, unsure. Bella was spluttering and trying to speak but Clan shoved her behind him. "Maybe you guys can party without her. That sounds like a plan," Clan was saying with cold menace to Ned, who lifted his hands as if in surrender.

"Hey man, chill out. You want to muscle in on the chick, no sweat," he smirked and then ducked back out before Clan could reply. Clan turned to Bella with a telling look.

"That's the guy you wanted to spend the night with?" he said cuttingly.

"One of them, actually," was her catty reply. "I hope you're happy for embarrassing me. But if you think I'm going to let you get away with it, you're joking. I'm going right out to tell Ned that I..."

She turned angrily away but he was twisting her round again. Next thing he was kissing her for the second time that night, far less gently and with more hunger than ever. His arms were like steel bands wrapped around her, molding her to every inch of his hard-muscled frame. She stiffened for a few moments, and he growled against her lips, "Kiss me back, damn you. This is what you want, isn't it?" He seized her lips once more, and it was a moist invasion, full of heat and sweetness. Her mouth was more yielding and responsive this time, as she moaned in desire at his delicious onslaught. He broke away a few moments to say huskily, "Let's get out of here."

Bella could hardly believe this was happening. She'd dreamed about it for so long it seemed like it would always be just part of her imagination. Clan had driven like a fiend to his place, barely taking a second to glance her way or even speak. She kept looking sideways at him and wondering what he had in mind. He hadn't said much since he'd kissed her so passionately in the hallway.

They had reached his home but she barely had time to look around before he caught her in his arms again. And this time his kiss was downright savage, stealing her breath as his tongue brushed hers with erotic intent. Just having him alone, touching and kissing her made her tremble almost feverishly. His hands smoothed upwards to work on her zipper, and she suddenly balked.

"Clan," she said breathlessly, forcing her lips from his with difficulty as she gazed up into his fiercely blazing eyes. "If you're doing this to try and stop me from doing something crazy I don't want to be here."

"I'm doing it because I want to," he pointed out in a harsh, lust-thickened voice. "And because if I don't have you right now, I'm at the risk of going crazy."

Bella had to bite down the smile that tilted her lips and didn't demur when his sure fingers unzipped her dress and sent it pooling to the floor unhindered. She had a strapless bra, which he promptly unhooked. Now all she had on were a pair of lacy black panties, and for a few moments he simply gazed at her. Bella knew from his expression that he had no complaints about her high, proudly tipped C-cup breasts, her pinched in concave belly, and shapely, well-toned hips. She stood quite still when he hooked his thumb into the knots of her panties. He pulled them free, revealing her smooth-shaven pussy with the tiny landing strip pointing straight to her clit. He let out a groan as if in pain. "Fuck, Bella, you're so beautiful!" As he spoke he was already tearing off his clothes like they were choking him. And now it was her turn to watch.

He was magnificent. All rippling, solid male flesh, his pecs and abs carved like something out of a fitness magazine. At last he was tearing off his boxers and she looked down and her mouth instantly started to water at the sight of his massive, thickly veined cock as erect as a mast, the purple tip shaped like a marble mushroom. She gasped breathlessly, ready to just fall on her knees and take that fabulous monster cock in her mouth.

"Oh, Clan," she breathed, unable to say more. He seemed glad at her reaction, a slight grin lightening his features for a moment.

"I've practically carried it like this all night, watching you," he growled, pulling her close for their first heated skin-on-skin contact. "Damn, Bella! You almost killed me dancing and flirting with those fools, you know that?"

She shrugged, still in tease mode as she said coyly, "Well... I guess I was desperate. Considering that the only man in the room I wanted wasn't interested, I decided that any will have to do."

"Thank goodness I made you change your mind," he said, his hands busy at her tits, which filled his large palms nicely. "You'll never have to think of pulling that crazy stunt again, after tonight. I promise you that."

With those words, he swept her easily into his arms, carrying her off to the bedroom. He lay her down on her back and began to work his way over her shivering body: her lips, her throat, and her breasts; he kissed and licked at her, finally latching his mouth onto her nipples one after the other. She moaned beneath him, sinking her fingers through his hair as she pulled his face even closer against her breasts.

The moisture between her thighs seemed to flow like a tide as he suckled on her breasts, sometimes gently and sometimes not. He bit and sucked as hard as she could bear, and she cried out in pleasure-pain to let him know she loved every bit of it. It felt especially good when he intensified the pleasure by slipping his free hand down her navel to sample her wetness with his fingers. He groaned deep in his throat in delight to find her pussy so slick and swollen for him. He skidded the pad of his thumb against her hardened clit, making her hips jerk in response.

She was moaning out his name now, over and over, her fingers reaching between them to grasp at his cock which was throbbing against her thigh. She stroked him with immense enjoyment, loving every hard, pulsing inch of him. The coil in her belly twisted in anticipation for the moment when he'd fill her to the hilt with his gorgeous fat, long cock. She also wanted to have him in her mouth so bad that she was panting. He seemed content to lead the way, as he chose that moment to lower himself to settle his face between her widely parted thighs. Gripping her just beneath her knees, he shoved her legs way back till her cunt and ass crack were bared to his ravenous gaze. And then he told her how much he wanted to eat that pussy and tongue that clenching little sphincter. She shuddered just to hear him say it, her fingers clutching the sheets in breathless excitement.

And Clan didn't disappoint; he took his time to thrill her with his tongue, laving her with passionate tenderness one minute and then with ruthless pressure the next. He stroked his fingers past her distended pussy lips, shoving his way deep into her walls and making her almost sob with ecstasy. On and on, round and round, in and out, he finger fucked her and sucked on her, eating her out like he'd gladly be at it all night. And Bella wouldn't have complained; it was the best feeling ever to have Clan's face in her pussy like that. Better than she'd even imagined it would be. And then when he began to rim her crack, she was sure she was in heaven. She was soon begging him to let her have a taste of his cock, too. He turned so that he was on his back and she was sitting with her pussy on his face while her own head was poised over his groin. She cooed with pleasure as her fingers wrapped around his burgeoning cock, right before she bathed his cap in lollipop licks, humming as she tasted his delicious pre-cum. Now that they were in the 69 position, they could feast on each other to the max, filling the room with noises of their slurping and sloshing.

Bella had never enjoyed sucking a cock so much; everything about Clan's made her want to keep her mouth on him for hours. She masturbated the base of his shaft with firm strokes, while she shoved the rest of him up into her face, twirling her tongue all over the cap and ridge and simply giving him the full works. He began to thrust into her mouth, and she gladly took in more inches, gagging a couple of times before she found the perfect depth and rhythm. At the same time, he was eating her pussy and making her whole core shudder like a steam engine. There was no way she could last a minute longer if he kept tonguing her clit like that, with three fingers punching into her tight pussy at the same time. She could feel her mouth vibrating on his cock and knew she was giving him mutual pleasure with the way his groans punctuated the air.

She couldn't help it; moments later she was gushing into his mouth, lifting her mouth off his cock as she arched and squirmed, cumming so hard her whole body seemed to vibrate with the force of it. He held her thighs in place, lapping every cum drop with his tongue and humming with delight, telling her how fucking good she tasted. Moments later, she fell to the side, dazed.

"You okay, baby?" he asked softly, planting a kiss on her forehead as he brushed the damp hair back. Her reply was to grasp his cock firmly.

"Not till you top that fantastic pussy eating by fucking me hard doggy style. I need that thick fat cock slamming into me from behind, now."

"With pleasure," he rumbled, taking hold of her hips and flipping her on her belly. Her face was shoved into the pillow as her ass was pushed high in the air. She felt him settle on his knees behind her, and she tucked in her knees, curving her bottom upwards so her pussy was more prominently accessible. She was so slippery wet that he didn't even need any more lubrication; he simply rolled on a condom and the next moment, was shoving into her in one hard, ferocious thrust.

Bella felt like he was tearing her in half with that thick-rimmed cock of his bashing into her. And she loved it! Her greedy little cunt took every deep, almost punishing thrust, her ass wiggling every time he slapped into it. It was the hottest fucking she had ever had, everything she'd hoped it would be and more. He built up a steady rhythm, hitting her hot spot with such unerring accuracy that she knew she'd be coming again in record time.

She gritted her teeth to hold it back, feeling him lean forward slightly to bite on her shoulder with a deep groan.

"I can't...damn it, Bella, I won't hold on for much longer," he said on a harsh breath, shoving into her so fast it was like each jab was blurring into the next.

"Don't hold back, baby," she told him, equally breathless. "Give me all you've got. Come for me, Clan. Come inside me."

Her words were like a trigger, setting him off so strongly that he pounded into her with such ferocity she could feel him mashing into her cervix. She screeched at the sweet pain, arching her back as she climaxed in waves the next minute. At that same moment he was roaring and blasting into her, finding his own release as well.

Had she passed out? Bella couldn't say for sure. All she knew was that she opened her eyes to find herself now lying on Clan's chest, his hands stroking her hair. She snuggled closer to him, inhaling deeply his delicious, manly scent that was all him.

"I feel achy all over," she purred, glancing up at him with dancing eyes. "That was one workout you gave me, honey. Sure beats a threesome anytime."

He tugged her hair back, making her yelp through her smile. "Were you serious about going off with those guys?"

Her eyes looked more mischievous than

ever. "Well, yes. But not for what you think," she added quickly when he seemed ready to yank on her hair again. "I'd only convinced them to take me out to the beach and go skinny dipping or something equally crazy. I'm surprised they agreed."

"Yeah, right," he muttered. "Like any guy would say no to the chance of getting into your pants."

"But you did," she pointed out with a pout. "And besides, I never would have let them do anything. I just wanted to make you jealous."

"You did more than that – you made me homicidal," he growled, lifting off the bed a little to grab a hot, angry kiss. "The only reason I kept holding back was because of Kirk kept remembering the promise I made. Well, that's all broken now."

She frowned slightly. "What promise?"

"That I'd stay the hell away from you," he muttered wryly. "I guess he suspected I had a thing for his hot sister, well, ever since you turned eighteen anyway. I had to give him my word I'd never mess with you."

"Hmm...Well, since this was my idea, I think you can skip the guilt trip," she teased, leaning her elbow on his chest.

"Hey, this was what I wanted, too," he told her firmly. "And I'll have to convince Kirk one way or the other that unlike his other pals, I have good intentions."

"Not too good, I hope," she cooed, smiling tantalizing as she bent her head lower to his lips. One of her hands already began snaking down to his belly and beyond to wrap possessively around his cock. He was already hard as a plank. "Hmmn...insatiable, aren't you?"

He growled in reply, quickly to lift her by the waist and straddling her across his hips. "Need to let you see, baby, that you'll never need another guy but me."

"Oh, definitely," she agreed as she settled her ever dripping pussy on his waiting shaft, sighing as he swelled even thicker, deep inside her twitching wall. There was no doubt that Clan, and only Clan, would do quite well.

2 GONE WILD

He was striding across the room to where she was, and for a few moments, she actually wanted to believe that the gorgeous smile on his face was for her.

Gina couldn't say she knew that much about men, but the tall, darkly handsome hunk making his way towards her had to be the hottest male she'd ever seen. Wavy chestnut brown hair, dark grey eyes, chiseled face, and he looked like something out of a gentleman's magazine. And he was dressed like it, too, from his classically cut dark suit to the tip of his well-shined shoes. He was certainly out of place in the highly pink and frilly cake shop she co-owned with her best friend Tully.

Tully was standing right behind her, and it seemed she was the one the hunky stranger was smiling so genially with. His eyes twinkled with appreciation as they looked past Gina to the slim, shapely woman standing just behind her.

Gina knew Tully was a very beautiful woman. She had the hourglass figure that came naturally without any need for enhancements, high double-D boobs and hips that seemed to flare in a perfect curve no matter what she was wearing – even the sack of an apron she had over her jeans and t-shirt right then. She had long, curly dark hair reaching to her waist and thick-lashed eyes that never needed the help of mascara. In short, she was a walking bombshell.

And yet, Gina had never really had to feel jealous of her best friend. Even though in college Tully had got all the main attention from boys and Gina got pretty much overlooked, it had never really been a bother. Gina was comfortable enough in the shadows; no one tended to bother her. And she knew she was pretty enough, a bit too skinny but at least she kept her body healthy and in shape. Her hair was a nice shade of golden blonde, and she'd been told her blue eyes were really pretty. She'd also been told by Tully once before that if there was one girl in the world she could trust alone with her man, it was Gina.

Well, that was a compliment, right? Gina mused out of nowhere, as Tully moved from behind the counter and went ahead to shake hands with Mr. Hunk, as Gina secretly tagged him.

"Hello, Clark. I wasn't really sure you'd be

able to make it," Tully said warmly, and Gina saw her reach up on her toes to kiss the man's jaw. Gina's curiosity deepened as she wondered who he was and why Tully had never mentioned him. Was he Tully's new catch? Gina knew that her best friend and partner went through guys like clothes on a rack – here today, gone the next. And immediately she was on to the next, even more gorgeous male admirer.

"Hey, for you Tully, anything," he said in a voice like crushed gravel. Gina realized she must have been staring at him because he suddenly looked up and pierced her with his grey, fathomless gaze. She swallowed and wanted to look away but couldn't. She was normally a level-headed girl and wasn't bowled over by every handsome fella who crossed her vision. But there was something about this guy that got her forgetting to be sensible. And now she was making an utter twat of herself by gaping at him.

"And this must be your partner you told me about. Gina, right?"

Hearing her name so unexpectedly from those sculpted lips of his made Gina blink in surprise. Tully turned and beamed. "Oh, yeah, Gina, come over let me introduce you two. Gina, this is Clark Evans – an old friend of my brother's. He's offered to take a look at our books and work out the figures we've been having problems with. Clark, this is Gina Felton, as you know. She does the real work around here," Tully said with a teasing smile.

Well, she was certainly half right, Gina thought as she forced herself to move from the counter and walk the few steps over to them. Gina was the one who prepared the confectionaries: the cakes, pastries, and pies that made their shop so popular. But Gina had to admit that it was Tully who had turned it into a fiscal success with her head for business and money. However, there seemed to have arisen some kind of problem with the accounts or something lately.

"Gina," Tully turned to the slim woman next to her, "Clark is a whiz kid auditing executive. He offered to help us out with things and he's here to check everything out. I'll be with him in the back office."

"Sure," Gina murmured, and when Clark swept past her with a brief nod, she couldn't help following him with her eyes. They disappeared into the office area and Gina turned away in self-irritation. She wondered what the heck had come over her.

Seriously girl, you need to get laid soon.

The thought crossed her mind in an instant and she had to stifle a giggle behind the notepad she'd been clutching. If anyone she knew even guessed the things going on through her mind right then, they wouldn't believe. Gina knew that most of her friends thought she was the innocent, goody-goody type. Well, it was the truth that Gina didn't really enjoy partying and clubbing like most chicks her age. She was only twenty-four but she took her job and business very seriously, never really making time for anything else.

But that didn't mean she didn't have feelings. That certainly didn't mean that she was immune from having the most lustful thoughts for a certain Clark Evans she'd only just set eyes on.

She kept thinking of the image of his clean-cut, handsome features and the way his expensive looking clothes fit his tall, lithely muscled frame. But then it wasn't just his looks, she decided; the moment she'd set eyes on him, she'd felt a strange, magnetic essence he exuded so effortlessly. He had an unmistakable male presence that she was sure many women had fallen victim to – and without him even trying.

Well, he'd certainly caught her attention, Gina noted as she forced herself to focus on the task of properly displaying the fresh batch of chocolate-covered cake balls. They had a few staff who worked in the medium-sized shop, but that was at the cash register and then back in the kitchen. Besides, Gina loved to handle the display and window dressing with all her best creations. She loved what she did and it showed in every bite – or so her customers told her. Pushing the thoughts still lingering in her mind of the hunky Clark Evans, Gina focused on the task at hand and tried not to wonder too much just what those two could be doing back in the office.

"So, do you like her?"

Clark looked up in surprise at Tully's question. He'd been browsing through the computer screen pages showing several figures in front of him. But he didn't pretend not to know what she meant. "Tully, I barely shared two sentences with the woman and certainly spent fewer minutes in her presence. I'm not sure how you expect me to answer that question..."

"Oh come on, Clark. You can't deny that she's lovely," Tully pressed, sitting on the edge of the desk. She'd known Clark since they were teens; he was just a few years older than she was, about her brother's age. On a good day she liked to tease him especially about his many conquests, but today she was more than half serious. "And I can tell she thinks you're something. I've never seen her blush like that around anyone. She was practically ogling."

Clark huffed, not replying. He was used to getting female attention and basically ignored it if he could help it – except when he had an interest in pursuit. He had noticed the woman called Gina looking him over, and for a moment he'd felt a flash of awareness – but then stamped it down. He could tell she wasn't his type. Her pretty-blonde looks, scraped back hair, and fragile-looking frame...she had the air of the untouched, Vestal virgin about her. And from the little Tully had told him about her...He shook his head inwardly. Clark liked his women with a lot more fire in their veins. The type you weren't afraid would break in your grasp if you so much as handled them a little too rough. No, Clark decided, he didn't do fragile.

"At least ask her out," Tully went on cajolingly. "She really is a nice girl. And I don't think she'd gone on a decent date in months. All she thinks about is work. Besides...something tells me you guys are actually quite suited. Only, neither of you know it yet." She grinned suddenly even as his scowl deepened. "That's why you need me to point out the obvious. Besides, you're single, and so is she."

"What makes you so sure she'll agree to go out with me anyway?" Clark asked, trying to quell his dark look.

"Oh, she will, trust me," Tully said with deep feminine self-assurance. "She definitely will."

Gina's mind was still in a whirl as she prepared for her dinner with Clark that evening. She could still remember the moment he'd asked her out – and how promptly she had responded. She hadn't even blinked or thought of how wildly improbable it would be that a man like Clark would even want to take her out.

He'd emerged from the inner office with Tully, who suddenly said she had to make a phone call and asked Gina to please see Clark out of the shop. Gina had been courteously leading him to the exit when he'd paused in his stride and asked her if she'd like to go out to dinner that evening. She'd been so surprised yet thrilled that it never even occurred to her to refuse.

Just what do you think you're doing girl? She asked herself as she stepped out of the shower and put on some underwear. You agreed to go out to dinner with this totally hot guy who had probably been put up to it by Tully. Gina wasn't dumb, she'd considered that possibility. Tully was always bugging her to go out on more dates and had even threatened to "fix her up" with someone soon. Gina had been aware of all this and still she had agreed to go out with Clark tonight.

Maybe I have a point to prove – to myself at least, she thought, as she opened her wardrobe and stood staring for a few moments at the slinky dress hanging there. It was black, but it was in no way plain. In fact, it was the most expensive, daring, and sexiest outfit she owned. It was one of those dresses you'd buy because it looked so fantastic, but even as you hung it up, you knew you'd probably never get to wear it. But you felt sexy just having it in the closet, knowing it was there. Gina never dreamed she'd have the nerve to wear it, but tonight...she felt that she could swing it. No way she wanted to look frumpy or outdated when she met Clark for dinner soon.

Why she wanted to make all this effort was beyond her. She was definitely attracted to Clark, more than she'd ever been to any guy she'd just met. And for some reason, she wanted to make a great impression on him. When she was finally dressed and was dabbing on some perfume, she looked at her reflection and thought, I look wild...and pretty darn hot.

Definitely different from the way she normally looked, she knew. Oh well, it's about time I lived a little, she decided, as she left her apartment and went down to the cab waiting to take her to her destination.

What was it they said about first impressions, mused Clark? Well, because sometimes, they don't count.

He saw the woman striding into the restaurant and felt his breath stolen away. That was her? He almost couldn't credit his senses that this image of hotness swaying over to him was the same uptight-looking Gina he'd met for the first time earlier that day.

She had on a black, form-fitting dress that played sensuously over her slim frame, displaying her gentle curves to perfection. Her hair was a mass of tossed blonde waves, tumbling over her shoulders as if ruffled by a lover's hands. Her dress stopped just above her knees and displayed the most fabulous legs he'd ever seen. Her high heels made her look taller and even sexier if that were possible, thanks to their tiny black straps hugging her ankles. Well, well, well, he thought, rising to his feet as she was shown over to his table. Gina had definitely transformed and he wasn't sure what to make of it. She might look hot, but that was on the outside. Sexy clothes, nice make up, and hmmm...gorgeous scent, he noted, as she reached his side and he managed to word out a greeting. Yep, she definitely looked like a red-blooded woman, he decided. The only thing was, did the red blood really flow in her veins? Or more to the point, would he fuck her?

She smiled and placed her fingers in his for a handshake – and as his hand enclosed hers and he looked down into her blue eyes, a sudden flash of awareness zipped through him as they touched.

Hell yeah, I definitely would.

The moment he'd answered his own question in his head, he knew it was true. The notion became a settled fact as they sat down to dinner and actually got talking, getting to know each other better. Okay, so she was beautiful and smart, he discovered. She had interesting views and ideas about things he found relevant. She was witty and laughed easily. He liked that in a woman. As the evening wore on, he found his gaze narrowing as he looked at her and he couldn't help wondering that since he'd decided she was a woman he'd definitely like to bed, was she beddable. Would she be hot and wild in bed the way he liked them? Or would she screech and scamper off like a frightened rabbit once he stated his intent?

Only one way to find out...

The more time she spent in his company, the more she was convinced that tonight, given the chance, she was going to do something totally out of character. It was the way he kept looking at her, his grey eyes growing darker and darker by the minute. It was the way it felt sharing a conversation with him, finding that they gelled on so many levels. But the most important thing she discovered was just sitting there, looking at him, and hearing his voice, she was getting seriously damp. Like, she had to keep crossing and uncrossing her legs to ease the wetness forming in her crotch.

Because heck, the man simply oozed of sexiness. His hands, large and blunt-tipped, were so fine – and she was a girl who was into hands, totally. Just looking at his hands as they stood on the table, or held his glass of wine or cutlery, and she could just imagine those strong-looking fingers trailing all over her naked body. And that got her wet.

Her convictions grew stronger as once they left the restaurant, he asked if she'd like to go dancing or something. Good sign, Gina told herself: looked like he actually wanted to spend more time with her. A part of her though wanted to reply, "Dancing? No, not really. I'd rather just go straight to your place and fuck."

And she giggled to herself as she wondered what he'd say to that. Right then she felt hot wired, ready to simply implode if he so much as kissed her. But it looked like he was ready to play the gentleman; he was generally keeping his hands off as much as possible. Even his touch, as he led her out to where his flashy car was parked, was light in the small of her back. But when she looked sideways at him as they settled next to each other in the car, she could have sworn she didn't imagine that telltale glint in his eye. It told her he was simply drawing out the moment, torturing them both with the idea that, one way or another, they were ending up in bed that night.

Gina liked to dance. No one really knew that about her, but just because she never really went to bars or clubs with them didn't mean she couldn't shake it. She loved to listen to music and home and let loose; it was great exercise and it was uplifting to dance like crazy the way she did in her living room. Tonight though, when she arrived with Clark at some swanky nightclub, she allowed herself the luxury of actually dancing in public. The music was great, the atmosphere pumping – and then there was her very hot, very sexy date...so all that put together was really motivating. She got into "dancing queen" mode and just rocked, laughing gaily and just rocking it to the max. Clark moved great, too, which meant they had a fantastic time hitting the floor.

They took a break to have a few drinks and by then the mood had been set and locked. Gina looked over the rim of her glass at him sitting on the other side of her. They'd wined and dined, and now they'd danced, their bodies sometimes touching and bumping. It was becoming clear that they'd reached the level where they'd have to decide, my place or yours? However, Gina didn't really want to get her hopes up. He might end up wanting to play his cards the other way and just drop her off like a true gentleman.

But Gina didn't want to be treated like a lady tonight...

Clark was pretty good with signals. Most times, he could tell when it was right to go in for the kill. And as he drove them from the nightclub almost an hour later, he could almost tell for sure that he and Ms. Gina Felton were going to end up in the sack sooner than later. The only question now was whose sack? One way or another, neither of them would be sleeping alone that night...

"I had a great time tonight," he said, turning to her after he'd stopped in front of her apartment. He hoped his comment didn't come out as surprised as he felt. It was true, he'd had fun. Gina wasn't the boring, demur, and skittish female he'd thought she was. In fact, he could swear that if he reached forward and kissed her right then, she won't smack him in the face – she'd actually respond.

"So did I," she said with a smile that seemed a little shy. Oh no, baby, you aren't backing out now, he thought resolutely. He unhooked his seat belt and leaned across to where she sat still as stone. He slanted his face so that his lips were mere inches from hers. And then he kissed her.

It was light and filled with promise. He tugged on her lips and groaned deep in his throat when she pulled back on his. A little tentative, but he could feel the passion underlying her moist response. In two seconds flat, he felt his cock go hard as a plank. Heavens above, he'd been ravishing her right inside the car if something wasn't done – and fast.

"Invite me up," he said gruffly against her lips, his hands reaching up to tangle in her silky locks. Lord help him, if she went all virtuous on him and told him no...

"Have you got condoms?"

He blinked her question so unexpected and very direct – even for him. And then he smiled, very slowly. "No. It wasn't till you walked into the restaurant earlier tonight that I realized how much I'd like to fuck you. No offense, but when we met earlier today..."

"I know," she murmured, smiling to let him know there was no offense, "But the funniest thing was, I knew I wanted to fuck you the moment I saw you." Her smile widened into a grin, and she stuck her hand inside her bag. Moments later she was holding up the packets of condoms. "Good thing at least one of us came prepared."

He let out a ragged laugh, feeling his head spinning a little. "You're certainly full of surprises, Ms. Felton," he growled, catching her lips in one fast, hard kiss. "I can't wait to find out what else you've got in your goodie bag..."

Gina had heard the word "chemistry" used a lot of times, but had never really understood what it meant – between men and women, anyway. Until Clark took her in his arms and kissed her the moment the front door was locked behind them. Her body simply came to life at his touch. All night there'd been a force field radiating from him and drawing her closer, making her forget all her notions of how a "sensible" woman should act. No falling for the first hot guy you meet, and certainly no falling into bed with him. But with Clark, she was willing to throw caution to the wind and break all the rules.

They barely made it to the bedroom, tearing their clothes off on the way. Gina led them there, giggling as he grabbed her into his embrace again once the bed was in sight. But they ended up not getting to use it – not right then anyway. Now that they were naked, every touch, every kiss, and even lustful desire seemed intensified monumentally. Right there, in the middle of the bedroom, they locked lips, with their bodies Velcro-clung to each other. Gina savored the luxury of sliding her hands all over his body which felt smooth and chiseled like it was carved from marble. His chest was broad and hairless, his nipples hard as pebbles. She twisted them experimentally with her fingers and heard him groan deep in his throat.

"Yeah...I like it rough like that," he husked against her lips, and she smiled sensuously.

"Do you?" Her fingers trailed down his ripped torso to where his cock stood proud and thickly girthed as a flagstaff. Her grasp was firm, sure. He gasped as she began to masturbate him with steady, strong strokes. Her teeth nipped into his bottom lip, feeling his shaft lengthening and hardening even further in her grip. "Hmm, seems you do," she agreed with a soft chuckle.

Her humor faded quickly as passion took over. She found his touch just as hungry and exploring over her quivering frame. Moments blended into each other as he roved his hands from her throat to her thrusting breasts, their upturned nipples fat as coins, and pointed with pleasure. He rolled them beneath his palms, and she felt her breath catch almost painfully.

She loved her breasts being fondled, and Clark seemed to have the most sure, expert hands which caressed her with sensual precision. Her arousal pooled into telling moisture between her thighs; her knees felt weak beneath her. She released his cock and lifted her fingers to rifle through his hair, tugging at the roots till he groaned. Her tits spilled into his hands, fitting perfectly. She felt him caressing the mounds almost fiercely, thumbing her stiff nipples all the while.

Gina could stand it no longer; her half-year celibacy, as well as being so turned on by him since the evening had begun, had her virtually panting with lust. Her arms clung around his shoulders for support, as she lifted a thigh to wrap around his waist so that their privates brushed tantalizingly against each other. "I can't...Clark, I'm not sure I can wait much longer...."

"Neither can I," he confessed, his voice raspy. He reached down between them, laying his fingers flat against her smooth-shaven pussy. Gina bucked against his hand – shocked at the pleasure that blasted through her belly.

"Fuck!" She gasped, her legs parting of their own accord to give his searching fingers find her pussy lips which were slippery and swollen now. She felt his thumb tease her pebble-hard clit, and her fingers dug into the skin of his back, making deep ridges.

He didn't seem to feel that, more intent on sliding his way through her soft folds, dipping his finger tips in her vaginal walls and finding her tight and juicy. "Damn, Gina...," he let out on a groan, his lips sliding down her throat as she arched her back, tipping her breasts to be tasted by his roving lips.

"You feel so frigging good," he said, steadily finger-fucking her. Gina felt like giggling at the pun, but she realized he wasn't even joking. No, his breathing was ragged enough, and his cock against her felt so hard it seemed ready to break in half. She figured he was in as much earnest as she was. She almost couldn't bear it, the way he was shoving his fingers into her with sweet, powerful thrusts, mimicking what his cock would soon be doing. And damn it, she needed that meaty manhood buried deep inside her now.

"Clark...," she breathed out almost warningly, and he seemed to recognize her deep intent. He chuckled softly, taking his time. Still thrusting with his fingers, he bent his head to her tilted breasts and pulled on her nipples, one after the other. He nibbled and suckled, relishing the taste or her flesh in his mouth.

"I could eat you alive," he groaned, his teeth sinking into the curvy under swell of her firm breast. "Your body is so beautiful...and it's driving me crazy."

"You're driving me crazy," she wailed, barely able to stand with the needy passion pulsing through her body. She was ready to explode – but she needed that rigid staff of meat ripping into her before she'd let the volcanic emotions within her erupt. "Take me, Clark. Please."

"Magic words," he replied on a rasp, his hands grasping the cheeks of her ass and squeezing hard for a few moments. He released her only long enough to wrap on some protection, and then he was hefting her lithe body in the air, making her grip him round the waist with her legs. His cock homed in instinctively on her waiting slit, and once he found the slick opening, he surged right in without delay.

"Aah," Gina sighed, clenching her inner muscles upon his invading cock, which rocked so deep into her she was sure her belly vibrated with each thrust. "Yes...yes," she moaned on each downward drive, as he pumped her ass on his cock, his fingers clenched into her butt cheeks.

Her eyes tried to focus, and she saw that his were fixed on her face, watching her every expression. "You like that?" he husked, holding her gaze with his, which was narrowed and blazing. "And that?" His words were punctuated by his cock bottoming up into her pussy, his hands on her ass tightening.

"You bet I do," she managed to choke out, the most incredible bliss tearing up from her cunt and around her body. "Don't stop,

Clark...fuck me hard!"

"With pleasure," he said deeply, his hips picking up rhythm, pistoning into her like he was some fuck machine. He found her lips and took it in a forceful kiss, thrusting his tongue deep inside her moistness. It felt just as good as his cock shafting up into her greedy, tight cunt that enveloped him in its velvet walls.

It was hard for either of them to speak after that, every breath stolen by the pleasure of cock in pussy, flesh against flesh. There was the sense of here and now, now or never in the way they fucked. Gina, for one, felt all her senses zoning in on that rampaging cock that ground into her again and again. She felt the fountain rising and building right from her core, threatening to flood her with its tide. She returned his kiss as their tongues swapped and danced. It wasn't long now, she knew. She'd waited long enough for her release, and now she wasn't sure she wanted to hold it back. It felt much too good to resist, so she succumbed helplessly to its sweet, thrilling call.

"I'm coming," she screeched out of nowhere, surprising him as well as herself. His cock seemed to bulge and pulse within her at those words – and then it happened. In perfect sync, as if perfectly timed, he erupted deep within her as she spurted upon his cock. Wave after wave hit her and she held on tight to his shoulders, cumming in an endless rush.

"Aargh," he groaned, his own hands gripping her waist tightly as he hacked punishingly into her again and again. He tried to hold on to his erstwhile control, but her own spasms, the shuddering clash of her body against him, caused him to forget to hold back. He heard her moan in pleasure and pain and was sure he'd slammed into her cervix. Gritting his teeth, he forced his whole being back to earth as the last throes of his climax ebbed.

He led her over to the bed while his legs could still support them both. Spreading her gently down, he lay next to her, unable to take his eyes from her dreamy-looking face. He'd enjoyed watching her while he'd fucked her, had loved looking into her beautiful features, and see them filled with wild abandon. He thought of Tully and her prophetic words – and he thanked the Lord that he'd listened to her. Gina was the entire woman he'd dreamed he'd find; the woman who responded to him completely and gave all of herself without thought. This was arguably the best fuck he could remember having in ages – and she looked like it had gone great for her, too.

Smiling, he raked his fingers through her damp blonde hair, shoving it off her face. Her skin was deliciously flushed, and she looked so blissful that he couldn't help stealing another kiss. "That went pretty great," he drawled, his grin slightly cocky. "Glad I could bring out the tigress in you. Who would have thought, huh?"

She smirked, her fingers slashing down his bare chest, smoothing over the ridges and slopes. Damn, she was hot for him all over again. That probably had to do with him having the body of a Greek god, all bronzed gold and sculpted. "You're right though...I always had it in me – I just never met the right guy who could let it out. That really was something, Clark Evans. Wanna do it again – slower, this time?"

His lips parted in a feral grin, and the heated delight in his eyes almost scorched her shivering skin. "My kind of woman," he murmured, reciprocating her touch by cupping her boob possessively. "And slow is good. Great, in fact. We do have all night, don't we?"

"We have as long as you want," she returned softly, looking up at him with smoky eyes. She meant it; if they had to become fuck buddies, friends with benefits – or even fall in love...What ever it took, she wanted that cock for as long as she could have it. Now that she'd found someone who could take her to the fiery clouds of pleasure and back, she wasn't going to want to let it go so easily.

"Then we're in for a sweet, hard, and thrilling ride," he promised, tweaking her nipple into tingling sweetness.

"Ever had shower sex?" she asked on a purr, reaching up from the pillows to tug at that gorgeously full bottom lip of his. "Because I haven't. I want you to shove my face against the tiled wall and then slam that big fat cock into my pussy from behind till I gush all over your cock a second time."

"Fucking hell woman, you've got me hard as a plank again," he said with a groan, wrapping an arm round her waist. "It's a good thing I'm up to the task...something tells me that behind that angelic face of yours is a she-wolf with ravenous needs. Well...I always did want a woman with a sex drive to match mine."

"You'll find I match you in a lot of things," she declared, rising fluidly and swaying to the bathroom door. She looked over her shoulder at him, laying back there with a raging boner and his eyes following her every move hungrily. "Well, you coming or not?"

He flashed a devilish grin at her. "Oh I'm right behind you, baby," he said deeply, straightening from the bed quick as a fox. "But as for 'coming'...that I will save for much, much later..."

"Promises, promises," she cooed and squealed when he came up close behind her and spanked her wiggly ass hard. Hmm, thought Gina, that sharp smack gave her another good idea of what they could do the next time or the next.

3 SLICK NICK

Prologue

Ooh, he was slick, making his play for the two friends.

When Delia and her best friend discover Nick's ploy, they decide to beat him at his game....

Nick Freeman was hot, no doubt. Delia was all ready to fall, right into his lap, when she found out he was out for her friend, Lisa, as well. He'd tried to play them against each other, but they were determined to make him pay and leave him empty handed...

"Do you want me?"

Delia kept playing the same conversation in her head. It was always that one fantasy, and it hardly ever differed in plot, or conclusion.

The handsome, totally virile, Nick Freeman would ask her that same question every time, while his dark grey eyes were smoldering down into hers. His full-bottomed lips would be a breath away from hers and she'd flutter her lashes as she sighed in surrender.

"Yes...Oh yes, Nick," she'd reply and he'd kiss her, hotly and hungrily, ranging his hands all over her quivering frame. Right there, on his desk, he'd push her down on her back, lift up her skirt and...

"Delia!"

She was startled at the harsh sound of her name, blinking guiltily as her eyes focused on her boss, Mr. Winters. He certainly had a wintry look on his face right then. When had he come in anyway?

"I don't pay you to daydream, Miss Stone," the middle-aged, totally bald man said grimly, and Delia bit on her lip. "I walked in, just now and had to call your name thrice, before you even noticed I was there."

"I'm sorry, Mr. Winters," she said soberly, sitting up straight. "It won't happen again. Is there something you wanted?"

His eyes shifted at her words, the steam taken out of him by her simple apology. He told her grumpily, "I'm putting you on the Clayton team."

Delia had to blink once again, this time in shock. "What?"

"Don't give me the chance to change my mind," the grouchy man said, turning and leaving her small office.

Delia almost didn't remember to start breathing again. Working on the Clayton team was more or less like a promotion of sorts. Only the best hands at the firm were ever chosen to be part of it. Well, considering that Clayton Industries was their biggest client, it only followed that the team handling such a portfolio would have to be top-notch.

Yet, all that didn't interest Delia. What mattered was Nick Freeman, who was heading that team. Now that she'd be working closely with him, she could get a better chance at him.

She told herself to calm down. Nick had arrived at the firm barely two months ago, and she could count how many times he'd spoken to her on one hand. He'd been moved over from headquarters, in a bid, to inject new special spirit to this branch. From all accounts, he was some marketing whiz and an asset to the company.

"The man was an asset, period," Delia thought, dreamily, rising to her feet and straightening her skirt suit. From the first day he'd walked in and seen him, her nights had never been the same. He filled her darkest fantasies, with images of her being taken by him, over and over. Even during the day, right here, at work, she couldn't help a daydream, or two. She wondered if her boss, Mr. Winters, would blame her if he found out whom she'd been mooning over. She was sure even he would sympathize. After all, Nick Freeman had to be the hunkiest male alive.

A few inches over six feet, he had gorgeous, russet hair and the most piercing grey eyes. Always impeccably dressed, he managed to look like he'd stepped right out of some highbrow men's magazine. Yet, even in his sharp suits, one could tell he had a killer bod underneath. His lips, heaven help her, were just perfectly formed for kissing. She'd already kissed those lips a hundred times in her head.

Okay Delia, seriously. Behave.

Smiling at that imaginary voice in her head, she grabbed a quick look in her compact and decided she was quite presentable, maybe even somewhat hot looking. Delia was very modest. She had no delusions about her looks. She'd definitely been taking more care with her appearance since he'd shown up, however. In fact, all the other single females in the office had perked up since Nick joined the firm. Delia thought of her friend and colleague, Lisa, who worked as Mr. Winter's secretary. She was also of the conviction that Nick was totally hot. They'd shared a lot of dirty, wishful talk about what they'd do to him, if they ever got him into their clutches.

She was about to have the chance to meet him face to face, properly, for the first time. Taking a deep breath and tamping down the feeling of glee, she swept out of her office.

Damn, she was gorgeous.

Nick couldn't help thinking that the moment she walked in. Delia Stone... He knew her name well enough. He knew a lot about her, too, more than she realized.

"Hello, Miss Stone. Take a seat, please" he said, with a welcoming smile, indicating the chair in front of his desk.

"Thank you... and please, call me Delia."

"With pleasure. My name's Nick," he replied, settling back into his own seat." I take it the boss has informed you about coming on the Clayton team?"

She nodded, a pleased smile on her face. "That's why I'm here."

"Good. Because when Melissa White had to go on sick leave a few days ago, we realized we'd require someone to take her place. The first person I thought of was you."

He saw her blink those gorgeous brown eyes of hers in surprise. He decided he liked to look at her face. She had the kind of looks a woman has when you just know she's fun to be around, pretty, with dancing, bright eyes and a ready smile; nice hair, very dark and shiny, chopped into some kind of stylish bob. Then, from the neck down... Woah!

Nick would never forget the first time he'd seen her. He'd been here two days and was just about settling into the new state of things. She'd been coming from the opposite end of the same corridor he was striding through. It was a long stretch, so he had ample time to view her before they had to go past each other. All he could think of was, "Damn, I'd totally fuck her."

All she had on was a smart suit, the skirt was a bit short, which was the fashion. Yet, her clothes played off her killer figure to perfection. She was in no way reed slim, and Nick, certainly, liked his women with more than a bit of flesh on their bones. Her abundant bust was evident, stretching the camisole she wore beneath her jacket. At least a D-cup. Then came that delectable pinched-in waist and nicely flared hips. "Perfect hourglass," he thought, with approval. Her legs were long, with shapely calves and feet encased in very high, black patent pumps, Nick's favorite kind.

This appraisal had taken no more than five seconds, but the image had stuck in his head. He'd hidden his thoughts well, giving her a courteous nod as she'd finally brushed past him. He could still remember the warm, floral scent that had trailed faintly after her. He could recall how her eyes had brightened, a smile of pleasure crossing her face at his greeting. He'd been enchanted.

Now, looking across his desk, at her, and viewing her blank, surprised expression after his last statement, he affirmed his initial conclusion that he'd definitely want to fuck the delectable Delia Stone. The most alluring thing about her is that she didn't even know the effect she had on him. Partly because he was very good at concealing his thoughts and partly because, well, she didn't seem like the kind who figured every man with blood in his veins fancied her. Many of the other chicks in the office seemed to think they were the biscuit, strutting around just thinking he'd make his play. Yet, none of them remotely appealed to him. Not like Delia did.

Then, again, there was this one other girl....

"Why... Thank you, Nick," she finally said, smiling a little, shyly. "I didn't even think you noticed me or anything."

"Oh I sure did," he replied, his tone deep, eyes holding hers for a meaningful moment. He then added, "I know, for one thing, that you're very dedicated, with a great track record. I simply recommended you to Mr. Winters, and he wholeheartedly agreed. So, you see, it's all due to your hard work that you're now on my team."

"Oh," she said, and her eyelashes fluttered a little. "And here I was thinking this was just some ploy of yours to... I dunno, get into my pants, or whatever."

He grinned, knowing she was just teasing. But he wasn't, when he answered, "Is it going to work?"

She looked him up and down, coquette-fashion. Nick felt a familiar stirring in his loins, when she said, "I don't know. It might."

"Damn," Nick swore, with an inner groan. He'd throw her face down, on the desk, right then, if he thought there was time. He could just see himself positioned behind her cute, round ass, ramming into her pussy, doggy-style, while she moaned with every thrust. He'd fuck her so hard it would send files and stuff flying off the desk....

Shaking off those cock-hurting images, he smiled with deep charm, "Then maybe dinner tomorrow night will help you decide? I know a really nice Thai restaurant."

"I love Thai."

"Great. We'll make arrangements later," he said, glanced at his watch. "The other members of the team will be waiting in the conference room for today's meeting. Shall we join them?"

As he escorted Delia out of his office, he began to wonder if it was really a good idea, putting her on the team after all. He'd done it, partly, to get closer to her, but now, he was thinking, maybe she'd turn out to be too much of a sweet distraction....

Lisa looked up and couldn't help smiling when she saw that it was Nick standing by her desk.

"Hello, Nick," she said warmly. "You're here to see Mr. Winters?" She tried to rein in her enthusiasm as she leaned forward. She saw and spoke to him almost every day. Yet, she still hadn't gotten over her crush on him. Each time he was close, like now, a very moist patch spread between her thighs, making her want to cross, and uncross, her legs.

"Yes," he replied. His voice was still as gravelly as she remembered. "I just finished a meeting with my Clayton team. I'm sure Mr. Winters would be interested to know how it went."

"Of course. I'll let him know you're here," she said and in moments, rung up her boss.

"You can go in, Nick," she told him with a smile. Her heart tripped as he returned it. She could have sworn that one of his gorgeous grey eyes closed in a slight wink. Lisa felt the moist patch in her panties grow moister.

She watched him till Mr. Winter's door had closed behind him, then let out a deep sigh of longing. It really was pathetic of her, pining for Nick this way. Especially when she knew that more than half of the female population at the office did the same. Even her pal, Delia, who worked on another floor, had the hots for him. He didn't seem interested in any of them. She couldn't help wondering if he was in a relationship already. Or maybe he wasn't really into chicks.

She shoved that possibility to the side. She just couldn't let herself even consider that option.

By the time he reappeared, fifteen minutes later, she was far more composed. He paused at her table, once more and, when she looked up at him, he was smiling.

"New hairdo? It looks lovely," he said, tipping his head to the side.

She patted her hair. "Yes, actually... and, thanks, Nick. Nice of you to notice," she said, unable to remove the surprise from her tone. "I never really knew you had an eye for such things."

He leaned forward on the desk. Their gaze was almost level as he murmured, "I have an eye for a lot of things, and when it comes to beautiful women, I tend to pay close attention."

Lisa felt her belly lurch almost sickeningly. Was Nick flirting with her? The prospect seemed almost too good to be true. For the first time, in the two months he'd been there, he was actually treating her like she was more than just the secretary of his boss.

"That's... good to know," she breathed, staring wide-eyed up at him. She could have done anything he asked, right then. The handsome devil seemed to know it, as the next moment he was inviting her to dinner that evening.

It wasn't till minutes after he'd gone that she'd shaken out of her stupor, realizing she had promptly accepted to go out with him later that night at some fancy restaurant. She had a huge, triumphant grin on her face as she told herself she couldn't wait to break the news to Delia....

Both women were positively fuming.
It was their lunch break, and they were outside, taking a quick smoke, while they filled each other in on gossip. Lisa had wasted no time in announcing her new, soon-to-be, conquest of the hunky, Nick Freeman. Delia had gone rigid with disbelief. She spilled the beans about Nick asking her out to dinner for the next night.

"Why, that cad!" Delia cried, flinging away her cigarette and clenching her fists on her hips.

Lisa was looking at her accusingly. "Were you ever going to mention Nick asking you out?"

"What do you mean?" Delia frowned.

"You only decided to tell me about it after I'd brought up the fact that Nick wanted me to go out with him, to dinner tonight. You were going to keep it from me, weren't you?"

"What's that supposed to mean? I was definitely going to tell you. Maybe, not today...."

"I knew it," Lisa muttered. "You'd have dated him, behind my back, gloating all the while... really nice move, Delia. And to think we were pals and everything."

"Woah... May I remind you that Nick is the one to blame here, not me? Look, I didn't mean anything sinister by keeping anything from you. I just thought that, because you really liked him too, you might feel sort of put out. I was sparing your feelings, Lisa. I had the best intentions."

"So did I," Lisa said, deflating. "I wasn't trying to brag or anything when I brought it up. I was just so happy about the prospect."

Delia was shaking her head, angrily. "Look how he's making us go at each other. He really is a jerk. What was he planning to do, anyway? Have his way with you, tonight. Then, tomorrow would be my turn?"

"Despicable."

"Totally... we're not going to let him get away with it, are we?" Delia asked.

"No," Lisa replied, eyes narrowing. "He wants to have a go at us both... I guess we might as well oblige him...."

Nick could hardly wait to get the dinner over with. Sitting across from him was the very sexy, very eye-catching, Lisa. How come he'd never noticed how lovely her green eyes were? She'd worn an alluring satin gown, in a matching shade, and her hair was swept up in an elegant style. He could just imagine that lovely hair getting all mussed up.

"Dinner was delicious, Nick," she told him,

smiling when their dishes were finally cleared away. They were polishing off the last of the exquisite wine, after which Nick decided he was whisking her straight away to his place. Hopefully, she'd be of an equal mind. Then again, was Nick's cocky thought, "No woman had ever been able to say, 'no', to me." And, there was a special request he had to make of her, when the time arrived....

"I'm glad you enjoyed it," he said, with a slight, sensuous smile, lifting his glass in salute. "Let's hope you enjoy everything else I have in store for us tonight."

He saw her eyebrows rise, but he merely shook his head, not about to give her even a clue.

Inside his car, some time later, he casually asked her if she'd like to go to his place. She gave a shrug to indicate she wouldn't mind. He sent her a pleased smile.

"I must warn you, though, I don't live alone," he told her, as he drove them through the well-lit city streets.

She seemed surprised to hear this. "Oh? You have a roommate?"

"Something like that," he said, cagey as ever. He flashed her a reassuring grin. He didn't want her panicking and deciding to chicken out at the last minute for whatever reason. This was just step one of his plan, and it couldn't go awry, not with him so close to goal....

Lisa glanced, surreptitiously, at her watch. Almost nine pm, would Delia make it to his place on time? She thought of how the evening had gone so far. It had been such an effort not to act normal, like everything was cool. It was all so galling. She was, after all, attracted to him as ever. And tonight, away from the confines of the office, she'd gotten to know him better. It was hard, so hard, to be mad at him.

Yet, mad she was. He'd asked Delia out and he'd done the same to her. It wasn't flattering, in the least. Even if he was just messing about, with either of them, and didn't intend to go far, it still irked. No woman liked to be made a fool of.

Nick had a very nice apartment, very spacious and modern. Yet, Lisa was far too nervous to take note of the very masculine and elegant décor. She was more concerned about exactly what Nick had in mind.

"Would you like some wine?" He enquired, going across the living room to the fully stocked bar.

She shook her head. "I've had enough to drink already. A cup of coffee would be appreciated, though."

"That's great," an unexpected voice said. "Because, I make fantastic coffee."

Lisa swiveled round, to see a very gorgeous man standing in the doorway. Her eyebrows lifted high at the sight of him. He was dressed in nothing but a pair of low-slung blue jeans, and his body seemed like it was carved from marble—all smooth, hard planes. His striking face was framed by long locks of dark hair, and his square-cut jaw was shadowed with very sexy stubble.

"Hello," he grinned, dazzling Lisa with his white grin. He came forward, his bare feet padding silently to where she stood still a statue. "My name's Lawrence. Obviously, Nick didn't tell you about me."

"He...um... Mentioned, he had someone living with him," she spluttered, not sure she could say much more. Nick was standing behind the bar. She saw him smile at her expression, like he could read exactly what she was thinking. Lisa was certainly in a state of confusion. Whoever this Lawrence was, he was every bit as lethally sexy as Nick—only Lawrence had the upper hand at the moment, with him being half-dressed and all. Lisa swallowed with difficulty as she tried to rein her rampant female hormones in check.

"Hmm... that's a quaint way of putting it," Lawrence was saying in reply to her last comment. Lisa saw him hold out his hand, and when she placed her fingers in his, he raised them to his lips, gallantly.

"You're Lisa, I presume?" he inquired. "Nick has told me so much about you."

"Really?" She let out, somewhat breathlessly. "That's interesting, considering he never mentioned you."

He made a comical face as he released her hand with obvious reluctance. "I'll confess that we both like the element of surprise," he murmured, gazing down at her. She tried not to shiver beneath his smoldering gaze. His look had a meaning she could not yet dare define. Just what was up, she wondered.

"I'll go brew that coffee now," he said. "Let me guess... black, no sugar?"

"Perfect," she croaked and hoped she wasn't staring too hard at his nice, departing butt, when she said that. He looked over his shoulder at her, sending her a slight wink. Once again, she had to swallow.

Nick was smiling, teasingly, as he came to stand next to her and took a sip from his glass. "I hope you weren't too startled. I mean, he moved down here with me when I got the new position at the office. He's a theater actor, quite successful, but he's also laid back about a lot of things."

Lisa could imagine so, considering he was walking around shirtless, even with a strange female—her—around. However, she couldn't allow herself to be distracted and glanced at her watch again. Where was Delia? She was supposed to be here by now.

"I'm sure he is," Lisa finally replied, facing him with a tight smile. "But then, some men live quite free of certain scruples, don't they?"

He seemed to consider her enigmatic words for a moment, then shrugged. "I try to, at least, get by without hurting anyone. I'm no saint, but then who is?"

"Who indeed?" she murmured, trying to hold on to her irritation. Funny, he should talk about not hurting others, when he went about asking two different friends out. Lisa was positive he knew she was pals with Delia. He'd seen them talking together, more than once. So why had he taken the risk of being found out?

"That's why I was hoping you'd agree to a certain... arrangement of mine," he drawled, placing his drink to the side. Lisa's ears perked up. A what now?

"You see, Lawrence and I share more than just a flat," he continued, placing his hands on her waist and drawing her closer. Confused, she could only look up at him. "And when I told him I'd met two very charming, very sexy ladies, he was dying to get to meet you both. Tonight, I decided we'd spend some time together, see how it works. And tomorrow, I get to do the same with Delia. The only question is, which one of you would be amenable to our... proposition."

"Which... proposition?" Lisa asked, her head swimming with all the details. If he'd wanted to knock her for six, he'd chosen the best way to do it.

"We, Lawrence and I, get to fuck you."

He'd said it so simply. Yet, it had the strangest effect on Lisa. At once, her body responded, strongly, to the words and the images they evoked. "What?" She breathed, shuddering with a belly-hurting need that shocked and shamed her.

His smile was a little twisted. "A bit of an unconventional way to end a date night, but hell, Lisa, I've wanted you for weeks. And the thing is, I wanted Delia too. I just couldn't decide which I'd pick. Then Lawrence came up with the idea that I ask you both out and lay it on the line. We like to fuck women. Only we like to do it together, you, me, and him. I wish it could be rounded up to four, to include Delia, but I guess that would be pushing things." His grin was rueful now.

Lisa could hardly piece her thoughts together, but found herself saying, somewhat dazedly, "You never know, Nick. I mean... you'll get the perfect chance to ask her, sooner than you think."

"Huh?" He looked at her with a quizzical smile.

"Oh, Nick," she said, with an expressive sigh. "Gosh, why did you have to be so 'roundabout' with it all? I mean, we could have, all four, gone on a... a double date, or something, you, me, Lawrence, and Delia. As it is, Delia and I found out you asked us both out, and we felt you were being pretty slick. Now she's on her way here, tonight, in a bid to confront you." She grimaced. "We really wanted to make you feel pretty dumb. But now, Delia and I will be the ones who'll have cake on our faces."

Just as she finished speaking, Lawrence reappeared, bearing two mugs. He handed one to Lisa, a hopeful smile on his face as he turned to Nick. "Well? What's it going to be, buddy? Talk her into it?"

Nick shrugged, and simply turned to Lisa, his eyebrows raised. "It's all up to you, Lisa. I always thought you fancied me, and I was kind of hoping you'd fancy Lawrence as well. Fancy us enough to fuck us both tonight."

Lisa found herself taking a quick gulp of coffee and almost scalding her throat in the process. Her heart was racing, but she already knew that, even with it all being like something out of a Shakespearean comedy of errors, the whole idea totally appealed. Before she could reply, though, there came a knock on the door. Suddenly, she grinned. "Let me make a deal," she told them both. "If Delia agrees to join in and make it even, then, heck yes, let's do this..."

If anyone had thought, Delia would be in the least weirded out by everything; they were in for a surprise.

Once she arrived at the door about to spew fire and brimstone at "slick" Nick and came face-to-face with the hunky Lawrence, she got a little sidetracked. And when the whole truth got out about how Nick felt attracted to both her and Lisa and had been reluctant to choose, she let it be known that she could relate to that, because, right then, with both Nick and his utterly gorgeous friend, or roomate in the same room, she could hardly pick which one she'd like to fuck more.

Then, when she got the complete low-down on how it stood about Nick and Lawrence loving to have things a little crowded in the sheets, she was totally taken.

Hey, if the two fittest guys she'd ever met liked a bit of an orgy, no way she was refusing.

It seemed like such a clinical, businesslike proposition. These two, reckless females, agreeing to fuck these two virile hunks—one of them a complete stranger, which was the whole point. Nick liked the fact that they'd never met his pal before. It made it all the more random and kinky. Think about it, a foursome none of them expected—and heck, they were all grown. No one saw any big deal in trying out something different and exciting—certainly not the guys who'd done it a number of times before. There was always some willing girlfriend who didn't mind the idea in the slightest. However, Nick confessed to Delia and Lisa, much later, they'd never had it with two girls before, at the same time. So in the end, tonight was going to be a first for the guys too.

Lawrence was already half undressed, so all he had to do was take off his jeans. Both girls just stood there, staring at his totally naked, totally buff body, with no single trace of fat and, what looked like, plenty enough cock. They glanced at each other with obvious glee, which mounted, as Nick left the music player he'd been fiddling with and started to take off his own clothes.

The girls were enjoying the show. There was some jazzy tune playing in the background, and the Nick they'd never have believed could be so laid back did a bit of a sexy striptease, slowly, tugging off his shoes, socks, and trousers. Then he unbuttoned his shirt, revealing a broad chest, dusted with dark, silky hairs. Lisa and Delia were fairly drooling, at this point. He took his time, but he finally had all his clothes off, and he was just as hard and toned. Also, not surprisingly, hung like a horse.

"Oh boy," Lisa cooed, giving Delia that same look of, "are we dreaming?" Yet, there was no need for words. Somehow, they knew just what to do. Going to where the two men stood, side-by-side, naked as sin, Delia got to her knees in front of Nick, while Lisa knelt in front of Lawrence. Moments later, they each had a cock in their mouth, sucking with such dedicated enjoyment that Nick and Lawrence's moans of pleasure started to blend with the music.

Minutes later, both girls decided they wanted to swap, and they ended up getting a taste of each of the two magnificent cocks, springing right in front of them. Their hands worked, busily, on the shafts, as their lips and tongues slurped on the smooth bulbous caps. Soon, they were pushing both men onto their backs, on the floor, and Delia started undressing first. The moment she unhooked her bra, her massive tits bounced out, the nipples high and as taut as pebbles. She felt both men reach out to grope her roughly and she let out a groan, when Lawrence pinched her nipples within his fingers.

By this time, Lisa was wriggling out of her dress and was soon naked herself, leaning back on her elbows and spreading her knees wide, to reveal her completely waxed pussy, the lips glistening pink. In moments, Nick was diving between those legs, burying his face in her fragrant cunt. He guzzled away, his hands reaching up to massage her rounded C-cup boobs with their erect little nipples. His hands clasped the back of her knee, and he shoved it back, way back. This way, he could also rim her crack with his tongue, making her squirm when he poked a finger into her clenching sphincter.

Right then, Lawrence had himself straddling Delia's upper body, his cock positioned between her fabulous breasts. She cupped them in her hands and squeezed them together, while Lawrence's thick shaft shoved between the generous globes. He was groaning as he titty-fucked her. She was leaning forward so that her tongue came in contact with his cap every time he thrust. He was in bliss.

Nick could easily say the same himself. The taste of Lisa's pussy was like honey; he ate into her with hunger, sticking two wet fingers into her vaginal cave, fucking her steadily and making her cry out his name. His tongue found her clit and he tormented it as well, making her hips buck into his face as she covered his face in her juices. He couldn't stand it; his cock was on fire by this time and the taste and scent of her cunt had driven him past the edge.

Deciding he was past waiting, Nick reached for protection, got it on, and in moments had rocked his way into his first thrust. He surged into her pussy and felt her muscles clench around him like a sweet velveteen glove. Again and again, he pounded into her, feeling her wrap her legs around him as she lifted her bottom off the ground to meet his thrusts midway. Her hands raked all over his chest, grazing his nipples and driving him even further off the edge. He totally forgot to be careful as he slammed into her hot vibrating pussy. Everything went dark in his head, and all he could focus on was the pussy; the pulsing flesh wrapped around his own invading meat. It was fucking incredible.

Lawrence was virtually sitting on Delia's face by this time, his balls hanging over her chin. He'd fucked her tits, and now, he wanted to fuck her mouth. Fisting his cock in one hand, he guided it to Delia's parted lips, almost choking her, as several inches of cock got buried down her throat. Groaning, he withdrew, but only slightly. She kept her lips wrapped around his pole, her tongue busy on the inside, dancing on his cap which poked at her tonsils. He'd have busted his load right there in her sweet mouth, but he really needed to fuck her doggy-style first.

In the meantime, his gaze fastened on Nick who was humping fast in between Lisa's high, widely parted thighs. Lawrence felt his cock hardened even more at the sight of Nick's ass as he pumped into Lisa, again and again. Unable to resist, Lawrence reached out an arm and slapped that firm, tanned ass hard, just like he knew Nick enjoyed. Every time Nick thrust into Lisa, Lawrence would spank him, sharply, and make him moan. It felt so flipping hot.

Suddenly, inspired by the muscled firmness of Nick's ass, Lawrence lifted himself off Delia. Taking hold of her waist, he flipped her on her hands and knees, getting her to lift her wiggling little ass in the air. Then, he ground his face into it. Licking, eating, and slurping, he smashed his tongue and mouth all over her slit, sliding from her lips to her tiny ass crack. He growled his pleasure at how good she tasted, what, with her shoving back on his face and burying his nose within her generous ass cheeks. He felt like he was in some kind of heaven.

The only thing that could top that was him, finally, getting to fuck his cock into her ass properly. He rimmed her sphincter up good, widening her up, bit by bit with his fingers. She tucked her face on her folded arms and writhed as he fucked her first, with one finger then two, stretching her ass up. With his other hand, he stroked on her pussy, which was slick with her lust-sap.

Unable to resist any longer, he straightened on his knees and punched his long, hard, fat cock into her pussy first of all, giving the tight gash some fast hot fucking, before withdrawing and popping his cunt-juiced cock past her asshole. She moaned at the maddening flash of pleasure and pain that racked her body and made her thighs quiver, but she didn't stop him. She didn't stop him sliding in, deeper, past her tighter hole, which expanded slowly to his girth.

By this time, Nick had fucked his way up to his first climax, exploding deep inside Lisa's pussy as she shuddered against him in her own perfectly timed climax. For a few moments, they clung to each other, their breaths coming out fast and ragged. Soon, however, Nick slipped out of her spasming pussy. He lay back, positioned in front of the kneeling Delia who was grimacing in sweet pain, as Lawrence mercilessly fucked her ass.

She had her face right before Nick's parted thighs, and it just seemed the right thing to do to take hold of his still erect cock and begin to suck it free of cum. He moaned his delight at her thoughtful service, one hand reaching to squeeze her swinging tits brushing the ground beneath her. As she sucked on Nick's dick and got him rearing to go again, Lisa was now horny as ever, choosing to squat her sopping cunt over Nick's face and making him lick up all of her gushed-out pussy drops. Sitting hard on his face, she hardly gave him the chance to breathe in anything else but her hot, sticky pussy which he licked clean.

It wasn't much later that Lisa decided she was good and ready to get her taste of Lawrence's dick. Lifting herself off Nick, she went and knelt right beside Delia so that her ass was right in the air as well. Lawrence knew exactly what she desired. She wanted that cock out of Delia's sweet ass and into her juicy pussy. Lawrence was quick to oblige, groaning out loud as his dick sliced through her cunt and found it slick and syrupy. He fucked her good, building the tempo till she was all but pushed forward by his hard thrusts. He erupted deep inside her womb moments later, causing her to arch and screech as her second climax ripped through her.

They all went at each other like sex fiends; all through the night, it was like a marathon. The pussies dripped, while the cocks were in constant states of solid enthusiasm. Every hole was fucked and plumbed with relish, taking the wild, wanton girls, both to their own respective paradises. It seemed like such a perfect union, and even as they romped till there was almost nothing left, each knew that this would be far from the last time they'd be coming together for such a feast of flesh. Now that they'd found each other, there was no way they wouldn't take the opportunity, again and again. There would certainly be many, many more nights of abandon to follow.

"You still owe me some Thai dinner"

"It's a date."

4 RED HOT REVENGE

Nessa Brody had things all figured out. She'd come to the bar that night with a couple of friends to have fun, drink, and dance away her sorrows – and get laid.

Yep, it really was that cut and dried. No one would ever accuse her of being complicated. A very attractive career woman, she knew the stakes when it came to city life. She'd grown up in a small town, true, but she'd picked up a lot once she moved into the big league and started hanging with the movers and shakers. And the basic fact was this: life was no fairy tale. No "prince charming" was going to come throw you over his shoulder. You wanted something; you just went out and grabbed it.

And Nessa saw something she wanted right here.

Todd Walken had always caught her eye. They had mutual friends and always seemed to bump into each other at parties and bars like this one. He was always with someone else, as was she. But tonight, she'd come with her girl pals, while he was hanging out with a couple of guys. Would this be the perfect opportunity to get things on with him as she'd always secretly hoped?

He was standing several yards away, talking with one of his buddies. He was easily the tallest in his circle, with wavy hair so dark it seemed to have traces of blue in its depths. For now, all she had was his profile – and what a profile. Handsome in every feature, he was the kind of guy that would make a normal girl take a second – and third look. And for a hormone-blasted young woman like Nessa, well, he made her do more than look – he made her pussy twitch as she tried to imagine what it would be like to fuck him.

Right then, he looked around and caught her gaze. She didn't look away and smiled in the usual friendly manner. Not too much of a come-on in it, just a hint of warmth to let him see she liked him. So it sort of irked when he seemed to just look right through her and shift his gaze somewhere else.

"Well!" she thought, burying her nose in her drink. It was her fault, she decided, for thinking that just because she was attracted to someone that he'd even noticed her in return. He probably couldn't even remember her name, Nessa felt. They'd met countless times, and though they'd never really spoken, she always felt that given the chance, there could be a bit of chemistry there.

Wishful thinking, obviously, thought Nessa, as she turned her back to him and tried to pay attention to her own group. They were chatting animatedly over the loud music in the bar. It had been meant to be a kind of "girl's night out" for all three of them: a few drinks, some dancing, and then back home. Unless any of them got lucky and found someone totally hot to take home and chase away the nightly chills....

Nessa never thought of it all as being even remotely promiscuous. She couldn't even remember the last time she'd had sex. But when she needed to get it on, well, then she needed to. Now if only Todd would just walk up behind her and whisper in her ear how much he wanted her; then she'd count the night as perfect.

It didn't happen, of course. He didn't even ask her to dance, even though a couple of his other friends came over to do so. She had a few twirls on the floor, deciding to enjoy herself at least. There was some heavy flirting from her male partners, but she wasn't biting. She liked them as friends but wasn't into any of them. They must have sensed this, because each time, they backed down with good-natured smiles.

Feeling somewhat flushed, Nessa decided to take a few minutes to escape to the ladies' to freshen up. Repairing a bit of the damage caused by her enthusiastic dancing, Nessa made her way back. On the right side of her was the corridor leading up to the men's, and she heard a familiar voice say her name. This made her stop dead in her tracks as, without thinking, she listened to the conversation.

She recognized the voice who'd said her

name to be Peter, a guy she liked but had never dated, though he'd asked her out several times. Another voice replied to him, and Nessa instantly recognized it as Todd's. Wondering what they could possibly have to say about her, she inched closer to the corridor where they seemed to have paused after emerging from the men's room.

"She's been dazzling all night," Peter was saying. "I could hardly take my eyes off her. I really would have tried to ask her out again, but I'm certain now that she's got a totally different interest. I think she likes you, Todd."

Nessa could hear a teasing note in Peter's voice and held her breath for Todd's reply. "What makes you say that?" were Todd's disinterested-sounding words.

"Intuition, I guess. Besides, I went out with one of her friends, Sally, who mentioned something to that effect. Well? Are you going to make your move?"

"Sorry dude, but I think I'd pass. She's far from my type – and besides, you know it's just a week since I broke up with Jen."

"Fuck Jen," Peter said with a good-natured laugh. "She was far too controlling for you. Trying to tell you what you should wear, eat, and even where to go. And she even tried to transfer that dominating spirit to us, your friends. Trust me, you're far better off with someone like say, Nessa."

"Like I said, buddy, not interested. A bit too hard-edged for my taste."

"You can't deny thought that she's got the charisma, not to talk of the looks."

Nessa grimaced with annoyance when she

heard Todd chuckle scornfully. "Yeah, sure she's got the charisma...of an iceberg."

Ouch, Nessa thought, pressing her back against the wall as they seemed to approach where she stood. She fervently prayed they'd walk round the corner without looking to the left and find her standing there.

"Come on, Todd. Don't tell me you got fooled by her snow-queen façade," Peter was saying. By now they'd turned the corner from the men's room and were making straight back to the bar. Nessa heaved a sigh of relief as she watched their backs receding down the end of the hall. She could just catch Peter's last comment about her being "really nice once one got to know her."

They were gone; their voices had finally faded away. Nessa bit on her lip and wondered why she felt strangely hurt. She thought of all those times she'd wondered why Todd had never asked her out or anything. Well, now she knew.

And then she felt really pissed. What right had he to speak about her in that way? Fine, he was welcome to his opinion, but it still irked that he could call her "hard-edged." Which she totally wasn't! Nessa had never guessed she came across like that. In a world where women with a beautiful face and body were usually overlooked as brain-dead, Nessa had strove to make a way for herself in her field. And that had meant standing up a lot for herself. If it had in turn made her seem cold and unapproachable, then it was no fault of hers, but the fault of the person making such a perception.

The truth was, Todd didn't want to like her, she surmised. But why? Nessa had a feeling she just might find out one day– and prove him wrong about her not being his type.

"Oh no, here she was again," Todd thought with a strange lurch in his chest. For the third night in a row, he was bumping into the blonde, brown-eyed Nessa. This time she was dressed in some kind of silvery smock, well above her knees and halter-necked to give a great show of skin. Her beautiful hair was done up in an elegant ponytail, and the first thing that came to mind was how he liked his woman to tie her hair up like that. He liked when he fucked her from behind and could take hold of that ponytail and pull her head back so that her body almost arched in half and he could kiss her on the lips. Or when he had her kneeling in front of him and taking his cock in her mouth, the ponytail was just as great to keep her hair off her face so that he could watch her deep-throat his throbbing hard shaft.

He felt himself go hard at those images. Why did he always think of sex when he saw that Nessa woman? It annoyed him because he hated to lose control, even just mentally. No one could read his mind, thankfully. They'd be surprised to know that his apparent aloofness for Nessa was just a cover. He wanted her too much – and that made him stay the heck out of her way.

He stiffened when he realized she was walking straight for him right then. But all she did was turn to the bartender standing inches away, behind the bar, and ordered a drink. He had the first whiff of her perfume: something exotic, musky. A downright fuck-me scent that would get any red-blooded guy panting and in heat just being next to her. His eyes roamed over her delicate nape, which was turned to him. He had the weird feeling she was ignoring him, which was weird because she usually acted quite friendly while he acted the total jerk, if he remembered correctly.

Feeling strangely like making amends, he tapped her gently on the shoulder. "Hi."

She seemed to stop short, hesitate, and then turn to him with a wide-eyed stare. "Sorry, did you say something to me?"

His lips curved at her mockingly incredulous look. Okay, he got the point. He must have pissed her off once or twice by cold-shouldering her. But what did she want? A guy who always drooled at her feet like the other morons? Todd figured he had more sense than that.

But he didn't want her thinking the worst of him. "I said hello. We've never actually got to talk. You're Nessa, right?"

"And you're Todd," she returned coolly, taking the drink which the bartender placed before her. Todd quickly offered to pay for it, and she made a careless shrug.

"Well, if the niceties are over, I hope you don't mind if I go back to my friends," she said with a smile that didn't reach her eyes.

"I think I do mind," he said, surprising

himself as well as her. He gave her a charming grin. "I'm not used to an attractive woman running off the first chance she gets."

"Hmm," she nodded in agreement. "I guess you're more used to them slobbering all over you."

His grin widened. "That's funny – I was just thinking the same thing about you – but with men. I've seen the way they swarm around whenever you show up."

"What can I say?" she shrugged. "Some guys have good taste."

He had a funny feeling those words had an underlying dig somewhere, directed straight at him. But he chose to ignore it. Instead, he asked her, "Would you like to dance?"

Once again she hesitated, and then he could swear that a calculative look crossed her eyes for a second. And then she shrugged. "Sure."

He smiled, somewhat cocky. Then he took the glass from her hand, took a sip while he held her brown-eyed gaze. Her eyes narrowed speculatively. And Todd wondered, does she know the effect she has on me, and how much I want to just carry her off somewhere and fuck her brains out?

They danced to the hip-grinding slow tune that was playing in the dimly lit bar right then. Other couples moved around them, but Todd felt like they were in their own little world for a second. He'd wanted to feel her close in his arms, wanted to find out if he hadn't imagined that spark he felt any time she was near. It took moments of having her body wedged into his, for him to discover that he'd been fooling himself all along for even doubting her desirability. If there was ever a woman he'd want to have on-the-spot sex with, it was Nessa. Right there, on the dance floor. No foreplay, no teasing, just a straight-up fuck. To lift her up on his flanks, position her over his cock, and just drive straight into her while she bounced her pussy up and down on his pulsating shaft.

He went hard as a plank just thinking of it. She had to have felt the solid ridge pressed against her belly. Todd was thankful at least that the club wasn't brightly lit. And he wondered what she'd say if he suddenly suggested they leave, right then. Just find the nearest motel and fuck each other senseless.

As if she read his mind, she leaned back, looking up at him through sultry eyes. "That had better not be your Blackberry poking me in the stomach, sweetheart. Wanna get out of here?"

"Yes," he heard himself croak. She led him out of the bar, and when they got out in the fresh night air, Todd felt himself start to get a bit of cold feet. This was Nessa, right? Did he really want to get it on with her?

Heck yes, his cock told him. Damn the consequences, he decided. He'd fuck her, and then he could worry about the repercussions. Right now, he just wanted to push his misgivings aside and just let things flow.

"I know somewhere just minutes away," he suggested, stopping in front of his low-slung automobile. "Discreet, classy."

"My kind of place," she purred, getting into the car. He smiled in triumph and joined her.

It really took them just under ten minutes to get there. He booked them a room, and in record time it seemed, they were alone in the pristine though impersonally styled bedroom.

Moments later, it was like unleashing the dragon – or whatever had seethed between them all those months they'd skirted around each other. Now, with no one and nothing around to stop them, it seemed pointless to stand on ceremony. They undressed each other with expert, record speed, tumbling to the bed in a tangle of limbs. Their lips meshed and dueled in kiss after kiss, while their hands roamed boldly over every naked inch.

She was just as beautiful as he'd imagined – even more so. He cupped her melon-sized breasts and groaned at how firm and yet fleshly they felt. He bent his mouth to grab one light pink nipple in his mouth and nibbled. She moaned and squirmed underneath him, grabbing his cock in her hand. As she pumped her fist around his burgeoning staff, he guided his free hand between her parted thighs and forayed her slick, waiting pussy.

No doubt about it, she was soaking wet. It made his head swim, especially as he could almost smell her delicious juices wafting up to tease his nostrils. Short of breath like he was running the marathon, he tore his lips from her nipples and slid down her concave belly to the shaved V between her legs. Her pussy was tightly furled, like the petals of a rose bud.

He heard her gasp as his fingers parted her swollen folds to expose her inner secrets to his hungry gaze. Unable to wait a second more, he tasted her. Slid his tongue flat against her slit and slurped. She bucked against him, grabbing fistfuls of his hair and urging him every step of the way. If there was one thing Todd liked, it was to eat pussy. And Nessa's had to be the most scrumptious cunt he'd ever had the pleasure of chomping. He dove in and ground his face into that pussy, chewing, licking, and lapping, his thumb stroking her erect clit all the while. Not letting up with his tongue, he then shoved his fingers into her tight vagina and began a hard, fast rhythm of fucking. He just loved the sounds of squelching as her sodden cunt clenched and unclenched on his ravaging fingers.

He finger-fucked her fiendishly while she moaned out loud, her thighs quivering. Moments later, he could taste her gushing on his tongue as she came with a shrill cry. Her whole body shuddered for a full minute before her breath slowed and she looked like she was back down to earth.

Todd didn't give her much of any recovery time, not when his cock was so painfully hard it looked like he'd explode any second. Kneeling close to her head, he fisted himself while his other hand took a grip of her ponytail and urged her face up to take his pole-straight shaft in her mouth. Her lips parted willingly, sucking on his pre-cum-tipped cap. She licked on it, her head bobbing steadily as she took in more and more inches of his hot, throbbing dick. He groaned so loud the sounds vibrated against the motel room walls. His hands on her head tugged her closer, causing her to gag on his meat each time. But she didn't stop, intending on pleasuring him as he had her.

Todd was tempted, so tempted, to spurt his cum in her hot, giving mouth. And yet, he found the willpower to hold back just on the plateau, pulling away from her lips with a growl. "Fuck baby, that was good," he rumbled, tugging on her ponytail and making her look up at him with her flashing brown eyes. "I've wanted this so long I may not hold back...and sometimes, I may forget to be gentle. Once I get my cock inside your pussy, Nessa, it's going to be one long, hard ride."

"You won't catch me complaining," she purred, pushing him on his back and straddling him. "Cause I don't do gentle, either. I like it rough, sugar. So give me all you got."

"Now that's what I want to hear," was his throaty reply, his fingers digging into her waist as he arched up and embedded his cock within her moist cunt. She enveloped him like a velvet glove, clamping him inside her wall of flesh. He groaned, looking up into her blissful face. Her boobs swung invitingly just above him, and he grasped one and then the other, massaging it with rough, punishing fingers. She moaned, throwing her head back as she danced her hips upon his flanks, pumping herself on his driving shaft. He could feel her stretching around his width as he seemed to broaden deep within her. She slammed hard on him again and again, making him go balls deep, just how he liked. Damn, she was such a great fuck, he couldn't help thinking that maybe she was the best he'd ever had. Her pussy was so tight yet so giving, and she had the sexiest breasts, which fit perfectly in his palm.

She'd told him she liked it rough, and he hadn't forgotten. He slapped experimentally on her breasts, just sharp enough to sting but not bruise. Her moan of delight told him he had the green light. Pinching hard on her nipples, he shoved his cock up her pussy as far as it would go. She cried out in sweet torment, balancing on her feet so she was now crouched atop him, giving him even deeper access up her cunt.

Looking down, he could see how her pussy clung to his pole, her pink flesh almost seeming like it was welded to his rock hard meat. Taking his hands to wrap around her throat, he tightened his grip and felt her blink as for a few moments; she had a sensation of choking. He squeezed harder, and it seemed to set her even more aflame. She rode him even faster, her hands holding on to his wrists as he dug his fingers in her delicate neck, almost cutting off her oxygen. It was only for a moment, but it got her so close to the peak that he felt her pussy walls clench on his cock in spasm after spasm. The next moment, she shuddered into her second climax.

Letting go of her throat, Todd quickly switched their positions, keeping himself deep inside her even as he drew her beneath him. She was still gasping from the exertion of her release; and once again, he didn't allow her to get fully back down to earth. Taking hold of the back of her knees, he shoved them way back, placing her feet on his shoulders as he rocked his dick harder and faster within her now sodden pussy. The sensation of her slippery, tight cunt vibrating around his punishing thrusts soon had him blasting into his own explosive eruption. He ground into her, unable to hold back the growls coming from deep in his throat. He didn't think he'd ever come so hard, or for so long before. He pumped rope after rope of cum up her squelching pussy till he was sure he was drained dry.

And then he wanted to do it all over again....

He woke up an hour later to find her getting dressed. Grabbing for her, he was surprised when she drew further back, reaching for her coat.

"Wouldn't have thought you were the fly-by type of lover," he teased.

"Well, you'd know all about types, wouldn't you?" she returned, eye brow lifted mockingly. "That was great sex, Todd. But that was all it was."

"Woah," he said, with a quizzical smile, as he straightened, reaching for his boxers and pulling them on. "Sure, it was great. Great enough for me to think maybe we'd better not let a good thing go to waste. Now that we know we're so sexually compatible...."

"Trust me, there's no point. Considering I have the charisma of an iceberg..." she said, shrugging and holding his gaze meaningfully.

Suddenly, her attitude made sense. Todd looked sheepish for a moment. "You overheard what I said?"

"Every word," she said, tossing her hair carelessly. "But I guess I had to prove a point that you, like most guys, don't know shit about what you really want."

"I always knew I wanted you," he confessed. "And so I hid behind a mask and told myself it was all wrong – we wouldn't work. But now, hey...I've seen the light, totally. Not only are you my type, you're near freaking perfect." He grinned wolfishly. "Any woman that can fuck like that gets an 'A' in my book."

"Thanks for the vote of confidence," she murmured, heading for the door. "I'll keep that in mind if I ever decide to change my mind and give you a second chance."

Somehow, even with her walking out, Todd knew this was far from over. There was that teasing glint in her eye that told him that though she'd had a bit of her revenge, she wasn't done with him yet.

"I'll hold you to that," he told her with a hopeful grin. And then she was gone.

5 HOME IMPROVEMENTS

Preface

Crazy things happen when you least expect them. Like when a simple visit from a hunky home designer could turn into a pleasure fest for two very, very hot-blooded people.

The moment Fiona opened her front door and saw Riley Swank, she decided she just might require his services in a whole new different way entirely. And she soon discovered that he certainly had the right-sized tools to do a commendable job....

Fiona could not believe her eyes. The most virile, gorgeous, and totally edible guy she'd ever seen was standing outside her doorstep. She'd rushed to open the door to the ring moments ago, expecting to see Cheryl, her best friend, only to come face to face with this hunk of a male.

The first thing she thought was that he'd definitely got the wrong house. What would a tall, blonde, gym-lithe guy dressed in jeans and a denim shirt be doing in front of her doorway at 9 AM in the morning?

"Are you...looking for someone?" she asked, trying not to seem like she was drooling. Damn, but he was sizzling! His dark-blonde hair was swept over his forehead in thick, wavy locks. He had a chiseled, golden-tanned face and eyes so blue they made her just want to fall into them. And his lips – oh my, they were shaped just for kissing. Simply looking at those lips made her think how she'd like them running all over her body, on her nipples, between her legs....

"I'm from the home improvements company – HomeProv. You rang a week ago to schedule an appointment?"

At last, his words registered and she forced herself to stop staring at his gorgeous mouth as it formed the sentences. Even his voice was sexy: deep, husky, like gravel beneath the tires. She shivered in her light robe. She'd only thrown it on seconds before opening the door, thinking Cheryl was back from the grocery store. They'd been planning on doing some baking and had needed a few extra items. Cheryl had volunteered to go to the supermarket since Fiona had only just recovered from a terrible flu and she was still a bit under the weather. But at the sight of Mr. Gorgeous here, she felt right as rain.

She hugged the lapels of her robe tighter

around her, aware that it gaped a little from being at least a size too small. She'd had it for years; it was her favorite kimono style robe and it was pure silk. And now she couldn't help but notice how his bedroom-blue eyes swept quickly over her straining assets. Fiona knew she was racked, and most of her ex-boyfriends had told her that was the first feature they got to notice about her. She mostly felt offended when they'd said that, but for some reason, when the hunk in front of her flicked his gaze appreciatively over her D-cup kimonoed boobs, she felt certainly glad she had enough for him to look at.

But he didn't gawp. He brought his gaze right back up to above chin level, schooling his features into calm courtesy. "I'm Riley. Riley Swank. I know we told you last time we were booked up for appointments, but today we got a client who cancelled, so…" He was cocking his thick dark brow quizzically, and Fiona suddenly realized he was expecting her to actually speak, say something.

"Wow, that's great," Fiona croaked, forcing her brain to function. HomeProv was a prestigious though small home improvements firm. They'd been recommended by a colleague and she'd been looking forward to having someone come over and work out some improvement ideas for her bathroom. They were hideously expensive, but Fiona had heard they were worth every big buck. She'd been so dismayed when she'd been told last week that they couldn't make an appointment to see her till next month and now this surprise.

"Maybe I should have...called first?" the guy called Riley said hesitantly, looking at her with that same questioning expression, and Fiona knew she'd better get her act together if she didn't want to seem like a psycho.

"No...yes – I mean, that's fine," she blurted, then smiled cheerily. "It was just that I wasn't expecting anyone. Well, except my friend who should be back soon."

He nodded understandingly. "If this is an awkward time, I'll understand. We were just glad we could work you in especially since you said a friend suggested you to us. That's okay; we can send someone on Monday."

"Someone else?" she asked casually.

"Yes, I'm afraid I will be out of town on another assignment. That's why I rushed here today; I saw the photos and the plans you had, from your file, and was eager to see what can be done before I left. But no worries, my partner is just as capable to..."

"Today will be fine," she said at once, smiling at him once again. If she may never get the chance to see him again, she wasn't going to blow it. She couldn't help wondering how old he was. He looked young, maybe no more than twenty five. Fiona didn't want to feel like such a cougar because, hey, she was only twenty eight and well kept for her age. She'd been told by her envious friends that she still had the same figure from her first year in college. Well, give or take a few inches, she thought to herself, tugging her tight kimono once again.

"Do come in, Mr. Swank," she said, turning and walking on into the house. He came in after her, shutting the door behind them.

"Riley, please."

"Then you must call me Fiona," she replied, smiling over her shoulder at him. She liked the way his gaze was shifting all over her booty, which wasn't bad either she knew. Hmm, the guy sure knew how to check a lady out without making her feel objectified, she thought. Any other strange man look her over like that, she'd have felt like smacking his face or, at least, felt like bristling in anger. But she liked to have Riley look at her. She liked it a lot.

"Would you...like to go up with me and look it over?" she asked, turning to face him in the spacious living room. She'd had the house done Mediterranean style, and the décor was fresh, reviving, and clean. The only thing was now she wanted to do something more modern with her main bathroom, which was upstairs.

"If you don't mind," he murmured, and she nodded and then headed up the stairs, leading the way. Once there, she waved her arms round expansively. "As you can see, I simply feel like it brings down the tone to the whole place," she said. "I really want something totally different and alluring."

He was nodding, looking around at the very clean, large-sized bathroom. "What matters is that the bathroom has a great ground plan which is always important as a basic for us to work on. I can definitely think of several ideas that would turn this into just the right mix of comfort and modernity. This sink, however, needs to be..."

"No, don't touch it," she yelped in warning,

rushing forward. But she was too late; he'd bumped his knee into the enamel, and the next thing, water came gushing out from a dislodged brick in the wall.

"What the..."

"Sorry! Oh my gosh, I forgot to warn you about that," she was wailing, as she joined him to try and wedge the loose brick back. It took several moments, but soon it was closed up again. By then, they were both soaked through.

Dripping, she turned to him with a sheepish smile. His light denim shirt was now clinging to his lithe, muscled body, outlining every carved contour. His blue jeans were now dark and wet and tighter, it seemed. And there was a very huge, tell-tale wedge growing right in his crotch.

Her smile disappeared, shock and lust rushing right through her as she realized what had happened. His eyes seemed fixated on her body, locked on her now sodden robe. She looked down and saw that she could as well have been naked. Her kimono, now wet, was practically see-through, and her large, firm breasts were traced perfectly, their rounded curves jutting proudly. To make matters worse, her treacherous nipples were sticking out, fat, hard, and high-profiled. The rest of the robe was wrapped tight to her curvy hips, even outlining the shape of her mound, revealing that she was wearing zero underwear. Her swollen cameltoe was so embarrassingly obtruding behind the wet robe that she felt herself blush furiously.

She bit her lip and stared up at him, the

atmosphere charged with so much electricity that it was crackling. She swallowed convulsively at the dark, hot lust that turned his blue eyes almost black. He was staring at her like he was about to tear her into pieces, just grabbing her and devour her right there in the flooded bathroom.

There was a moment of clarity, as Fiona told herself to just laugh things off, apologize, and then rush out to get changed. Or just rush out, period, before she was ravished on the spot by the horny-looking home improvement guy.

But then she glanced down at his crotch again and lost focus. The moment of clarity passed, never to be remembered. The jeans were doing nothing to hide how massive his cock was, the length reaching down at least nine inches. She could even see the outline of his cap, slightly tapering like an arrowhead. She felt a different kind of wetness gather copiously between her thighs.

"I think I'd better..." he said in a strangled voice, as he seemed to recover enough to try and move out of the bathroom. Fiona had the impression that he had figured they were both in a dangerous position and one of them needed to make the move for some damage control.

Certainly dangerous for them both, she mused with a lurch in her belly. Because neither one knew who was going to jump who.

And because, damn it, she was ready to "rape" him if she had to. Rip off his shirt, wrench down his jeans, and suck on that massive, jean-clad cock, get it all slobbered up and then straddle it till it felt like it would come right out of her throat. Her imagination was already running wild at what such a girth and length could do to her own tight canal. She'd never had one so big and she felt her own cunt clenching and unclenching in hunger and recognition of a true pleasure-giver of a cock.

"Yes," she finally agreed, her voice throaty. "I think you'd better."

But he wasn't moving out the door; he was moving straight for her. They collided into each other like a violent clash of cymbals, lips meeting in a fierce, magnetic kiss. Riley pushed his hand right past her robe to cup her breasts, making her moan against his lips. She, too, was just as forward, as her own hand groped down the front of his jeans as if to make sure that her eyes hadn't deceived her.

Nope, they hadn't. He truly was built like an ox. Her pussy vibrated in kinetic response as her fingers trailed down the length of his cock still imprisoned by the wet jeans. The next second, her hands were desperately working on the button and zipper until the hot, throbbing member popped out like a huge mamba.

Fucking hell, Fiona thought in deep feminine delight, as her hands wrapped lovingly around his huge cock. He'd pushed her kimono off her shoulders by now and had her breasts in the open, and he began to knead them hungrily, stroking the thick nipples and squeezing hard.

"I've never seen such beautiful breasts," he groaned, breaking the kiss to gaze down at her tits which he was fondling passionately in both of his big hands. "I feel like fucking my cock between them and then coat them in cum when I'm done."

Fiona moaned out loud at the prospect, her fists masturbating his huge cock. "And I feel like taking this big fat dick in my mouth and sucking it," she confessed. "I don't even know what's come over me..."

"Neither do I," he growled. "But the second you opened that door and I saw you, I wanted to fuck you. I was so afraid of what I'd be tempted to do if you let me into the house. And now that this has happened, I want you to know that you can stop it. At any time." His face had a painful grimace, as if making the promise was like ripping his own arm off.

"Do I look like I'm about to stop anything?" she challenged, eyes blazing up into his. He sighed deep and raggedly in relief.

"Boy am I glad to hear that. But...what about your friend? You said you're expecting her back soon..."

"Any minute now," she agreed, pushing herself closer up against him so that her hard nipples rubbed against his solid chest. Purring, she added, "Which is why we have to get this show on the road pronto."

The sense of urgency seemed to add even more excitement to it all. Now that they knew how little time they had, they were frenzied.

He was ripping out of his clothes, which took like three seconds. Then they stumbled out to Fiona's bedroom, and somehow she lost her robe along the way. Both naked, they tumbled unto the bed, their bodies still slightly damp.

Riley immediately went for her tits again, this time bending his head to suckle at them hungrily and making them both groan. He rubbed and pressed them roughly, pulling strongly on her nipple with his lips and teeth. Fiona almost shed tears of pleasure at the sensation. His other hand dipped low to stroke her hairless pussy with its swollen, slick lips. He shoved his fingers in three at a time and began fucking her with them in deep, hard strokes.

"Oh fuck," she sobbed her whole body on fire with ecstasy. She fisted his cock at the same time, rubbing her hand all over and spreading his plentiful precum so that it lubricated her palm. He was moaning in approval, even as he nibbled on the full, firm flesh of her breasts.

Moments later, he pushed her on her back, and Fiona readily let him straddle her high on her waist so that she could come face to face with that horse cock of his.

"What a beautiful monster," she breathed, cupping the sides of her breasts together as he slid his cock into her cleavage. He grunted with pleasure as he pumped his shaft between her gorgeous tits, and hungry to taste him, Fiona leaned forward so that she could flick his pointed cap with her tongue each time he slid forward with his hips.

"Arrggh," he growled, throwing his head

back as he titty-fucked her faster. Fiona loved to feel that big hot meat shoving in the middle of tits, his hands molding and squeezing them lovingly. His cock was well lubed by precum as well as her enthusiastic blowjob which had him coated in saliva. He was sliding in and out smoothly, his pleasure evident from his deep moans. Fiona could swear his monstrous cock was growing even larger by the second and she felt so aroused and excited by the obvious pleasure she was giving him.

He kept groaning loudly with passion and she guessed he was very close to spurting his sperm. The next second, he was pulling back with a deep gasp.

"Damn, can't cum just yet; I need to fuck this wet juicy looking pussy of yours," he said enthusiastically, taking his cock in his hand and moving his weight off her. Fiona had no objection to that suggestion. She'd never felt her cunt pour out so much moisture before; she was like a busted tap down there herself.

Reaching for her bed-side dresser, she quickly unearthed a condom from the pack she always had in the bottom drawer. She waved it in the air and he took it with gladness.

"My kind of woman...always prepared," he said with deep approval, as he sheathed his massive member. Fiona really hoped the condom would hold, seeing how it seemed incredibly stretched. She wondered absent-mindedly if there were such things as extra-large condoms. Well, since she'd never come in contact with a guy this huge, she'd never had cause to ask. After today, she swore she'd definitely do some research just to make sure.

Wanting to feel the utmost penetration from that cock, even if it killed her, she lay on her back and widened her legs. He settled eagerly between them, lifting one of her ankles over his shoulder and lining his long, thick dick in front of her quivering pussy.

"Fuck me Riley," she gasped, as he slowly ran the tip up and down her wet slit. "Rip me in half with that beast of a cock."

"Aah, baby," he sighed, shuddering with pleasure as in one quick motion, he thrust into her. Fiona screamed. The intrusion was terribly sweet and painful, so much that she felt her entrance literally seem like it was ripping. Just like she'd told him she liked it.

"Don't stop," she screeched in protest as he made to withdraw and roll off her. "Are you crazy?" And to buttress her point, she grabbed his ass cheeks and pushed him into her deep.

"Damn, Fiona," he said on a gasp. "Most women can't take so much of me up them...are you sure it's okay? Can you handle it?"

"I'm sure as hell going to try my darnedest," she swore through gritted teeth, feeling like her belly was being ruptured as he thrust into her again. It felt so good it hurt. Pleasure like this could change a woman's life forever, Fiona thought dazedly; it'd make her never see cocks the same way again. Having something so big, hot, and meaty inside her beat any kind of the best sex toy a woman could buy.

As he fucked her in a steady, fast motion, he bent his head to her upturned tits and latched his mouth to a nipple. He used just the right suction to get her moaning and bucking into his mouth, just as her hips pushed up to meet his pounding thrusts. Her pussy clenched on him tight and then released, sheathing him like a breathing velvet glove. He was groaning loud against her breasts, his hips beginning to move so quick it made her eyesight blur. Having that huge pole of meat pistoning in her at that measured pace, with his hungry sucking at her breasts, became too much for her. Seconds later she was crying out that she was coming. Convulsive shudders rocked them both as Riley, too, gave in to his own release as if he'd been only waiting only for her signal.

He was still hard as a plank, still buried deep inside her, when Fiona tumbled back down to earth. Blinking her eyes into focus, she stared up at his smiling face, his hair plastered to his scalp. "I wasn't going to last much longer," he admitted with a boyish grin. "I'm happy though that I was able to satisfy you first, because I was ready to bust my load the second you grabbed me inside that tight pussy of yours."

"And that pussy is never going to forget your cock in a hurry, that's for sure. I feel like it's stretched out of shape now," she joked, moaning as he slowly pulled out. She felt him experimentally run his fingers down and into her sodden, sensitive vaginal walls. She couldn't help moaning again.

"Still feels snug enough to me," he said with husky approval. "But perhaps after ten or twelve times of having my cock in you, there'll be a different story." His smile was teasing.

"Most of my exes were always worried about that. That's why I'm kinda single now. My last girlfriend was really tiny."

"Well, it's really strange, because I'm single too," Fiona said with eyes widened playfully. "And I'm far from tiny. Have you ever heard of kegels? Those exercises will keep me as tight as I need to be around this huge pussy-pleaser of yours."

He groaned out loud. "I knew it; you really are my kind of woman."

The doorbell rang shrilly, surprising them. Kissing him quickly on the lips, she told him he could take a quick shower. "That'll be my friend Cheryl. I think I'm going to get rid of her somehow and come right back up for second helpings."

Riley grinned wolfishly, watching as she quickly shrugged on a clean robe, and he said, "You can bet I'll be here gladly waiting..."

6 WRONG BUT SO RIGHT

Chase wasn't sure what he was doing here knocking on Mika's door – about to face her again after so long. Was he such a masochist?

But ever since he'd heard she was back in town, he'd been curious. He wanted to see her again, especially since the news had spread of her broken engagement from that mega-rich actor boyfriend of hers. It had been all over the gossip mags – not that he read them, but he'd seen glimpses on the newsstands and heard details from friends. It looked like the town's golden girl had returned to lick her wounds after being dumped. Mika had always easily been the most beautiful girl in Newton – she'd also been the most sought after. All the guys had wanted her, and before she'd left for the big city lights, Chase had been the lucky guy who'd won her.

But then, he lost her.

Remembering how Mika had dumped him, just the night before she was to leave for New York three years ago, was enough to make him wince and want to turn back. And yet, he seemed unable to do it. He did want to see her really bad. Not to gloat, no. A part of him had always wanted to remember the time when she'd been the sweet, lovable Mika. And it was that Mika that he wanted to reach out to today to make sure she was okay. That was the only reason he was there.

Or was it?

He rang the bell of the house, which used to be her parents' before they died. It was a car crash, and Mika was devastated to be left on her own so unexpectedly. And then it was a few months after that when she told him she wanted to leave home and make a way for herself, far away from Newton.

And now she was back. He wondered if it wasn't too late to just turn around and walk away. Just forget about seeing her again. What made him think he could face her, even after this long?

But it was too late to leave; she'd come to the door, opened it, and gasped.

"Chase!"

He smiled, surprised at how happy she looked. His eyes were fastened on her face; it was just as beautiful as he remembered – even more so. Her dark hair was swept to the side to fall over one shoulder, the tips just touching the swell of her breasts in the tank top she wore. His eyes roved down to her bare legs, exposed by the brief shorts she was wearing. Her body was still perfect, too, he noted. She was a year younger than he was, and her 25-year-old body looked fit, lovely – and sexy as hell.

"Hello, Mika," he returned, shoving his hands in the pockets of his jeans which suddenly felt too tight. The sight of her looking so hot and not in the least as shattered as he'd thought she would look was doing something to his treacherous loins. "Welcome back."

She made a face. "Thanks. I guess like everyone else, you wanted to see for yourself how I'm taking my latest humiliation."

"Look Mika," he said with a sigh, "Far be it from me to come here looking to gloat. I just thought you needed a friend, especially now that you're back in Newton."

"Friendship, Chase?" she retorted with a smirk, folding her arms. "Is that what you're offering now?"

He sighed again, angrily this time. "You know what, I was dumb to come here," he said shortly, turning to leave.

"Wait."

He paused and then looked back round again. He saw her face was pleading, her smile wry. "I'm sorry okay? I don't want to be a bitch. I just...well, seeing you again, after everything..."

"I just wanted to make sure you're okay," he said, facing her again. "Whatever happened between us, I always felt that at least, we didn't part as enemies. And that if you ever needed my help, I'd be there for you."

A thoughtful expression came over her face just then, and she suddenly smiled dazzlingly, holding the door open wider. "Want to come in?"

She made him some coffee, and they talked – a lot. About how she'd met her ex, Lionel Black, during some fancy dinner party. He was an A-list actor, but she'd caught his eye easily. He'd pursued her for months until she finally agreed to date him. And then six months later, they were engaged, only for him to dump her just two weeks ago for some starlet who'd costarred in his latest movie.

"It was like crashing back down to earth," she said numbly, her forefinger rolling round her saucer. They were seated on stools in her white, pristine kitchen, their cups of coffee on the table between them. "I always wondered what a guy like Lionel saw in me anyway. I was just an assistant to a film agent – and yet he wanted to be with me. At least, until something better came along. Gosh, I was so dumb."

Chase didn't like the unhappiness in her voice. He reached out a hand to grip her shoulder. "He's the dumb one. To have a girl like you and just throw it all away...." He shook his head with fury.

"But that's what I did to you, wasn't it?" she asked softly, staring up at him with her big green eyes. "You loved me, wanted us to get married. But I threw it all away chasing after my grand dreams."

He shook his head at her. "You were never

really happy here, Mika. You always felt choked in this town. I understood that I couldn't tie you down and that you'd only be fulfilled if you followed your heart."

"And what good did that do?" she asked bitterly. "I'm back here, licking my wounds. I hooked up with some guy who turned out to be as shallow as I was...used to be."

She sighed deeply and turned her head to his hand which still lay on his shoulder. And it was then that Chase realized how deeply his fingers were digging into her flesh, caused by his anger at how beaten down she seemed. Quelling his inner annoyance, he made to move his hand, but she lifted hers to cover it. "No, don't," she said softly, looking deep into his eyes. "It's good to feel your touch again. I missed that a lot, among other things. I also missed how much you cared."

Chase shook his head. "Look, uh...I'm not sure we should keep bringing up the past, Mika. It's best we keep it where it belongs, behind us."

"You married?" she asked, tipping her head to the side.

"No."

"Is there someone in your life?"

"Not right now," he said in a clipped tone, not sure he liked the direction the conversation was taking. He knew Mika; she liked to toy with emotions. It made her feel powerful when she did that. He knew she'd claimed that she had changed, but he could never really trust her.

"Mika," he went on, "I'm not sure why you really came back to Newton. Maybe you felt this was home and this is where you could find some peace, or closure. Whatever the reason, I'm sure you never had me in the picture."

"Maybe I did," she said calmly, her fingers trailing lightly over his knuckles. He tried to move his hand away again, but she held it fast. And to his utter amazement, she began to lead it down, lower. Soon, she had his palm over her breast. The first sensation of that soft, firm mound, even through the fabric, got him rock-hard in seconds. His eyes flew up to hers somewhat in confusion.

"I've thought about you, Chase, a lot, especially since I got back. I kept hoping that one day I'd open the door and you'd be standing there. If there was one thing I missed about this town, it was you."

"Mika...," Chase began in a warning tone, with a voice that sounded strangled even in his own ears. She was massaging his hand over her left breast, holding his gaze all the while. Damn, she wasn't even wearing a bra, and he could feel the hard nub of her nipple thrusting into his palm behind the thin material of her top. He gritted his teeth, fighting off the urge to rip the top in half and grab those tits of hers he could remember were so full and deliciously rounded.

"You were always the kind to help a person in need, Chase," she went on in a soft, mesmerizing voice. "And heaven knows I need you now. I need something hard... and solid... and full of heat. For what it's worth, you were the one man I knew who could fuck me right. No other guy ever came close to pleasing me just how I wanted. Not even Lionel. And every time he made love to me, I always thought of you, Chase – and how stupid I was to walk away."

"Mika, I'm not sure I know what you want…," he half-groaned. Of their own volition, his fingers groped around her flesh, cupping her, stroking her. She smiled sensuously, her eyes darkening with pleasure.

"You know what I want," she returned, her free hand stretching out to fall on his crotch, where she found his cock straining against his trousers. Her smile widened. "Hmm…and something tells me you want it too. Well, Chase? Are you going to make me beg? Because I will if I have to."

Chase felt his jaw grind with the exertion he was putting on himself. His heart told him to leave and just walk out the door. Mika was so good at this, using someone, taking advantage when she could and then leaving them hanging dry when they least expected it. She wanted some kind of consolation fuck; he knew that now. She wanted to have him romping with her to gratify her sense of worth. How the hell was he going to give her that satisfaction of knowing that she could just ask and he'd jump right in and give her what she wanted?

"Mika…," he rumbled his eyes fierce as they held hers. "I don't think…"

"Then don't," she cut in, sliding down from the stool and standing in front of his parted thighs. She pressed herself into him, wrapping her arms round his neck right before she kissed him.

Chase was rigid for a second, the touch of her lips almost hypnotic, going through him like a laser. Damn, she tasted so good, he thought, as her mouth ground into his, seeking, tasting. He parted his lips and she dove in with her sweet tongue, driving him insane with her bold, searching thrusts.

Her hands slid down his chest to his belt buckle, and she began to unfasten until he gripped her wrists and tore his lips from hers. "No, Mika...this isn't going to work –"

But she ignored him, her smile slightly mocking as she bent on her haunches. Unable to do anything but watch, he felt his grasp on her wrists go limp. She got the belt open, then his zipper – and then she was freeing his cock, popping it out and cooing when she saw how hard he was. Her hands gripped the base of his turgid member, which looked like a monster inside her small, delicate fingers. Chase groaned, hating himself for being too weak to stop her. Even when she began to lower her head to the tip which dripped with precum, he still couldn't do a thing about it. Couldn't do anything about her putting her mouth on his cock and licking at him like a lollipop.

"You were saying?" she purred, looking up at him with eyes gleaming with hot feminine lust. But before he could reply to her taunt, she took him in her mouth again, slurping on him with a mix of tongue and saliva and lips. He felt his thighs buck into her face – felt himself grip her scalp and shove her closer on his shaft, making her gag. He couldn't help that it felt so good. All he wanted was to make her take it all and to choke on his dick. He wanted to give her all she asked for, and more.

She moaned as his fingers raked into her hair and guided her into a fast, hard rhythm, face-fucking her so deep that he could feel his tip bumping the base of her throat. Moments later he let up and she got to draw in some air, and then he was shoving cock into her mouth again in a punishing deep throat.

"Is this what you want, huh, Mika?" he said hoarsely as he watched her lips wrap lovingly around his cock. Drawing her head back, he withdrew his shaft, this time guiding her head down to lick his balls. Cupping them in his hands, he made her stuff them in her mouth and suck on them. "Fuck yes. This is exactly what you want."

Chase knew he was right. Because he remembered just how she liked it. She liked the man in control, acting rough, treating her like she was there only for his pleasure. He remembered it all. After fucking her face for as long as he could stand the torture without exploding, he finally popped his cock out again.

"Come on, baby…. I need to taste that pussy – find out if it's as juicy and sweet as I remember," he growled, drawing her to her feet and then lifting her up to sit on the kitchen table. He helped her out of her shorts and panties. He then spread her legs wide. Her pussy was smoothly waxed, with not even a trace of hair. His cock reared at the enticing sight, and he resisted the almost animalistic urge to shove himself deep into that hot-looking pussy. But he wanted this all to last as long as possible – he wanted to give them both their fuck's worth.

He pushed her knees apart and drew them high, got his tongue on her slit, and lapped at her juices until she moaned out loud. Her clit was hard and pink, and he sucked on it too, loving how she squirmed beneath him. Yep, she sure tasted just as sweet. At that moment Chase forgot everything else, about how wrong this was, to fall so easily back in her net and give in to his never-forgotten need for her....

Chase hadn't realized how much he'd missed her – missed her molten, honeyed pussy till now. His tongue lashed at her clit and core, stabbing through her slit and mimicking what his cock so longed to do: fuck her senseless! She moaned and rocked beneath his mouth, fingers grabbing his hair and tugging at the roots. He reached up and fondled her breasts, pinching her tight little nubs till she cried out in pleasure–pain.

Finally, after endless minutes, she drew him up and kissed his lips passionately. They were both breathless when they drew apart, and she looked up at him with a teasing smile. "Well? Was the taste to your satisfaction?"

"Oh, yes, indeed," he rumbled, bending his head to nibble momentarily on her pointed nipples. "And yet...I'd still need to taste it with my cock to be able to make a...proper estimation."

"Then why wait," she let out, gasping

blissfully as he pulled on her nipples with his teeth. "I need that big fat dick deep inside me now."

A deep growl escaped his throat, and he hefted her forward, his hands cupping underneath her bottom and lining her cunt up before his rearing cock. His eyes held hers compellingly as, in the next moment, he surged into her without another word.

"Oh!" she cried out, her eyes widening at the powerful intrusion. Her pussy seemed to stretch and vibrate around his spreading width, moans of delight spilling from her mouth. He began to fuck her in strong, swift strokes, building up tempo within seconds.

"You like that, don't you," he grunted, thrusting into her twitching pussy with the force of a bull. She cried out again, louder this time, her lips parted in grimace of bliss. He didn't tear his eyes from her face, but watched every expression that played there, her moans like music to his ears. Again and again he pounded into her, reaching past to her most sensitive, most aching corners. He never slowed, even when he felt his cock slam deep, so deep he was sure his tip had reached her cervix. Her eyes widened and she let out a shrill cry, but she didn't stop him; instead, she dug her fingers into his ass and drew him deeper still.

"Yes...yes!" she gasped again and again and threw her head back as the ecstasy built to feverish proportions between them. Chase couldn't hold back for much longer; he was finally caught up in her. Being buried in her pussy again was like a fantasy come true –

and he knew now that for every day she'd been away, he'd missed her. She'd hurt him – and probably would again, given the chance. But for now, all that mattered was her sweet, velvety pussy wrapped around his cock and her soft, willing body writhing against his. He told her in a hoarse groan that he was coming – and she was ready. She wrapped her legs around his waist, welding them together like perfect jigsaw pieces. And then she too cried out, announcing her own impending release.

They came together, bursting through the surface as their bodies pumped into each other. He spurted all he had in that pussy, and the pussy was only too glad to swallow it all greedily, clutching on him till there was not a drop left. And when he slumped down against her on the table, her breathing was just as ragged as his, and her satisfied smile just as wide. And even as the memorable pleasure washed over him, he warned himself that this must never happen again.

But something told him he was just deceiving himself....

7 HOT STUFF BABY

Preface

Casey had never really been used to getting male attention. And then suddenly not one, but two hot, totally fabulous guys wanted a piece of her. It became obvious she would have to take her pick, but Casey simply couldn't seem to choose. It soon made perfect sense that she might as well have them both....

Hank and Will shared looks as Casey came into the room. Was she beautiful? Yes – and she probably didn't even realize it, but she was sexy as hell, too. Hair scraped back in a bun, blouse buttoned up and skirt reaching past her knees – but still she had it. Just that hint of fire in her eyes, that promise of pleasure in the tilt of her breasts and hips.

She was woman, and they wanted her.

"Hello, Miss Smith," they said, shaking her hand in turns. She seemed almost shy as she looked up at them both. They realized that, together, they might look intimidating to any woman. They were both very tall, powerfully built guys – rugby playing and regular grueling workouts had much to do with it. They had also been told they were quite good looking; they definitely had more than their fair share of admirers. Hank was admired for his golden-boy looks; blonde hair, grey eyes, and a hint of Brad Pitt about him – but handsomer. Will was darker, swarthy almost, and ladies seemed to swoon any time he turned his dark blue gaze on them. He had gleaming russet hair and a slash of dimples on his cheeks when he smiled. Many women had found that smile – among other things – too hard to resist.

Will put up that smile now and saw her blush slightly in awareness. He indicated she take a seat. "I'm glad you finally decided to select us, Miss Smith. You'll find that we're the best company to handle your new venture."

"Please, call me Casey. And your firm came highly recommended by my brother."

Ah yes, Casey's brother, Tommy. He'd been their good friend in college, and now he was some fancy plastic surgeon in Los Angeles. They'd handled some financial work for him too. Nice of him to have put in a good word to his sister about them. Will couldn't help wondering what else her brother had told her. Probably warned her off getting personally involved with either of them, Will figured.

"Of course, Tommy – yes. He's a great friend and also one of our favorite clients. Hopefully, soon you will be, too." Will was grinning at her with his usual charm – but he hoped he wasn't laying it on too thick. He didn't want to scare her off. They wanted her too bad to let that happen.

Hank came forward, a file in his hand. "We've got some projections mapped out for you, ideas we think will go great with your own plans. It's certain we'll have your bookstore up and running in a month."

He held her earnest gaze with his own deep grey stare and could swear he saw her swallow. Was she nervous – or was it just simple feminine consciousness, telling her that he desired her? He'd wanted her for weeks, ever since she'd shown up at their firm in a bid that they handle her new project. They'd been going through preliminary talks, just to see if they could work together. Hank had taken one look at her and had decided he wanted her too. Will and Hank had been best friends since high school and now were also business partners. But it wasn't only their work they had in common; in fact, they happened to share a lot of things – even their women.

And they couldn't wait to get their share of Casey....

The next few weeks passed in a whirl for Casey. She didn't have much of a head for business; all she really knew about was books. And opening the bookstore had been a dream of hers for many years. She loved books, and even with the explosion of electronic publishing, there was still a great market for her kind of books. People would, in their heart, always still love paper and ink, to feel a real book in their hands, to turn a real page. Besides, she was dealing mostly in first edition books, basically. Those ancient classics, still bound in their original back covers, but well preserved.

She was really glad she'd got the two friends on board. They really knew their stuff and had everything rolling in record time. Casey found it such a secret thrill to be working so closely with them in the following weeks. It wasn't just their looks – it was everything about them. Their quick-fire way of thinking up ideas and mapping out business strategy, their utter confidence in what they were doing. A confidence they projected straight to Casey. She found herself coming out of her shell more when she was with them. They made her relax around them, befriended her, and made her feel far more than a client.

Too bad Tommy had told her to keep it strictly business. She could remember what he'd told her even as he'd handed her their card. "Hank and Will are great guys, the best I know. But they're devils when it comes to women. Between them, they broke enough hearts in college that it seemed almost like a crime. I don't want my sister to fall into either of their traps, so look out, sis."

Well, she was looking out. But it was hard as hell. Being around them, whether it was in a business environment, or when they were out having lunch or even dinner, she tried to keep her cool. Casey wasn't so used to male company; she knew she was nice looking but she'd managed to reach the ripe age of twenty-four without getting too hurt. She found she liked male attention though, and they both gave her enough of that. They were always charming, even flirting. And she couldn't help but wonder if either of them ever made a play for her, which would she choose?

Oh stop it, Casey. Like these guys even saw you that way. Sure, you hang out with them when it isn't about business, but they're just being nice to a friend's sister. You're in this new city, trying to establish a business on your own. They might even feel sorry for you.

And yet, Casey was sure there was more to it. She wasn't that inexperienced to see that at least, they both found her attractive. This prospect was even more solidified when, one weekend, Hank invited her to watch a movie with him. She'd happily accepted. And as the evening had worn on, she'd enjoyed his company immensely. She had also enjoyed the very delicious kiss he gave her when he dropped her home a few hours later. She'd longed to invite him in, had seen it in his eyes that he wanted it, too. Her whole body was screaming at her, telling her she was crazy to watch him walk away back to his car. She had a very sleepless night after that, aching at the memory of the deep, eating kiss they'd shared. When a man kissed a woman like that, he certainly wanted to be more than friends.

But what did she want?

That was exactly the same question she had to ask herself when Will invited her out to dinner, just three days after her movie date with Hank. She'd seen no reason to refuse. But then the dinner turned out to be in a very romantic, very expensive Italian restaurant. Romance and excitement was in the air; she couldn't help feeling she was falling under a spell with Will. Like Hank, he kissed her, this time in the car as he stopped them in front of her house. She kissed him back just as eagerly. To her dismay, she found she wanted him just as much as she'd wanted Hank just three days ago. Her body had that same screaming sensation, like it wanted her to just succumb to Hank's caresses and take it even further. As far as actually inviting him up into her bedroom and asking him to fuck her. Just throw off all her clothes and ram his cock deep inside her...

Blinking in amazement at such filthy thoughts, she pulled away from Will's tempting lips and had stumbled out of the car with a hasty "thank you and goodnight."

She was up in her bedroom when she heard him drive away. And then she hugged her arms around herself, walking to the mirror and looking at her own reflection. Her long, silky brown hair styled in long bangs which framed her slightly long, angled face. Her green eyes, thickly lashed, her pert nose, and full-bottomed lips – which some had told her was her best feature. As she stared at herself, she wondered how possible it was that a woman like her – pretty yes, but maybe slightly above average looking, could attract not one but two gorgeous hunks. She'd gone out on dates with both of them, and both times, they'd let her see how much they wanted her. All she'd have needed to do was say the word.

But she hadn't. She'd managed to back away from both of them. Not because she hadn't wanted it too. She'd wanted it probably more than either of them. But the weirdest thing, Casey realized as she stared at the face in the mirror she suddenly didn't recognize, was that she wanted them both. She couldn't choose – didn't want to have to choose. And it was crazy. How could she have fallen for two men at the same time?

"Damn, Hank, kissing her was like...heaven. It was all I could do to keep my hands off her, to let her walk away last night."

"It was the same for me," Hank told Will, chuckling deeply. "I mean, we were at this movie and all I could think of was her sitting so close to me, her sweet floral scent teasing my nostrils and making my cock hard. And then when we got to her door and we kissed, I could have sworn she was going to invite me in."

"But she didn't," Will reminded his friend with a smile. "She shut the door in your face. Just like she ran out of my car like the devil was after her." He sighed deeply. "Think we've scared her off somehow?"

Hank shook his head. "No. It was just a kiss, Will. Not like we pawed her or anything."

"But dammit, I wanted to," Will groaned.

"Wanted to grab her tits beneath her dress and just squeeze, hard. All I could think of when she was near was how much I wanted to rip her clothes off and fuck her like crazy. And yet, I had to settle for just a kiss."

"We both did. Will, she's opening the store in a few days. Very soon, we'd have no reason to see her as often as we do. Unless she picks one of us and decides she wants to date him. But somehow, I have a feeling she may never take her pick."

"That's where we come in," Will said deeply, looking up at Hank with dark, purposeful eyes. "We'll have to convince her that she doesn't have to choose. That she can have us both."

A wide grin spread over Hank's face as he pushed his hand through his thick blond hair. "And you know what, I have a feeling she'll think it's the best idea ever..."

The evening didn't turn out as harrowing as Casey had expected. Her store was officially open; her friends and family had come around to help her celebrate. She'd picked the prestigious Crown hotel for the occasion, and it had been worth all the trouble.

And the best thing about it all was Hank and Will had been so kind to play hosts, of sorts. They were so charming and handsome, each striking in their own way. Her heart pounded every time her eyes fell on either one of them. They were a naughty girl's dream duo. Yes, it was true a man's deepest fantasy was to be in bed with two – or more – women. Well, if a girl had ever had such a fantasy herself, then Hank and Will were the best candidates to bring such a wicked wish to life.

There was no doubt that something was in the air that night. She'd danced with Hank and then Will. They'd each held her close with a special look in their eye. She knew something was up that night; she just wasn't sure what.

Tommy and his wife had been there to congratulate her, and he'd pulled her to a corner at one point in the evening. "Well?" he asked, staring deep into her eyes.

"Well, what?" she'd asked, half-exasperatedly. She could only guess what he was getting at.

"Did you manage to stay out of their trap?"

"What trap?" she said, then sighed heavily. "If you mean Hank and Will, then I promise you that they've been nothing but saints where I'm concerned. Nothing untoward ever happened. For heaven's sake, Tommy! One would think I was twelve again."

He smiled. "It's for your own good, sis. I haven't known a woman yet who's been able to resist either of them. I was so sure you'd have been a conquest of one of them by now."

Casey had bitten on her bottom lip to quell the retort that had sprung from her lips. What would her brother say if she told him she so much wanted to be "conquered" – and not just by one of them!

But she kept such wanton thought to herself. The celebrations drew to a close, and when the last guest had left the ballroom, she found herself left with Hank and Will.

"Tonight was fabulous, guys," she told them warmly. She couldn't help the affectionate smile that crossed her lips. "It's great you two offered to help; I don't know how I'd have managed."

"But the party's not over yet," Hank told her, grinning. "Casey, you were too busy wondering if the night would be a total success that we didn't think you really had any fun. So we've planned to sweep you upstairs for our little surprise."

Casey swallowed, surprised the way her heart began to trip within her chest. "Upstairs?"

Will glanced at Hank. "We rented this totally gorgeous suite. There'll be champagne, some music...." His eyes glowed laughingly down at her.

She found herself wagging a finger up at them. "If I didn't know better, I'd think you both wanted to whisk me up to this so-called gorgeous suite to seduce me."

"Busted," Hank murmured, holding up his hands playfully.

The smile died from her lips as she stared up at him, then at Will. "I...I'm not sure I should, guys. I mean, I always wanted to keep it strictly business between us. I'm not sure I should let things go further."

"We were hoping you'd come to know us enough to trust us, Casey. I could never hurt you, and neither could Hank," Will said, his voice deep, throbbing. He took her hand in his, and for a moment, she felt that electricity, that surge of energy that made her head feel suddenly light. Heaven knows she trusted them, wanted them both. But did they realize exactly what they were asking of her?

"Let me get this straight," she said with a shaky laugh, "Exactly what's going to happen if I go up with you guys?"

It was Will who replied. "Whatever you want," he said with a casual shrug. "We'd never dream of forcing you to do what you didn't want to do. But if you let us...then we'll show you just how much we've both dreamed and hoped to have you in our arms. And yes, Casey, we both want you. We were thinking you'd have to choose – but then as the weeks wore on, we realized that maybe you had the same notions as we do. That it would only be perfect if we shared the passion...together."

Together. Yep, she'd asked them to give it to her straight, and now she'd heard it with her own ears. They were grown adults, so certainly there was no need for a façade. They'd pussy-footed around long enough. And well, Casey decided with a jolt that she was sick of holding back, too. If she was going to do something wild, crazy, and stupid, then she might as well do it with the two most gorgeous men she'd ever met.

"Oh. So...," she began, eyes dancing up at both of them, "What are we waiting for?"

Casey had already had three glasses of champagne and still she felt nervous. They were in the hotel suite, which incidentally was quite opulently decorated. There was champagne on ice, some exotic fruit in a bowl, and two hunky men seated across from her watching her every move like they were ready to eat her alive.

Casey couldn't help laughing a little weakly. "Wow – this is nerve racking," she began. She rose to her feet and began pacing the room. Just beyond the door, she could see the bedroom, with its massive silk laid king-size bed. She gulped convulsively and then turned to find Hank had arisen to stand close behind her. He held out his arms, and she went into them, sighing as he embraced her warmly. Over his broad shoulder, she saw Will watching. He too had stood and was sipping on his glass of champagne, his dark eyes gleaming.

"How long...how long have you both known you wanted to...to..." She found she couldn't finish, and buried her face in Hank's jacket.

He chuckled, holding her even closer. She felt herself relaxing within his tender grasp, felt her heartbeat race in an erotically charged dance. The depth of his physical strength was imminent in his powerful, firm arms, and she felt buried in his affection and warmth. She'd never been hugged like this before, and it was as calming as it was arousing.

"Fuck you?" Hank finished softly, his lips in her hair. "Almost from the first moment you walked into the door two months ago."

He pulled her back to look down deeply into her green eyes. "And you? How long have you realized you wanted this, wanted us both?"

Casey stared up at him, unable to speak for a moment as she felt the unmistakable ridge of his cock burgeoning against her belly. That single evidence of his desire was just as strong as the hot, searing lust she could find in his steady gaze. "I...I'm not sure...I think maybe from a few weeks ago. I never really wanted to let myself believe that I could get either of you, not to speak of both. But I realized, whenever I dreamt it was of you and Will, touching me, making love to me..."

Hank groaned, and drew her up, till the tips of her toes were all that were touching the floor. He swooped down and covered her mouth in a kiss, so hot it tore through her like a flame. Her head went dizzy as he ravaged her mouth with his tongue and lips. When he tore his mouth from hers, his breathing was ragged. "Casey...we don't want to hurt you – we know you haven't done anything like this before. Just tell us...how do you want this?"

She glanced over at Will, who still held back, looking reigned-in like he was keeping his emotions on a leash. Casey knew that all she had to do was say the word, and he'd leap forward, join in the blazing circle that encased her and Hank. It was true; Casey had never been in a "threesome" before. Sex for her in the past had been pretty tame – and lame. So the last thing she wanted was to be treated like glass.

Gazing up at Hank, and then over at Will, she said clearly, "I want to be fucked – really hard, by both of you. So hard that I won't be able to walk straight tomorrow morning."

It seemed she was right about Will; at her words, he came forward in a trice, wrapping an arm around her and ripping into her mouth with a kiss that held so much hunger in it. The taste of his lips was just as intoxicating as Hank's, and she kissed him back with the same deep need. She could feel their hands all over her then, stroking her neck, her shoulders, and her breasts. Her dress was a simple, elegant purple frock, held up by two tiny scraps. It took moments for Hank's deft fingers to unzip it and send it pooling to the ground.

Will had his hands in her hair as he went on kissing her ravenously; he loosened the intricate braid and caused her long, streaming locks to fall over her shoulders. She moaned against his lips, her whole body set aflame by the sensation of being kissed and touched by their strong, bold hands.

"Oh," she sighed, gasping for air. Hank had slipped behind her and now cupped her breasts through her bra, his fingers firm as he stroked her, squeezed her. Will broke from her lips and she struggled to breathe normally, which was impossible, not when his heated lips were trailing down her arched neck. The first touch of his lips on her skin was electrifying. She could swear her pussy clenched and seethed, hungry for something she could not as yet define.

It was happening. Her fantasy was coming true at last. There was no way she could back out now; no way she could even want to. She was about to indulge in a night of wicked, mindless sex with two of the sexiest men she'd ever known. And nothing was going to stop her....

There was music playing in the background somewhere, something jazzy with lots of horns. It didn't register too deeply with Casey; she was more lost in the pleasure she was experiencing at that moment. Lying in the capacious bed with Hank and Will on either side of her, naked, bronzed. Perfectly contrasting with her paler skin, all pinks and whites.

Their hands were everywhere, and she was touching them too; Will's chest was broad and sprinkled with the same dark hair on his head; it felt silky beneath her fingers, and he moaned as she tweaked his tiny nipples with her thumb and forefinger. Her other hand snaked over Hank, whose body was just as magnificent, though hairless and smooth. Her fingers danced down his six-pack abs and she felt him suck in his belly as she moved dangerously closer to where his cock reared proudly.

She'd taken a shy glimpse of both their cocks once they'd undressed earlier; needless to say, she'd lost her breath. They were both huge, with thickly veined shafts and purple, marble-like tips. The one difference may was that Will's cock had a certain inward curve, and she'd felt a shiver in her belly as she'd thought of how that slightly bent cock would feel inside her pussy – or up her ass.

Before the thought of having any cock up her ass should have made Casey shudder with fear, but instead it made her eager, made her feel even wetter. Her most deeply buried fantasy was to be double-penetrated by both of them: one hot, pulsing cock in her cunt and another hot, throbbing cock in her ass. The very images made her head spin.

Hank took her chin in his hand and turned her to him for one more bone-melting, voracious kiss, just as Will snaked down her quivering body to suck at her nipples. She groaned loudly against Hank's lips, and felt ready to explode when Will intensified the sensations by dipping his hand low, to finger her pussy. The pleasure was almost too much to bear; Hank's lips kissing hers voraciously, tongue against tongue, saliva-swapping kiss after kiss. Will's mouth latched over her thrusting nipple, teeth nibbling passionately while his thumb danced on her clit. With his fore- and middle-finger, he tested the depths of her cunt and found her dripping so much there was a "squishing" sound as he stroked in and out of her.

"Oh!" she moaned, breaking from Hank's lips and throwing her head back as her whole body was set ablaze. Once Will's deft, probing fingers had penetrated her, she'd felt ready to shatter into a thousand pieces. He finger-fucked her steadily, pulling on her tits with his free hand and nicking her nipple with his teeth. Moments later, he moved his head from her tits and bent instead to her outstretched legs, which he parted even wider.

Hank took over worshipping her breasts, and he proved to have a rougher, more demanding touch than Will. His breath was raspy as he dug his fingers into her breasts and fondled them with strong, almost punishing, caresses. His teeth raked over her left nipple, sinking in deep and making her shudder at the sweet pain of it. It was a good thing, though, that she had Will to distract her, as he began to tongue her pussy with obvious delight.

Casey was writhing and twisting on the bed now, her fingers clutching the sheets as she tried to endure the indescribable pleasure of feeling her breasts and pussy being tormented at the same time. It was the best feeling in the world to have two eager, hungry males feasting at her treasures. Will ate her pussy for what seemed like endless minutes, getting her into a fever pitch of ecstasy that she knew it was only moments before she'd erupt in waves upon his mouth.

As if sensing her impending climax, Will withdrew his mouth from her dripping honey pot, and positioned himself on his knees between her wide open legs. He grabbed her ankles and drew them wider apart. In that moment, Casey knew that the time had come. Will was going to take her, make her his. With Hank's hands molding her tits and his lips sucking on her nipples fiercely, she was almost too dazed with pleasure to do more than wait, with bated breath, for Will's cock to pierce into her.

She could feel the large tip of his knob rub against her slit again and again, wetting himself on her juices. It was already too much for her; the surface stroking had been just the thing to push her right over the edge. Crying out loud in ecstasy, she came in a massive rush, her whole body shaking like a leaf. It was Hank who held her tightly, calming her with a kiss, just as in the next moment, Will jammed into her swollen-lipped pussy.

From then on, Casey was lost in a blissful void. Will fucked his way deep into her, giving her no chance to recover from her first, tumultuous climax. It was to be the first of many.

As Will shoved his throbbing cock deep

inside her again and again, stretching her tiny walls to the max, Hank lifted himself on his knees so that his cock was lined close to her mouth. She looked up adoringly at him, and then at his cock, which was as magnificently hard as ever and dripping with pre-cum. Her whole frame was rocked by Will's powerful thrusts, and she had to take a grip on Hank's cock so that she could hold it in place for her sucking. She drew his cap into her mouth and heard him moan, his hands rising to tug into her falling hair.

"Oh yes, baby, suck it," he groaned, throwing his head back. "Suck it hard."

She obliged, egged on by his passion-drugged voice, as well as that rock-hard cock pounding her pussy. Will was grunting like an animal; she could feel him watching as she bobbed her head on Hank's dick, lapping on the cap and then licking around the veined shaft. Her hands cupped his balls, finding them tight, full. She moaned at how delicious it felt to hold those beautiful sacs in her hand.

"Dammit Casey, your pussy is so hot and tight and wet," Will said, his teeth gritted. She moaned in response, unable to speak thanks to the particularly deep thrust he shoved into her, almost ripping her in half. She hummed around Hank's cock, her hand grasping the base and pumping just as Will pumped almost viciously into her.

"I can't hold back, honey," Will rasped, arching his back and burying himself balls-deep within her. For the first time, Casey felt enough of the pain to actually scream, her mouth lifting from Hank's dick. But the pain was gone in a second; Will put a hand between them and fiddled her clit; the pleasure washed in again and he rocked himself into a fast, grueling rhythm. Moments later, he came into her with a toe-curling roar.

He pulled out and shifted up to kiss her on her lips as she tried to catch her breath. "That was beautiful, Casey," he said softly, gazing into her eyes. "Ready for more?"

She nodded, eyes wide and shiny with amped-up lust. She kind of guessed what "more" was because she saw Hank reach for the lube standing on the dresser next to the bed. Will stroked her face lovingly. "I'm sorry I was a little rough just now. I lost control...."

"And I loved it," she replied, planting a quick kiss on his lips. "I loved the feel of you ripping out my pussy and then coming deep inside me, filling me with your hot sperm. And I know I'll love it too, when Hank does the same thing to my ass."

"Boy, am I glad to hear that," the man in question said deeply, back to the bed as he lubed up his cock enthusiastically. Casey almost couldn't bring herself to look at it again, in case she lost her nerve. She'd never had a cock up her ass before, and certainly not one the daunting size of Hank's. But then, it was what she craved: to have a big, fat hard cock penetrating her asshole.

"I'll be careful, baby," he promised, kissing her as tenderly as Will had done moments before. He gazed down at her with his dark grey eyes, and she let him see with her smile that she trusted him implicitly.

"I know," she replied, and without a word,

turned on her belly. She drew up her knees, lifting her bottom in the air as she supported her weight on her elbows. Right before her, Will had laid back, legs spread wide as he masturbated his now hardening cock. She moaned at the sight of him getting hard again as he watched Hank bend to lick at her exposed sphincter. The sensation of Hank rimming her asshole was enough to make her knees wobble; he ate her ass for as long as he dared. He'd waited so long already that she could sense that all he wanted to do was ram himself up her cunt.

But he'd promised to be gentle, which he turned out to be. Breathing harshly, he finally straightened and knelt behind her. He bent to kiss her back, saying softly, "I hope you're ready baby."

"I've been ready for weeks," she told him, glancing back with a smile filled with lust and anticipation.

He nodded; his smile almost a grimace of pain as he guided his cock close to her asshole. He seemed to remain frozen as only his cap touched the thin membrane, and Casey remembered to stay still as well. To distract herself, she reached forward and grabbed Will's dick, which was as rigid as a plank again. Without thinking, she clamped her mouth over his shaft, sucking on him and making him buck with pleasure. This, caught up with blowing him, she got lost in the moment, not even flinching when she felt Hank lube her ass crack.

"So tight...so fucking tight," she heard Hank groan, as his tip pushed through the thin membrane of her butt hole. She forced herself not to go rigid, but kept her rear muscles lax, hoping she wouldn't feel too much pain if he forgot to be gentle and just pushed straight into her.

But Hank didn't forget; he took his time, inch by inch, rocking his way into her ass. Only the harsh sound of his breathing and his deep, feral grunts told her how much control he was exerting. Casey felt the pleasure build up along with the pain as he penetrated her slowly. That feeling of being filled to the brim was familiar. She'd felt it earlier when Will had fucked her pussy. And now, her asshole was going to get the same belly-punching treatment. She could have easily died and gone to heaven right then.

"Oh...oh," she moaned around Will's thrusting cock in her mouth. Hank was halfway in; she could feel him. And already it was almost as if she was being torn in two. She loved it, loved the way her muscles stretched and yet clutched to his throbbing cock. Having a cock up the ass was the best feeling ever, she realized. And the only thing that could top it all was to have Will in her pussy at the same time.

As Hank paused, keeping still as his cock throbbed inside her butthole, she looked up pleadingly at Will. "I need you in my pussy, Will," she confessed.

He looked at her doubtfully. "Are you sure, baby? We're both large, Casey. Are you sure you can take us both?"

"I can try," she said and saw him glance up at Hank, who nodded.

"We'll take it slow, at least for starters," Will said at last, as he slipped beneath both their bodies till the tip of his cock was touching her soppy pussy. Taking her by the waist, he gazed up at her as she straddled him, Hank's cock still buried inside her. "You're really sure?" he asked her, and she nodded enthusiastically, only for her cry of pain to fill the room as Will surged into her for the second time that night.

"Shit," he groaned, as if in pain himself. Her walls closed tightly around him. It was instinctive, and yet even Will felt it. With them both deep inside her, they could feel that thin layer between her ass and pussy that separated their cocks.

Will lowered himself to whisper in her ear that he could come out if she wanted, but she shook her head vehemently. "I can take it. I can take you both. Fuck me, guys. Just fuck me like crazy."

Her words pushed them finally over the edge – there was no stopping them now. Hank sank all the way in, making her screech in pleasure-pain. At the same time, Will humped his hips and fucked himself up into her pussy that was still slick and sloshed with his first cum. Both men picked up a rugged rhythm, dancing in perfect tune in both her ass and pussy.

Casey loved every minute of it, a fact she couldn't hide as she gave into thrust after thrust, her whole frame rocking along with theirs. She cried out their names in turns, almost insane with pleasure as her holes seemed set on fire by their ravaging cocks. As if she wasn't already in too much pleasure, Will reached up to grab one nipple in his mouth, just as Hank bent forward behind her and managed to get his fingers between them to touch her clit and stroke it into perfect stiffness.

She almost blacked out right then. No one had the right to receive so much ecstasy as she was enjoying right then. Every nerve end in her body had been struck alight like a matchstick. And she was burning down to nothing; it was going to be moments, she realized, for her climax to arrive.

She succumbed to it willingly, just at that second when both cocks rammed into her and punched perfectly into those deepest, sweetest spots in her cunt and ass. It was certainly far beyond anything she'd ever felt in her life. She exploded in the most powerful climax of her life.

Both men seemed to lose whatever shred of control they had left as they saw her come so powerfully. Hank was pumping her ass in a frenzied back-and-forth motion; now that she'd come, her tightness had eased somewhat and he didn't have to move so slowly any more. He pounded into her just as thoroughly as Will was doing, and his quickened rhythm finally pushed him off the brink. He exploded into her ass with rope after rope of cum, her hole constricting on his cock as if to wring him dry. In the next moment, he felt Will grind into her as his own climax smacked into him. Their jerking movements made the whole bed shake and caused the woman between them to flop about like a ragdoll. They spent themselves inside her till there was nothing left, filling the suite with their satisfied grunts and growls.

Minutes later, they all fell exhausted into the bed, keeping Casey between them as they wrapped their arms about her. Her body went on shuddering for long moments, and both guys shared guilty, sheepish looks. They were wondering if they had been too hard on her, especially in those last moments when they'd climaxed. Would she be turned off a threesome for good? Had they hurt her enough to make her never want any more of their own fierce kind of fucking?

To their mutual surprise, she finally sighed and leaned up on her elbows to gaze down at them both with a happy, wide smile.

"Wow. That was...perfect. So when can we do it again?"

8 CALL MY NAME

Preface

One night with a handsome stranger and she never got to know his name...

A half-drunken dare had Kiera falling into bed with the most gorgeous guy at the club that night. The next morning, he was gone and she never even got to know who he was. All she had was the memory of one night of unforgettable sex. And then she shows up at work the next day to discover that her stranger lover was her new boss, Rake Evans. Talk about wild first impressions!

"I'll take the blond one."

Kiera shook her head at her best friend's words. She and Beth had that little game they played together: they both got to pick the guy they'd most likely want to fuck, given the chance. It was fun, most of the time – especially whenever they came to the bar without dates. Like tonight.

It was just the two of them on a Friday night, feeling like having fun without the constraints of a boyfriend or any male companionship. If they were lucky, they'd get drunk, get to dance with a lot of hot guys, and then go home to their beds.

That's so lame, Kiera thought to herself, shaking her head humorously, her eyes fastened on the two guys she was ogling with Beth. One of them was dark haired, the other blond. And they were both fit as hell. Beth had picked the hot blond one, so Kiera figured she'd pick the hot dark-haired one. The two men were talking easily with a few other friends of theirs, apparently. Kiera emptied her glass as she wondered, what if? If games were real, she could really get what she wanted. What if this tall, broad-shouldered, handsome dark stranger could be hers for the night?

She smiled self-deprecatingly. Girls could dream, surely.

"Hmmm, then the dark one's mine," she murmured, head feeling light from all the booze. Kiera wasn't one to go overboard with alcohol, but she and Beth were celebrating, sort of. Beth had just broken up with her boyfriend, and they'd felt like closing things down with a bang. But then Kiera wondered whether, to make it truly official, they should actually end the night with a real bang. Nothing like a random, good hard fuck to get one's mind off some ex. It had been Beth's ex, true, but if Kiera had to make the sacrifice as well, and get a hot cock in her pussy tonight, then she'd gladly do it. Anything for the cause.

"Look, I need another drink," she said to Beth, who nodded in encouragement.

"So do I. Make it a double for me."

Kiera returned with the drinks soon after and found Beth with some guy, giggling as he was whispering something in her ear. Handing Beth the drink, Kiera nodded to the man, and then stopped short as she realized who it was. The dark-haired guy. Her guy. He was dressed in a formal suit, the shirt unbuttoned at the neck, like he'd come here straight from work. He looked even hotter close up, with dark blue eyes that seemed to glow in the low-toned lighting of the bar. Very early thirties, very successful looking, and very fuckable, Kiera surmised, taking a huge gulp from her drink to calm her rampaging hormones.

"Hey, meet my friend, Kiera," Beth said, tipping her drink in her mouth and then giggling like a school girl for no reason. Kiera figured Beth was getting to the point of being tipsy.

I'm hardly sober myself, she noted, smiling in a friendly way to the guy, raising her eyebrows questioningly at Beth to finish the introduction.

"Oh, and Kiera, meet um...ah..." And then she waved her hand dismissively in the air. "Fuck it, I can't remember. I'm wasted."

The man chuckled, holding out his hand to Kiera. "I always wanted to meet a girl named Kiera," he said, his voice deep and charming.

Just behind him, over his shoulder, Kiera caught Beth's face, which was almost comical as she made very sexually themed faces. From mimicking a blowjob to rolling her eyes as if in a swoon, she mouthed, "Go for it."

"That's nice," Kiera murmured, ignoring Beth's earnest, humorous looks and smiling casually at the man standing in front of her. He was looking at her with a certain speculative glint in his eye – and she wanted to believe he was attracted to her as she undeniably was to him. He was so much man candy, totally the type she could see doing something wild and wicked with – like a one night stand.

Heaven knows I'm drunk enough and horny enough to do it, she thought with an inner giggle, as she placed her nose in her glass. How did he happen to even be here with them, Kiera wondered. It seemed so weird; five minutes ago she'd been checking him out, though in a joking way. She'd never in a million years thought that they'd actually get to meet face to face.

"And what did you intend to do when you met her?" she asked, picking up from his last comment. His grin widened, and Kiera's belly fluttered at the way his handsomeness was upped to irresistible mode. She was helpless, and wanted to simply go limp and say, "Take me, please." He was that fucking sexy.

"That would depend," he replied deeply, "On what she'd be willing to do with me."

"I...," Kiera began, staring up at him in confusion. Her heart was pounding so hard at the look in his eye, the timber in his voice. It seemed almost too much to believe that this hunk of gorgeous maleness could possibly want her. To think that she had, barely ten minutes ago, been "picking" him for herself.

Suddenly panicking, she blurted out, "I need to get some more drinks." Wanting to escape the unsettling feelings the stranger was evoking deep within her, Kiera rushed off. But then she felt his hand on her arm, and he said, "Allow me."

He was gone and only then could Kiera let out a ragged breath. Woah! She'd never been so sexually attracted to a man before. His eyes, the way he looked at her, even the casual way he'd touched her – was so deeply arousing.

"Oh my goodness isn't this so freaking wild?" Beth gushed, shaking her forearm. "That's the guy, Kiera! Remember, the one with the blond? He's the one you picked!"

"I know," Kiera cried back in glee, turning to her friend. "How weird is that? What happened anyway?"

"It's crazy, but when you left earlier, he came up to ask about you. He definitely likes you, Kiera. Maybe he saw us checking him and his friend out earlier or something, I don't know. And I don't care! This is just too much of a fantastic opportunity, Kiera!"

"So what am I going to do? He'll be back any second."

Beth stared at her like she was dumb. "Why, what do you think I'd do? Kiera, I know we were just goofing around, but when he came over like that, I so wanted to get him for myself – but then I remembered that you picked him, so I had to give over for the sake of fair play." Beth was grinning.

"Thanks," Kiera said wryly.

"Woah, wait a minute," Beth said slowly, "You're chickening out, Kiera? Too scared?"

"No! I mean – maybe! I never imagined he'd come right over and –"

Beth was shaking her head at her in utter disappointment. "If it had been the other guy, I'd have snapped him up in a heartbeat. Kiera, for some reason, this fabulous guy has all but fallen into your lap, and you're getting cold feet? Wow. Never thought you'd be the kind to throw away a perfect opportunity out of fear."

Kiera folded her arms. "Trust me, I'm not afraid. Afraid I'll make a fool of myself, though."

Beth smiled, and then poked a finger in her chest. "I dare you, Kiera. I dare you to do something really wild and crazy for once. We keep saying we would and we never do. But after I broke up with Luke, I swore to myself that any chance I got, I'd live life to the fullest. So what are you going to do? Because if you don't make a move, I will."

And then giving Kiera a meaningful look, she turned and moved into the crowd, dancing and laughing gaily.

"Here we are," a deep gravelling voice said behind her, and she looked up at her handsome stranger. He looked around. "Hey, what happened to your friend?"

"She went off somewhere," Kiera said, smiling up at him with dancing eyes. "So I guess it's just you and me, gorgeous."

Her words seemed to make him smile, and

he leaned forward to say in her ear, "I think that suits me quite well, sexy. But you never really answered my question."

Kiera frowned slightly in confusion. "What question?"

"About what you'd be willing to do with me," he drawled, lips tilted in a cocky smile. Kiera liked it when a guy got cocky once in a while – especially if he had the looks and charm to go with it.

"I've already let you buy me a drink," she returned, eyelashes battering. "I could spare a dance or two..."

"Where are we, the eighteenth century?" he teased, and then his eyes blazed down at her. "I think you know what I really want, don't you?"

"I'm not usually good at reading minds," she purred, looking up at him from the rim of her glass as she sipped, "But in your case, I think I do know what you want." And then she giggled like an idiot. "I'm just not sure if I should play along so easily. I could have sworn you had an eye for my friend. You did whisper in her ear, too."

He grinned wolfishly. "That I did. But only to tell her that I thought her friend was gorgeous and that I'd like to have you all to myself. To her credit, she didn't seem to look too stumped."

"No, she's a really good friend, Beth," Kiera said, her words slightly slurred. Oh boy, she maybe should have eased up on that last glass. But she'd downed it all, and put the glass shakily on the nearby table. And then she stumbled into his arms, giggling when he caught her easily.

"Can I tell you a secret?" she asked, looking up at him and forcing her head not to swim since she had to crane her neck way back because he was so tall. He nodded with an indulgent smile, and she continued in a hushed, smiling voice, "We were both checking you out earlier, and the other guy you were with, telling ourselves which one we fancied more. I got to choose you – and I was wishing to myself that somehow, we could get together or something."

His grin was so feral it made her catch her breath. "That's funny...I was thinking the exact same thing. And trust me, I noticed you first. The moment you walked in with your friend an hour ago, I already knew I wanted you like mad."

"So what are you going to do about it?" she cooed, tugging on his lapels with a flashing look in her eyes. At the back of her mind, she thought of Beth's dare. Kiera knew then and there that her friend was right; fuck caution. If one had just a single life to live, then it might as well be lived to the brim....

Be careful what you wish for, they said. Well, Kiera was glad for this wish, at least.

Him, in her bed, kissing her with such fierceness that it stole her breath away. How they'd managed to get to her place so fast was beyond her – or maybe it was just his very speedy driving. They'd left the bar in a mad, lustful rush. And now here, in the bedroom of her apartment, he was peeling off her clothes slowly, carefully. She was breathing so hard she could hear the thumping in her ears. She wanted to tell him to fuck her wildly, ravenously. He was a perfect stranger, but she didn't need to be handled like glass. She wanted to be fucked, hard.

I really must have had too much to drink, Kiera thought with a fiendish laugh, as she pushed him down on his back, surprising him. She was acting like a wildcat, she knew – but she couldn't help herself. Here was the sexiest guy she'd ever met, lying in her bed. She wanted to make this a night to remember.

He looked up at her with a slanted grin, as she straddled him and taunted sensually, "Where are we, the eighteenth century? You don't have to be gentle with me, mister. I'm a big girl, you know." And with that, she peeled his shirt off him, revealing his broad, hairless and rippling torso.

"Hmmm, nice," she murmured, her fingers working quickly at his trousers. Soon he was kicking those off too. In moments, they were both naked, tumbling over the sheets, lips merging in hard, eating kisses. He touched her all over and set her ablaze. Now that she'd let him know what she liked, he obliged her with enthusiasm. He slid his lips in a heated trail down her neck to taste her thrusting nipples, the buds pale and pink and hard. He sucked on them roughly, making her gasp in pleasure. His touch was firm, his strong hands raking all over her body, squeezing on her breasts, biting into her flesh. She shuddered with a thrill that coursed through her right down to her pussy which dripped between her thighs.

Not easing up on his feasting on her breasts, he probed his way down her belly to her nest of curls, finding her cunt lips slick with juices. He hummed, his teeth biting into the under swell of her breasts. Just as hungry to touch him, she slipped her hand around his hot, throbbing cock, feeling her belly curl at the thought of that chunky pole of hard, strong flesh stabbing into her. She wanted it so bad she was moaning over and over.

He drew his mouth from her breasts, and she let out a cry of protest. But then, he was pushing her knees wide apart and burying his face between them. Moments later he had his tongue lashing at her pussy, and she was moaning all over again, head thrashing from side to side. He was merciless, almost punishing in the way he ate that pussy, his fingers skewering into her and punching in and out like a piston. It didn't take long to have her bucking against him as tide after tide of ecstasy pounded through her, especially when he took her stiff, throbbing clit into his mouth and sucked hard. That got Kiera crying out and pushing his head even closer between her legs.

Kiera knew she had never felt such pleasure before, and the thrill was intensified by the fact that here was a perfect stranger, making her experience and do things she'd never have dreamed of doing or experiencing. He sucked long and passionately on her pussy, making her thighs quiver and causing her to get so wet she could hear the squishing sound as he finger-fucked her.

And when the pleasure got so much that she erupted in a chorus of screeches and shudders, she knew she wanted to do the same for him, too. Making him lie on his back again, she knelt beside him and took his throbbing shaft into her hands. He filled her palms and made her purr with erotic anticipation of having such a huge, sweet cock all to herself. She was practically drooling as she gazed at the stiff, purple-tipped rod that seemed to pulsate within her palms. Kiera masturbated him firmly with her fingers, stroking his balls in turn. Then, unable to resist any longer, she took him into her mouth, sucking on his cap and tasting the salty-sweet pre-cum. Her whole body vibrated in answering pleasure as she heard him groan in approval. Using all the expertise at her disposal, she pleasured his cock hungrily and eagerly. His hand had reached out to stroke her pussy as she sucked on him, and if anything, that gave her great incentive. He thumbed steadily on her clit as she rolled her tongue all over his shaft and balls, sucking on every inch of his manhood till he was bucking fast into her mouth.

Over and over, she tried to take more of him in her mouth, but he was too big, making her gag each time. She pumped on his cock with her fist as she wrapped her lips more firmly around his saliva-slick shaft. All she wanted was to keep sucking that dick and never letting up. But with a deep, animalistic groan, he finally pulled her away. "Enough, baby. Or it'll be over much too quickly." And with one of those slanted smiles of his, he covered her mouth with a kiss, pushing his tongue deep into her mouth. And then, without warning, he drew away and flipped her on her belly.

She giggled, wiggling her ass in the air as he forced her head down into the pillow. He knelt behind her on the bed, keeping her knees parted as one hand gripped her waist. He bent to whisper in her ear, "You were saying something earlier about being a big girl. I always thought big girl liked big cocks."

"They certainly do," she moaned, feeling his fingers sliding over her slick pussy lips. She arched her bottom even higher, and yelped when he entered her with one hard, powerful thrust. He grunted with pleasure, and her walls instinctively clutched at his invading cock even as the slick tunnel stretched to accommodate his throbbing width. The sensation of being filled to the brim was so strong it made her shudder. He drew back as far as the tip, and then suddenly, rammed straight into her again with grueling force. Kiera couldn't help screaming out loud again.

"Sure you can take this? And this?" he grunted, fucking her deep, each thrust like she was getting a flagstaff shoved into her. Kiera moaned into the pillow, her cries muffled. She'd never felt so deeply and thoroughly pounded before; she could feel him in corners of her cunt she hadn't even known a cock could reach. Lost in bliss, she pushed back into him, letting him bury himself balls-deep in her again and again. It all felt so good she never wanted it to end.

And then when the time came and he reached round to stroke on her clit with his fingers, she was sure she'd implode. The steady strumming on her fuck button, as well as the solid pumping from his thrusting cock, sent so many shockwaves through her. It wasn't long before she was screaming for the umpteenth time that night and gushing herself on his dick. His own growl of pleasure was deep and loud as he rocked faster into her, bringing them both to a tsunamic climax. She could feel that powerfully hot cock pulsing deep inside her, and her knees quivered in reaction to the utter bliss of it all.

Shattered beyond belief, she fell against the mattress, too dazed to move or even think. And when he lay beside her, breathing hard, she barely had the presence to say on a shocked, pleased gasp, "Damn, that was so fucking hot. The best." And then she must have passed out.

Epilogue

Kiera woke up the next morning, surprised she didn't have a monster of a hangover after all she'd drank last night.

Must have been thanks to all that fantastic sex, she realized, smiling impishly. When she'd awoken, her lover was gone. She'd felt a twinge of regret, especially since she hadn't even known his name, and wanted to kick herself for being so dumb not to even get his phone number.

But then she thought, was there a need? That night had been wild and forbidden.

Mostly due to a dare by Beth, but still, Kiera knew she shouldn't have acted so wantonly. It was probably best, she decided, that she never saw her handsome, sexy lover again, whoever he was.

She got to work, dressed smartly in a suit and crisp blouse. No one could guess by looking at her, that she'd allowed a perfect stranger to fuck her senseless the night before. It was a wonder she could walk straight, she realized, giggling to herself. As she appeared at the office, she saw her assistant waiting for her.

"Good thing you're here, Kiera. The new boss has finally arrived. He flew in yesterday, and is now waiting to meet you in his office."

"That's great," Kiera said, taking the file her supervisor handed to her. "Nice that Mr. Justin Parker is able to join us at last. It's been weeks since we've been expecting him from headquarters. I must remember to make a good impression."

And with a nod to her assistant, Kiera made her way to the new boss' office, which had been prepared specially for his arrival. Newly decorated and well appointed, she was sure he'd find it to his satisfaction. Taking a deep breath, she knocked on the door. A deep voice told her to "come in," which she did.

He was standing at the window with his back to her, and the first thing she noticed was how very tall he was, and how dark was his hair. He was looking down at a file he held in his hands.

"Good morning, Mr. Parker. I'm Kiera Nelson, and it's good to have you with us. I hope you like your office – " Her words stopped short as he turned around and she caught the first glimpse of his face. "You!"

Her hot-blooded lover of last night, her dark stranger, was standing there, looking at her with that slanted smile of his. "Well well, Ms Nelson. I hear it's a small world – I'm sure now that's true, it really is."

"I don't understand," Kiera gasped, blushing to her roots. "What are you doing here? How...what?"

He shrugged. "I'm as surprised as you. I saw the name just now, 'Kiera' – and I kept wondering if it was the same person – in fact, I think I was hoping it was. And I'm glad to see I was right."

Kiera's hands were pressed to her cheeks. Suddenly, every phase of the night came flashing back, how she'd been somewhat drunk, yet fully willing and even forceful in her need for him to take her. Which he had, many times through the night, till she had fallen into an exhausted sleep.

"You...you're glad?" she said hesitantly, eyes widening. "You mean, you aren't going to fire me?"

His expression was surprised. "Why should I? It's not like you did anything wrong. Besides, I was a very eager co-participant, if I recall." He flung the file to the desk and strode up to her.

"Last night was...well, unforgettable. I left wondering if you'd ever want it to happen again. I felt sure that it was something you don't usually do – falling into bed with a total stranger. I could tell it was your first time."

"It was," she said, still blushing furiously. "I could say it was Beth that put me up to it, but I wouldn't be completely honest. I...everything that happened last night was because I wanted it to happen. I wish now though that I'd thought to ask your name!"

He chuckled, reaching out to cup her face. "And then you'd have known who I was, probably. And then you'd have hidden behind some façade. No, Kiera. I'm happy I met the real you last night. The sexy, giving, and totally uninhibited Kiera. I wouldn't have had it any other way."

"Letting my new boss fuck my brains out the night before we officially meet is not exactly the kind of first impression I'd have wanted, but..." She paused, her eyes flashing gleefully up at him as he pulled her closer for a moment. He kissed her lingeringly, causing the breath to seize in her throat as the same wild-fire lust he evoked in her came rising to the surface again.

"Trust me, Kiera," he murmured as he drew back moments later, "In this case, it was the best kind of first impression as far as I'm concerned...."

9 MORE THAN ENOUGH

Preface

Ellen knew that Josh was in no mood for love. He'd never really gotten over losing his fiancé three years ago, and she could get that. After all, his fiancé had been her best friend. But she'd always thought he was a great guy: really cool and really, really sexy. She wanted him like crazy and figured that if she at least could give him some kind of comfort, then it would be more than enough. Comfort of a very erotic nature, that was!

Ellen was pleasantly surprised to receive that call from Josh. He was never really the outgoing type and even when he'd been with Vanessa, her best friend, he'd always been distant though an overall nice guy.

But now Vanessa had been dead two years, in an ill-fated car crash. Josh had promptly withdrawn into his shell and Ellen had been disturbed by it because she really liked him. Okay, more than liked him. She'd always had the hots for Josh and had actually met him first before her friend Vanessa had. But Vanessa had been the kind of girl who knew what she wanted and would go for it. And while Ellen had dithered over her attraction for Josh, her friend had swept him off right under her nose.

They'd been dating for just three months when they got engaged, and Ellen had truly been happy for them. And it had been devastating when Vanessa died, just a few weeks to the wedding. Ellen could understand why Josh wouldn't really want anything that would remind him too much of all that. So why was he calling her up now?

He'd kept in touch with her over the years, mostly phone calls and once in a while, they'd meet for dinner or drinks. She kept wishing she could tell him how she felt about him, how she wished that for one night at least, he could give her a chance to show him how much she wanted him. How she could help him forget the pain, even for a moment. Her body melted for him, longed for his strong, male touch. He was so handsome, with his gym-hard body and dark raven hair. His eyes were a compelling grey, and he had that deep, sexy voice that would make any right-thinking girl decide to pull down her panties if he so much as asked.

Josh's phone call had been vague, but she'd understood that he needed some advice about a few things and was wondering if she could come over and see him. "I'll make you dinner," he promised. "I've been learning this new Paleo recipe and I'd love to show it off to you."

"Let's hope my stomach can survive the ordeal," she teased, secretly overjoyed that he wanted to meet her and also happy that he sounded so cheerful. Ellen knew she would readily risk a bout of food poisoning if it meant being alone with Josh even for a few hours.

She dressed carefully for the evening. She was only meeting him at his place but that didn't mean she had to be shabby. She struck off the idea of jeans and a shirt, and chose a flirty, elegant purple smock which went well with her dusky caramel skin. She pinned up her curly dark tresses into a lady-like style, and then slipped her feet into some killer strappy heels. Then she dabbed on a generous amount of her very sexy designer scent.

She took a look at her reflection and had to make a face. Okay, maybe she had overdone it a bit, but damn she hadn't seen him in months and was eager to make a good impression, and who knew, fate could be kind and somehow he'd start to notice her properly. She thought of her "lucky" pair of black lace panties which she was presently wearing; already it felt damp at the prospect of seeing Josh again and perhaps, getting that chance to carry out her fantasy of seducing him....

He opened the door to her knock, and in an

instant she felt her heart lurch. Was it possible he'd grown even hotter? He was lean and athletic and dressed in an open-necked white dress shirt tucked into dark chinos. He looked gorgeously tanned, and his hair swept over his forehead in a dashing new haircut. Ellen was glad now that she'd dolled up for the evening.

"You look fabulous, Ellen. Good to see you," he said with a big, infectious grin.

They embraced in the doorway, with the customary kiss on the cheek. It was all she could do not to jump him right then – just back him into the nearby couch and mount him like a wildcat in heat....

"You too, hon," she said, beaming as she handed him the bottle of wine she'd brought and went into the spacious apartment. "I like the way you wear your hair now."

"Thanks," he replied, looking pleased she'd noticed. "I decided to let it grow out of its buzz cut."

She turned to face him and saw his eyes rove over her body in a fleeting glance. Her stomach lurched as she told herself she'd never seen him look at her that way before; he'd always been above-board with his relations with her. But just now she'd had a glimpse of a certain heat in his gaze that made her think that maybe, just maybe, he might fancy her.

Ellen wasn't going to leave it all to chance this time. She'd made that mistake two years ago and Vanessa had ended up with the guy of Ellen's dreams. Now, Ellen vowed that she'd do what she had to do. And even if it didn't last beyond tonight, it would still be more than enough. At least she would be able to say that she'd taken the plunge.

The food turned out to be great; it was some new recipe from a certain diet he said he was now into, which focused on healthy eating practices from the ancient days. Ellen thought it tasted great though and told him so. They shared the wine she'd brought and got talking about how things had been since they last saw one another.

"So how are you, Josh? I mean really?" she asked quietly, as they got seated in the living room after clearing away dinner. They were nursing glasses from the remainder of the wine, and an easy, settled atmosphere had surrounded them. He was seated mere inches from her, and she couldn't help feeling this urge to throw her arms around him and kiss him hard, rake her fingers through his thick wavy hair and press her full breasts against him till her nipples hardened with delight.

But she reined in her ravenous hormones enough to focus on what he was saying.

"Good, actually," he said, a curved smile tilting his gorgeous lips. She could hardly tear her eyes away from them and wondered if he could read the desire blazing in her eyes. She really didn't want to scare him off by doing something drastic, but being this close to him was making her go crazy. She really didn't want them to be talking right then – she wanted them to be fucking. On the couch, against the wall, even on the Persian rug right there on the floor...it didn't matter. So long as she had his cock stuffed into her pussy she didn't care about the smaller details.

"I've been...thinking a lot about what you always used to tell me. You know, about trying to move on after Vanessa. That it's what she would have wanted," he said.

Ellen nodded firmly. "I know it is. Vanessa loved living, loved to seize the moment. She wouldn't want you to miss out on your own life just because she was no longer in it," she told him kindly. "And it's been so long since you've even dated. So...have you found someone?" she asked, hoping she didn't sound too crestfallen at the prospect.

He seemed to pause and then looked up at her with a direct gaze. "I think I have. I mean, she's been there all the while, a great friend, very supportive," he said, his tone deep and low. "It's been hard for me, keeping her at arms' length for so long when all I really wanted to do was..." He broke off and then shook his head with a smile.

"Go on," Ellen urged, though it was making her heart crack into pieces inside. If he'd fallen in love with some girl...

"Well, the thing is...I've desired her for a while, and I'm always on the brink of just coming straight out with the truth. But I was afraid she'd hate me. Think I'm crazy. After all, she was Vanessa's best friend..."

Slowly his words started to sink in and piece together, and Ellen almost went faint as the truth hit her like a blow. She stared at him, her lips parted in dazed wonder. A slow, sensual smile broke on his lips. His arm was lying on the back on the couch, and he began to lean forward into her space, his warm, fresh scent teasing her nostrils. She was too shocked to even move.

"Ellen...I want you," he told her softly, his lips now just inches from hers. She was gasping, her breath coming out in shallow, ragged spurts. If he so much as touched her now, she knew she'd combust, literally just catch fire.

"And it's been killing me to keep wondering if you could possibly...want me too." He'd slanted his head to trail his lips along her earlobe and just beneath it, making her shiver as indeed, she felt like her whole body become one huge ball of flame. For her answer, she simply clutched the front of his shirt and shoved him against her. The next moment, she was clamping her lips to his.

He groaned deep in his throat as she tantalized him with an open-mouthed, deeply erotic kiss. Her tongue dipped into his mouth and clashed with his wetly, and it just went into acceleration mode from there.

Looked like her "lucky" lacy panties did the trick after all, Ellen decided not long after. They certainly hadn't ever let her down, and tonight was no exception.

Josh turned out to be just the kind of lover she'd envisaged. Those silent hunk types, those cool-headed men with the staunch personas – they were usually the types who were pretty crazy in the sack. Well, Ellen did recall how Vanessa told her once or twice that

Josh was a heck of a lover.

And did thinking of Vanessa at that moment make Ellen feel even a little bit guilty? Not in the least. There was nothing wrong in two consenting adults finding pleasure and passion with one another as long as they weren't hurting anyone – living or not.

She wasn't sure how, but their clothes had found themselves strewn all over the floor. All Ellen had on were her black lace thongs which, for some reason, he wanted to keep on for a bit longer. She fell back readily as he covered her with his body, resting some of his weight on his arms as he bent to run his lips down her arched neck to her high, brown-tipped breasts.

In small, incremental steps, he devoured her tits, nuzzling his face in them and then nibbling on her stiff, dime-shaped nipples. She writhed and moaned beneath him, her hands snaking hungrily over his muscle-bound body with his rippling chest and six-pack. Damn it felt good to touch him, to twist his tiny nipples in her fingers and hear him groan in approval. And then, to slide her trembling hands down his washboard belly to where his cock reared proud and erect. He filled her palms amply, making her coo in delight as she spanned its thick, throbbing girth in her searching fingers.

His teeth sank into the fleshy curves of her breast, and she arched into his mouth, feeling her panties get damper than ever. Almost mindless with pleasure, she tugged on his shaft, stroking him firmly and trying to draw him close enough to her dripping pussy beneath its lacy barrier. He only chuckled and said something stirring, like "Soon baby, soon."

Well, it couldn't happen soon enough, Ellen thought in frenzied anticipation. Did he want her panting for him, reduce her to weeping for his cock to rip past that last scrap of modesty, and plunge into her waiting cunt?

But Josh showed her he couldn't be rushed. That he wanted to savor every moment of their coupling. His head was edging lower, zoning in on the v-shaped wedge between her wide open thighs. When he touched his fingers to her crotch, she couldn't help but buck into him with a cry of bliss. He stroked her through the lace, round and round, making her sob as she felt all the more tantalized, just as if he was touching her bare skin.

"Your panties are soaked through," he noted, his voice thick with lust and approval. Through half-lidded eyes, she watched him watching her, his eyes lifting to gaze upon her face and note every expression of pleasure that played on her features. "It's driving me crazy, knowing how much you want this. Want me."

"I've always wanted you, Josh. Always," she moaned, her hips moving of their own will as he thumbed her, caressing her swollen folds which formed a rounded camel-toe behind its veil of lace.

Her words made him groan, and he bent his head to her belly, to dip his tongue in its bowl. "You taste so delicious here...and here..." He punctuated his words with moist kisses on her belly, and then on the inside of her thigh, that most sensitive point closest to her pubic area. Next, he slipped his fingers beneath her panties and drew them to the side, right before he put his lips there and tongued her in one fast, hard lick. "Oh, and definitely here..."

Ellen was too blanked out by now to hear a word. His mouth on her pussy, his tongue pushing past her thong to lap at her slit, had sent her over the edge. She couldn't help herself; she came instantly, gushing right unto his waiting tongue.

"Fuck," she heard him growl deeply like he was in pain, and her whole body shuddered in reaction to what her pussy was feeling. He was licking at her wildly, eating up her juices which seemed to drench his lower face.

"Oh, baby," Ellen gasped, barely breathing, as she buried her fingers in his hair and drew him up for a rewarding kiss moments later. "That was...awesome. I can't wait to do the same for you."

"Damn, Ellen, you drive me insane," he confessed on a growl, cupping her face and gazing down at her. "I loved watching you cum, and eating it all up. And your beautiful skin...so soft and silky, and warm as chocolate...You are something special, baby. And I'm going to take the whole night to find out all the treasures you have in store..."

"You won't hear me saying no to that," she purred on a soft laugh. "But first..."

As she spoke, she slid to the floor next to the couch, positioning herself so that she was kneeling between his open legs. She was watching his face, which held a grimace of pleasure-pain as she wrapped both her hands around his cock and began to pump experimentally.

"Hmm…turnabout's only fair play as the saying goes," she said, eyes twinkling wickedly up at him as she lowered her mouth to his purple-tipped cap. She rolled her tongue round and round, lapping up his pre-cum and making him jerk and shudder and groan. Taking her time, she worked on his juicy fat cock, masturbating the length while she sucked hard on the marbled tip. In minutes, she'd managed to get more than half of the shaft buried in her mouth as she deep-throated him again and again.

He'd placed his hands round her head, gathering up the loose curls so he could free her face watch her go down on his cock. Yeah baby, yeah baby, he was saying over and over. Ellen had never felt so turned on sucking on a dick. She could go on for ages just sucking on his cock and licking his balls, and listen to him moan and grunt with pleasure.

Soon though, he was pulling her away, groaning regretfully. "Can't take much more," he said hoarsely. "I am so ramped up and I don't want to spunk in your mouth…not yet, anyway."

Ellen shuddered with delight at the prospect of Josh coming in her mouth; she'd love that, to taste his cum like he'd done hers. She vowed to remind him about it next time…

She felt like such a hussy for thinking about a "next time" – and a next. But was it so wrong? She knew she'd once told herself that even one night with Josh would be more than enough. And yet, here she was, already getting greedy. And he hadn't even fucked her yet....

They'd brought each other up to a fever pitch. The air was charged with hot, grinding lust, and it was only a matter of time before it ignited into a burst of fire.

Ellen needed that fire; she needed that heat to make her feel alive, feel like a woman. And right then only Josh's cock could give her that. When at last, he pulled her soaked panties down her legs and off her ankles, she was more than ready. He laid her beneath him on that Persian rug and he fucked her. Literally banged her brains out. From the moment he put on the condom and then slammed into her, she hadn't stopped screaming. With every deep, hard thrust of his big, fat cock, she cried out in pleasure-pain as she got stretched and stuffed by his pounding shaft.

Her fingers were digging into his ass cheeks as she held on tight to him, lifting her hips to meet his thrusts as he formed a steady, pumping rhythm. Her pussy clutched greedily at his rampaging cock, stroked him like a grasping velvet glove. Her very walls seemed to vibrate as they bore the delightful intrusion of that hard, stiff dick that seemed to be ripping into her very cervix.

He had braced himself on his hands to hold up most of his weight and still she felt crushed beneath him. He was so powerful, so incisive in the way he drove into her with a piston pace. He battered her swollen, pulsing cunt with that punishing cock of his, and she loved it. She loved that he wasn't gentle but fucked her like a tiger. He lifted his hand to her breast to squeeze hard, making her moan even louder as his passionate caresses meshed with the pleasure taking over her pussy and driving a tighter coil deeper into her belly.

"I'm coming, oh my gosh, I'm coming," she suddenly yelped, as her second climax erupted out of nowhere and slammed into her like a tidal wave. Her frantic confession, as well as the almost convulsive shudders that racked her body and pussy, finally drove him over the brink, as he too came in a long, vibrating rush.

It took several minutes for the calm to settle, and for their bodies to finally lie still. He lay down next to her, his breathing just as heavy and laborious as hers. She didn't resist as he pulled her closer so that she was half-lying atop him, their sweat-slick skin slowly cooling as the passion ebbed – but only for a moment. The next second, he was bending his lips to hers in a long, tempting kiss. His hands roved over her body to sink into the globes of her ass as he cupped them firmly.

"It was just as perfect as I thought it would be," he murmured against her lips. "And it was just as I'd told myself many times before...I always knew, deep down, that if we ever did it, then I'd never want it to stop. I'd want it to happen again and again."

Ellen's heart leaped to hear that, to know

that she was going to have some more of that hot, throbbing cock she'd come to crave like a narcotic fix.

"There's nothing...and no one, to stop us, is there?" she asked softly, her hand reaching up to comb back his hair as she looked into his dark grey eyes meaningfully.

"No...not anymore," he said with a simplicity that made Ellen sigh deeply in happiness. With those words, she knew that he was letting her know that he'd let the past go at last. There was nothing stopping them from giving and taking whatever life held in wait for those ready to grab it with both hands....

10 SLEEPING IN HIS BED

It had been a long, hard trip, travelling by air for almost four hours. Drake Cole was glad to be back home, and as he let himself into the quiet house, he wondered if his sister was awake. She'd started staying with him six months ago, after she'd begun going to the university here in the city. He hadn't minded her being around since she was great with the meals and keeping the house neat and tidy. One thing he had to complain about, though, was that she liked parties and had no trouble throwing them here in the house.

He couldn't help sighing with relief when he got home and found it dark and filled with peace and quiet. It was very unlike the last time when he'd returned unexpectedly from his business trip to find that Heather, his sister, was having a very wild party. It had been late at night and the place had been filled with scantily dressed guys and chicks, the crowd spilling out to the back where there was a nice-sized swimming pool. He'd been pissed off with her for staging a pool party without his permission, though she'd managed to cajole him with a very sweet apology as she promised it wouldn't happen again.

Looked like she'd kept that promise, he thought approvingly, as he walked up the stairs of the quiet house. It was past midnight and he was sure she was asleep. Sighing deeply, Drake decided he'd just take a shower, fall into bed, and then maybe sleep for a week.

He walked into his bedroom, throwing off his coat and heading straight for the bathroom. He undressed and took a quick, hot shower to warm him up for bed. He was towel-drying his hair when he returned to the unlit bedroom. Feeling much better after the shower, he threw off his robe and pulled back the covers, ready to just dive into bed and grab some much-needed sleep. He rolled unto the mattress with a deep sigh, pulling the covers over him and laying on his back with his eyes closed. It took seconds for him to realize that the deep, soft yet unmistakable sound of steady breathing was not coming from him.

"What on earth…"

He reached out and snapped the bedside light on, before turning to his side and pulling back the covers to find that someone was lying in his bed right next to him.

At first, he thought he must be dreaming, shocked to the marrow to find a scantily clad woman asleep in his bed.

She was curled away from him in a tight ball, and her slim, shapely body was clad in some kind of sleeping tee and tiny cotton knickers. Her hair was a cloud of raven dark curls, spreading over the pillows next to her. Once the lights came on, she moaned and shifted to lie on her back, blinking in surprise. When she glanced Drake's way and saw him staring in shock, she sat up with a beaming smile.

"Oh, hi," she said in a sleep-huskied voice.

Drake was trying very, very hard not to freak out. What the hell was a very beautiful- and sexy-looking girl doing lying skimpily dressed in his bed? He couldn't help remembering that he was stark naked since he never wore any clothes to sleep. She looked to be around his sister's age, maybe twenty-one or twenty-two. As he stared at her, he began to suspect he may even have seen her once or twice, coming around to visit Heather. Heather had a lot of beautiful, sexy young friends, but he generally kept out of their way. He was at least ten years older than any of them, and at age thirty-two, he was always careful not to make a fool of himself. A serious man of business, he hardly had time for relationships, and it had been a while since he'd had a young woman in his bed and certainly not a strange one.

"I'm sorry, what are you doing in here? And who are you?" he asked, bunching the covers as much as he could around his midsection. He couldn't help his eyes straying from her face to her chest as she lay propped up by her elbows, unconsciously thrusting out her unfettered breasts. They looked quite perky and rounded beneath her thin, clinging t-shirt. He could even see the outline of her silver-dollar-shaped nipples and he absent-mindedly marveled at how hard and big they were.

"My name's Zoe—and sorry you had to find me crashing in your bed," she said drowsily, stifling a huge yawn. "I'm a friend of Heather's and was meant to have a sleepover, but Heather was snoring too damn much so I had to find a different room."

She was smiling humorously, and Drake noticed she had a really cute, white smile, with nice teeth which had a very slight and pretty gap in the middle. Her full-bottomed lips looked quite inviting and sensuous. Drake was feeling very, very confused. He was a naked, red-blooded male, and here was a gorgeous, very sexy young lady in his bed—one who didn't seem in the least alarmed by his appearance. She seemed even glad to see him.

He thought of her words and had to agree to himself that Heather did tend to saw logs at night especially after she had a late, heavy dinner. However, that didn't give her friend an excuse to come into his room and take over his bed. He knew his annoyance really didn't have anything to do with what she'd done though. He was actually more pissed off with himself and how his body was responding to the sight, smell and feel of having such a delectable body this close, and so unexpectedly.

"I'm really sorry this has happened," she

repeated with a rueful smile when he didn't speak. "And Heather did say you were coming—but when you didn't show up by ten she thought maybe you missed your flight and wouldn't make it anymore. That's why I decided to use your room. She doesn't even know I'm here, okay? She was fast asleep when I left her room. I'll just go back now...." She made to slide out of the bed, giving him a glimpse of her endless golden legs and pretty feet which she was about to swing to the floor.

Drake didn't realize when his hand shot out to grip hers. "No, stay," he said earnestly, surprising her. She looked up at him with quizzical eyes, and he quickly retrieved his hand. "I mean, you can stay in this bed. I'll just go...crash in the living room. There's a couch there I can use."

She was shaking her head firmly. "I can't let you do that. I mean you just got back from a very stressful trip and need a decent rest. I honestly couldn't ask you to take the couch, Mr. Cole. I mean Drake. Can I call you that?" she asked with a sudden shy smile. He nodded, finding that he liked the sound of his name on her lips. He was feeling so horny looking at her, with her pretty elfin face and hair mussed with sleep. In fact, his cock was getting uncomfortably hard just lying there next to her, and he had this sudden urge to do something really base, like seduce her.

She certainly looked like she'd be game. Drake knew a bit about women to know certain signals they unconsciously or consciously gave out. This chick called Zoe seemed much too comfortable around him, and she wouldn't be that way if she didn't trust him or maybe even liked him. He decided to pursue this line of reasoning with some digging.

"So...Zoe, you're Heather's pal—which means you're in her class?" he asked casually.

"Well, yeah, but I'm a year older, which makes me twenty-two," she said, suddenly wrinkling her nose as if she felt that age difference made her feel more ancient.

"You're a nice-looking twenty-two, trust me," he said with a stiff smile, wanting to say much more but didn't wish to scare her off. He actually felt like telling her she was in fact a very hot, sexy and arousing twenty-two year old. His last girlfriend had been closer to his age, a grown and accomplished young exec with a woman's body, big tits, spreading ass and thick thighs. He hadn't minded the extra flesh because he liked a bit of cushion in a woman. But looking over Zoe's lithe, youthful and obviously well-kept body made him think he wouldn't mind the idea of fucking someone slimmer in contrast. Maybe it was the refreshing shower, or maybe it was just the sight of a hot young chick in his bed, but Drake felt far from tired or sleepy. In fact, his cock was hard as a plank and he was glad for the thick covers that concealed the tent rising between his legs. He licked his dry lips as he met her wide, innocent-looking gaze.

"Why, thank you, Drake," she said, her voice a little breathy. "I always did think you're very handsome, yourself, although a bit forbidding. You don't remember me, do you?"

He shook his head. "Not really. I'm sure I

must have seen you before, but Heather has so many friends, I..."

"It's okay," she said sheepishly. "I remember you, though. I was here last month to study with Heather, and I was making a sandwich in the kitchen for a snack when you came in to get some beer from the fridge. You seemed to be watching a game in the den with your pals and when you saw me you gave me a friendly smile then you left to go back to the game."

He suddenly recalled that day; two of his friends had come by to his place to catch the Lakers game, and he'd had to get some extra beers from the fridge. There had been a girl there but he'd hardly noticed much about her, too distracted by the game probably. He wished now that he'd been more observant.

"I'd been coming around but that was the first time you'd ever looked at me or smiled at me. I felt really glad that day," she confessed breathily, then grinned. "I guess I used to be a little scared of you, just like most of Heather's friends are. And since we also seem to be nursing crushes on you..."

"W...what?" he said on a surprised laugh.

She shrugged, her cheeks growing pink. "Forget it. I really shouldn't have said anything. It felt nice sleeping in your bed though; I felt so warm and cozy in the covers, and I could swear I could pick your scent inside them. But I guess you'll want to catch some sleep now after your long day, so..."

She made to leave again, and once again he reached out to grab her hand. This time he didn't release her immediately; instead his fingers stroked up her bare forearm. He looked into her clear, beautiful green eyes, his heart pounding with the anticipation of what he wanted to do. But he still couldn't be sure he wouldn't get smacked in the face, or worse, send her screaming as she fled the room. The last thing he wanted was to do something she'd find distasteful. A young woman telling you she had a crush on you wasn't the same as saying she'd want to fuck you. He knew that, so he decided to tread carefully.

"Look, maybe neither of us has to leave. It's a large enough bed, big enough for the both of us. I don't mind sharing," he said with a teasing smile. He saw her eyes flicker down his bare chest, and he wondered if she knew he was totally naked. He decided to give her fair warning. "The only problem is, I don't sleep with pajamas on; I find clothes uncomfortable when I'm sleeping."

She chewed on her bottom lip, something like a gamble jumping in her eyes. He didn't know what it was, till she stuck her fingers into the hem of her shirt and said, "In that case, let's make it fifty-fifty," she purred, her voice smoky. Drake swallowed, his brain freezing when, just like that, she pulled the t-shirt off over her head. She flung it away, leaning back again so that her sweet bouncy breasts were thrust invitingly in front of his wide gaze. She smiled wickedly at the look of unmistakable need that darkened his face. "I don't much like clothes myself," she added, straight-faced. "Should I stop there, Mr. Cole?"

He knew what she meant; she still had on her frilly, somewhat girly cotton panties on.

Looking at them made his hard-on ache fiercely. His fingers were itching to grab her medium-sized tits with their gorgeous, almost invisibly pink fat nipples. He wanted to grab her in his arms and kiss his lips all over her slightly tanned body, from her neck to the tip of her coral-painted toes. In short, he wanted to fuck her all night till they both passed out.

He felt like such a toad for thinking this; he'd always thought he was much too sensible and controlled for such behavior. He'd kept away from Heather's friends precisely for this same reason: he wanted to keep his dignity intact. But here Zoe was, half naked in his bed, looking available for the taking.

Her calling him Mr. Cole, though in a teasing manner, reminded him of the age difference and how he was a decade older than her. And yet, she was gazing at his body with evident admiration and longing. Drake was glad that he always made time for staying fit, and kept himself as gym-solid as possible. He was sure he had as good a body—maybe even better and broader—than any of her university jocks.

"Well, Zoe, I wouldn't lie and say I don't like the idea of you taking it all off—because I do," he said lightly, "But I'm not sure how it's going to work out if I have a totally nude and sexy young woman lying next to me. It's not going to do great for my sleep patterns, I assure you."

"So...just what would it take for you to get a good night's sleep, Mr. Cole?" she asked in the same conversational tone. She reached out an arm and let her small, soft hand rest on his bare shoulder. Her fingers dug in experimentally, as she pouted with a thoughtful expression. "I do hear that a nice massage can take away the kinks from a hard day." As she spoke, she was caressing firmly on his shoulder, watching his face as he closed his eyes briefly at her touch.

"Or, maybe the kink's right here..."

His eyes flew open as she said those words and slid her hand from his shoulder, down his chest and past his belly to delve beneath the covers and grasp his cock. He shuddered in sweet, shocked delight, staring into her dancing eyes as a new, hot wave of lust ripped through his body. She stroked him in her firm, bold grip, pumping up and down on his shaft. He almost exploded there and then.

And there he'd been, afraid and worried about taking advantage of her. Yet here she was, taking charge and turning him into jelly right before her.

"Hmm, I seriously doubt you'd get any sleep with that to worry about," she said, edging the covers away and exposing his rock-hard cock which she was fisting in her hand. He stared down at her small fingers wrapped around his dick, and felt himself grow even harder and longer. He'd never been so deeply aroused before; his shaft was throbbing and the veins were standing out like angry ridges.

"No...sleeping would be out of the question," he croaked, looking back up at her. "What would you have in mind to...help me with that?"

She smiled teasingly, giving him the "naughty, naughty" look. Well, Drake knew he was being naughty, but so was she, grabbing his manhood like that. It was enough to give any man ideas. Yet he wanted her to spell things out right here and now. He wasn't about to start something and then have her act the tease and stop him. Or worse, end up accusing him of trying to rape her or something. She had to lay it down on the line before he let things get to the point of no return for him.

"Well...," she said thoughtfully, still masturbating his cock with her fingers. "I could suggest a bit of hand relief...or maybe a nice, wet blowjob...or maybe I could let you fuck me for as long as you want. Do you think that would help?"

"Oh, definitely," he said, nodding his head vigorously. "A nice hard fuck will put me out like a light afterwards. And I don't mind the "hand relief" and blowjob rolled in, as well. Just so there'll be nothing left to chance, I mean."

She was shaking her head at him teasingly, but she seemed to find his reply very satisfactory. "That's all settled then. I'll give you my patented hand and blow job—and then you can put this big monster right inside my pussy. I must say I do love the way a cock feels in my hand, my mouth...and my cunt." At that, she leaned forward and met his lips in a kiss.

They lay side by side and were kissing

lingeringly, not rushing it one bit. He rolled his tongue into her hot sweet mouth, and she opened up to let him plunder and explore. As their lips clung moistly, their hands were busy. She was still stroking his cock and also his balls and it felt so, so good, because she used just the right amount of pressure. His hands were busy kneading her perfect tits, twisting on the incredibly fat nipples. They were both moaning, though not too loudly so as not to draw any undue attention from his sister's room. It was down the hall and she was a deep sleeper, but it paid to be cautious.

Still kissing her hungrily, he let his right hand disengage reluctantly from her firm and bouncy boobs to slide past her concave belly to the junction of her thighs. As his hand fell on her crotch in their cotton panties, she immediately threw her legs further apart in invitation. His heart pounding like a sledgehammer, he stroked her over the fabric of her underwear, his fingertips tracing the mound of her pussy. He felt his whole body shudder; touching her was driving him crazy, and her soft moans of encouragement were music to his ears.

He caressed her continuously, rubbing and patting her pussy in small, circular motions. He could feel the dampness of her arousal spreading, and he could hardly keep from ripping the panties aside and fingering her furiously. But no, it felt so tantalizing to stroke and tease her this way and feel her thighs quiver in response.

She was moaning against his lips, her lower body bucking against his hand. Soon the area around her genitals was soaked right through, and she was kissing him more roughly, hungrily. Now that he'd got her all fevered up, he made her lay back as he broke the kiss and began pressing his lips all over her body. He trailed his way moistly down her neck to her shoulder blades. He simply wanted to worship every sweetly scented inch of her.

Her skin tasted so fresh and thrilling, the heat from her body making him harder than ever. He put his mouth to her nipple and suckled her, grabbing as much of her boob into his mouth as his hand kneaded her roughly. She was clutching his head in ecstasy, writhing and breathing hard and fast. He moved from one breast to the other, feasting on their flesh and nubs. He loved being able to do what he liked with her young, firm tits. He was also deliriously glad of the fact that she was willing and ready to let him do what he liked with her delicious body.

All thought of sleep vanished from his mind. He was lost totally in his desire for this sweet, sexually responsive young woman who turned him on like he'd never been before. Now that she was lying beneath him, limp with pleasure, he knew she was going to be ready to do what ever he asked. She would be hungry to take every direction and do anything she had to do to get him finishing what he started.

And finish it he would, he vowed, as he began to slowly roll down her drenched knickers. Once he'd taken them off her ankles, he spread them wide so he could view her beautifully trimmed pussy. Her outer lips were swollen and ripe-looking, and her little clit was hard and pointed. He'd never seen such a pretty vagina, so pink and tightly furled. He put his fingers to her slit and parted her to touch her moistened walls. She gasped and jerked, but otherwise stayed still as he explored her expertly. He guided his fingers slowly into her cunt and sawed them in and out in a pounding motion. She almost flew off the bed, but he used his free hand to grip her thigh.

"Easy, honey," he said with a soft smile, looking up at her pleasure-dazed face. As he finger-fucked her, he lowered his head so he could lap around her cunt region, sucking on her clit and licking up her dripping slit. She was shuddering convulsively by this time, and her obvious arousal, her copious moistness, made him feel ready to erupt in her hand which still jacked him furiously.

However, he thought it was a better idea to shift his position so that he could make her sit on his face, while her head would be in the direction of his crotch. She seemed to be quite well versed with this type of situation, as she readily straddled his face and bent over his torso before taking his cock in her mouth. He groaned with deep pleasure into her pussy, taking hold of her pert ass cheeks and pulling them farther apart so he could tongue her snatch and then upwards to her tight little bum hole.

Her whole frame was a shivery mass at this point, and she sucked on him like a fiend as he made her pussy feel like it was on fire. Her head bobbed enthusiastically up and down his now pole-straight shaft, one hand pumping the base while the other fondled his heavy balls. She sure knew her way around a cock, Drake noted with appreciation, as with her lips wrapped up and down his shaft, she worked inwardly with her tongue. He felt her warmth and wetness envelope his cock as she teased his cap with her tongue in butterfly licks.

When he was sure he couldn't take much more, he made her stop, and then brought her around so that this time she was facing him as she settled above his waiting cock. Her hands were braced on his chest, and she didn't even need to be asked before she slowly, painstakingly, lowered her pussy on him.

He slipped in easily, her walls so slick he had no trouble burying himself to the hilt in her tight, hot pussy. Both of them groaned at the first sensation of their most intimate parts being joined. Gripping her waist, he pumped upwards, willing to do all the work as he fucked her powerfully. She didn't complain, and in fact seemed to enjoy his somewhat rough shafting.

Again and again, he bottomed into her, watching her beautiful face as she grimaced at the deep intrusion. And yet the pleasure seemed just as strong, as she sighed and moaned with every thrust. His hands reached up to grab her enticing tits, and he could tell she was totally into their coupling with the way her pussy walls shuddered around his cock. He was ready for her, knew exactly when her climax was going to hit and picked up his pace, ramming through her like a fuck machine.

Being able to witness her cumming was just the right thing to get him blowing his load deep inside her. Her face contorted, her lips parted wide and she had to bite on her knuckles to keep from screaming as suddenly, she climaxed. Seconds later, he was bursting the banks, his balls emptying their contents into her cunt. They both bumped and ground into each other for a full minute as they combusted in unison.

There was no telling how long they took trying to catch their breath. She was slumped over him, her head lain on his chest. His arms were wrapped soothingly around her as slowly, calm settled within the bedroom walls.

Gently, he drew her down beside him, stroking the hair gently from her face as she sighed and snuggled closer to him. Her half-lidded eyes were looking up at him with a smile, and she looked just like an angel then, so happy, satisfied and thoroughly fucked.

"Wow, Mr. Cole...that was something," she cooed. "My pussy feels well pounded. I hope I can be able to wobble back to Heather's room on time, before she wakes up and finds me gone." She chuckled softly. "If she realizes what I've done, she'd kill me."

"What you've done? Baby, if anyone's to blame, it's me," he said firmly, cupping her cheek.

She seemed to blush guiltily. "Well, don't be

entirely sure of that," she said with a hesitant smile. "I have a confession to make, and I hope you won't hate me too much for it...Drake, I knew you'd be coming home tonight. I wanted you to return and find me in your bed."

He frowned in surprise and confusion, and she went on, "When you didn't show up as we expected, I took the liberty of checking online and discovered your flight was only delayed. So I had this crazy idea to be here, waiting. Heather does snore, but it's never bothered me much before, so that was a lie, too." She looked somewhat sheepish. "I always really, really wanted you, but I knew you'd never notice me or make a move unless I did something...drastic. Do you hate me now?"

Drake stared down at the beautiful, innocent-looking and highly sensual girl lying next to him. His expression was that of amazement. "Are you kidding? Hate you? Zoe, you've given me the hottest night I've ever had. It's like a fantasy for a man to have a young, willing girl ready and willing to please him. Finding you here, sleeping in my bed, was the best surprise ever. Don't ever forget that."

"Well, I feel much better now," she sighed happily, then threw her arms around him for a quick hug. "I hope we get a lot more sleepovers together, you and me. You sure know how to treat a girl to a good fuck. None of my college boyfriends can give me that good a work-over."

He grinned with pleasure. "Happy to have been of service and trust me, baby, this cock will be waiting any night of the week if that's what you want."

"Oh, I want," she assured him, before pressing one quick hard kiss on his lips and then slipping out of the bed. She picked up her discarded panties and t-shirt and quickly put them on. Blowing him a kiss and giving him one last mischievous smile, she left to return to Heather's room, shutting the door softly after her.

Sighing deeply, Drake glanced at the bedside clock and saw that it was almost five am. He was certainly glad that it was the weekend, which meant he could get some decent sleep. Smiling at the memory of what had just occurred, he settled deeply into the covers and was soon off like a light.

11 TO MY RESCUE

Prologue

Gina had chosen the worst night in the world to break it off with her faithless boyfriend, Hank. She hadn't really thought it out first but she'd been so mad after catching him flirting. The only problem was, now she was stuck outside the bar and had to get home before Hank showed up to cause trouble.

And then comes a perfect stranger who offers to whisk her away and out of Hank's clutches. At first, she's cautious, but then she decides to trust him, only to discover he was her next door neighbor, Brandon, a neighbor who was very intent on building warm and lover-like relations....

There was no way Gina was going to let Hank get away with this.

There he was, flirting with the waitress again. Every time they came here, he just had to embarrass her. She sighed angrily, wondering why she put up with this. She didn't even love him and that was what made the whole situation so galling.

"Sorry hon, there was such a long wait," he said cheerfully when he returned to their table minutes later with their beers. She shook her head and looked away. Obviously, he'd had no idea that she could see him easily from where she sat and had watched him the whole time chatting with the waitress and then taking her number.

"You know what, Hank?" she said suddenly, turning to face him again. "I think that standing so long in that line got you all hot and sweaty. Maybe this would cool you off." With those words, she picked up her glass and upended the contents on his head. As he gasped aloud in shock, she rose to her feet and shouldered her bag. And then not even waiting to say another word, she strode out of the bar, ignoring the curious looks she got.

Outside in the night air, she sighed deeply. She actually felt better now. Just seeing Hank's face when she'd dumped her beer on him was enough to make up for how angry and hurt she'd felt. It had been a reckless thing to do but it was worth it.

"Hey lady."

She stopped short in her stride, turning to find someone standing on the pavement next to her. A quick look told her it was a good-looking guy, a bit taller than six feet, and dressed casually in chinos and a check shirt. She tried to guess his age around maybe thirty. He had a nice smile, very charming. But she ignored him and looked stonily away.

"Oh, so it's like that," he said in a humorous voice. She found she liked it. Deep, gravelly, rough. Very sexy. She glanced his way again. His shirt fit his shoulders snugly, and detailed his narrow waist. He really packed those chinos well too, she noted.

"Yes, it's like that," she told him coolly. She'd been about to start walking when he showed up. "Look, I just had a bad moment in there, and I simply want to go home. It was nice meeting you but—"

"Oh, I saw it," he told her with a sudden grin. "The bad moment, I mean. But it wasn't you who got it bad. It was that guy." He thumbed over his shoulder, and she saw that Hank had stepped out of the bar and was looking round with a furious look on his face. When he noticed Gina, he shouted her name.

"Oh shit, he looks mad," she mumbled. His hair was plastered to his face and his expensive white shirt was ruined, discolored and sticking wetly to his frame. He was making his way over to them, and Gina couldn't help feeling a little apprehensive. Hank was on the huge side with lots of muscles, and she was getting worried that that his expression was in no way reassuring.

"I've got a car," the guy next to her said suddenly, indicating the vehicle parked in front of them. "You don't have to stand and take more shit from him."

Gina hesitated, but then she looked back at Hank who was striding quickly towards them. Making up her mind suddenly, she nodded to the guy. "Let's move it."

She scrambled in next to him and felt relieved how quickly the car got started, and they were zooming off just as Hank picked up his pace and tried to run up and catch them. But he was too late, and Gina could see from her rear view mirror how he stood in the middle of the road staring after them, his face a mask of anger.

In moments, they'd left him far behind and then he disappeared as the car turned the next corner. Gina found that she was laughing happily and turned to the man beside him to find him also smiling.

She sobered up a little though. "Thanks," she murmured, suddenly realizing she was in the car of a perfect stranger. She had allowed him to simply drive her off just seconds after meeting him. Now that was reckless; it looked like she was doing that a lot tonight.

"You're welcome," he said, his lips tilting up in one corner in a kind of lop-sided smile. He really seemed like a nice guy, but Gina knew it was better to be cautious.

"Look, you can drop me off at the next right," she said calmly. "I live not too far from here."

"I know," he said wryly, and she turned to him in surprise. "I live nearby too. Just moved in two weeks ago, two houses from yours. I see you go to work morning. And I recognized you when you threw your beer all over that guy."

"You mean we're neighbors?" Gina said in surprise, turning to stare at him. "How come I've never met you?"

"I'm a writer, and since I moved in, I was holed up trying to finish my latest—and long overdue—manuscript. I went to the bar tonight to celebrate finally getting it completed, and then you showed up."

"Hmm," she said, settling into her chair again. "Well, I'm Gina."

"And I'm Brandon," he returned, turning smoothly into the next street, which was theirs. "I've been looking forward to finally meeting you—I was thinking of showing up at the door to introduce myself as the new neighbor, maybe bearing a gift of home-made pie." He shrugged, flashing a grin. "I make mean pie. But then again, I think I like this way better—rescuing the damsel in distress and whisking her away to safety."

Gina tried not to giggle like a twelve-year-old girl. "Well yeah, it's an unconventional way to meet your next door neighbor, but I'll also admit it was cool. The way you maneuvered so easily out of that tight parking lot...and then sped off leaving Hank to choke on the fumes...." Her shoulders were shaking with laughter.

"That's your boyfriend's name? Hank?"

"My ex-boyfriend," she muttered, suddenly scowling. "And forget him; I should have dumped some beer on him long ago. I should have dumped him long ago, period."

Brandon paused, his gaze seeking out hers in the confines of the car. "Looks like you need some picking up."

She glanced over his way quickly, and saw his friendly smile. Saw the invitation in his grey eyes. In his very nice, warm grey eyes. Gina bit on her lip in confusion. She could feel the good vibes coming off him, but she could also feel the sudden sexual tension. She wasn't sure if she was ready for this right now.

"Look, uh, Brandon. I'm happy you helped me out tonight—you really did your part as a good neighbor," she began, smiling tentatively at her own attempt at humor, "But I just want to go in and..."

"Hey," he cut in softly, reaching out his hand to brush aside a strand of her long, raven black lock. His touch was light, but she could feel the uncomfortable intimacy in such a gesture. But then it only felt uncomfortable because she liked it. Uh oh, she wondered, was this how it felt to be attracted to a complete stranger? Even though he lived just down the road....

"Look, I've got a bottle of wine you might like to share. Very vintage red. Besides...I don't want Hank to come looking for you tonight when you least expect it," Brandon told her lightly.

Gina stiffened, suddenly realizing he may be right. Hank had a key to her place; he could easily show up and then start a fight or something. She'd really made a fool of him tonight and he may decide not to take it lying down. She remembered his face when Brandon had driven them off. He'd looked positively murderous.

She sighed heavily. "Oh, all right. But just

one glass," she said, wagging her finger. "I don't do alcohol too well. I only ever drink half of my beer anyway. Anything more and I usually have to get carried out of the bar."

He chuckled, she smiled. The chemistry was great, she realized. Coupled with the fact that he was very attractive and looked hot, he also had a way of being very easy to relax with. But Gina knew she'd better not relax too easily and put down her guard.

She followed him to his front door, and she glanced around the quiet, street-lit road. "You coming in?" Brandon asked her with a teasing smile as he stood behind his open door. She turned and looked up.

You can back away now, Gina, said her sensible inner voice. Just step back and leave. There's still a chance; then something made Gina decide, what the heck. It was just some wine and a bit of friendly conversation. Not like she intended to jump into bed with him or anything.

"Yeah, sure," she said at last, returning his smile.

"And then the guy finally said, "computer dating is fine—if you're a computer," Brandon said, finishing off the joke and sending Gina into another fit of laughter. Gosh, he was so funny. Thirty minutes after she'd walked into his house, and three glasses later, she was deciding that she'd never met anyone so funny. He made even the dumbest gags sound comic. She held a hand to her belly as she tried to quell the ache from all that laughing. Once she could breathe, she reached for her glass of wine and drank it down to calm herself. When he held up the bottle to give her a refill, she raised her hand in refusal.

"No, really. Or I'll just end up passing out on the carpet," she joked, though she did feel a little lightheaded. The wine was the best she'd ever tasted, and she'd ended up having more than she'd intended. But Brandon had been right; she had needed the picking up.

"So, have you ever tried it? I mean, meeting someone online? The so-called computer dating?" she asked curiously, tucking her feet under her on the couch. He was sitting on the other end, twirling the stem of his glass in one hand.

"Not really. I mean, you get to meet some people on the internet on one context or another—but I never tried meeting anyone or hooking. But now with being single for three months, maybe it's time I viewed the many options left open to me."

"I don't think the mode of meeting someone has a bearing on the relationship, or how it unfolds," she said thoughtfully, staring into her empty glass. "I mean, I met Hank at work. We were in the same department, at least till I got promoted. Anyway, I'm saying that even though I got to know him long before we started dating, it didn't make the relationship work any better. He still cheats on me when he likes, and still treats me like my feelings don't count. But that's all past tense now."

"I'm glad to hear that," he said softly, taking the empty glass she clutched in her hands, and placing it next to his on the coffee table in front of them. And then he turned to her, easing himself up to close the distance between them. Gina felt her body stiffen, especially when he placed his arm behind her on the top of the couch. "And I'm really glad I was there in that bar tonight. You see, I think it's really all about the right place, right time. It could be anyone, and it could be anyhow. But when it happens, you'll know."

He cupped her cheeks in his hands, and Gina took hold of his wrists, already shaking her head even as his face came lower. "Brandon..."

"I watched you for two weeks," he was saying softly, his lips just a breath away from hers. She felt mesmerized by the sound of his voice, her eyes tied to the shape of his mouth, with its firm, sexy curves. "Every morning, I looked forward to seeing you walk past on your way to take a bus to work. I'd be sitting in front of my window, working on my computer, waiting for you to show up. It always made my day—and I kept thinking, damn, she's hot. The way you did up your hair, the way you look so nice in a dress...I also used to see Hank come around, and I always told myself: that jackass doesn't even deserve her. And I kept thinking of the ways I'd make you happy if you were mine."

Gina swallowed with difficulty, feeling the air around them get charged with more of that sexual tension she'd felt in the car. Part of her wanted to give in, to find out where this would lead. Tonight had turned out pretty bad— maybe this could help make it feel right again, to lose herself in Brandon's arms, no strings attached.

She certainly felt attracted to him, a

sensation that had increased with every passing minute. And then there'd been all that wine, which had loosened her up into laughing at everything he said. If she kissed Brandon now, she knew they'd have sex. And after the way Hank had been treating her lately, she didn't even know why she was hesitating. But something made her pull away, and rise unsteadily to her feet.

"I...I've got to go," she said, backing away.

He nodded, a slight, regretful smile curving his lips. He, too, rose. "If you're sure you'll be okay."

"I'll be fine," she told him, making her way for the exit, relieved when he didn't try to stop her, though he came up after her to help unlock the door. She wasn't sure why, but she suddenly turned and gave him a quick, warm embrace. She was internally surprised how breathless that little hug had made her; the feel of her pressing herself against his body for those three seconds had been strangely thrilling. She could only guess what it would be like to actually get truly intimate with him.

"Wow, thanks," he murmured with one of his teasing smiles, and she saw how reluctant he was to let his hands fall from her waist. "But I was thinking that the knight actually gets a kiss at least, for staging the damsel's rescue."

"Huh," she huffed, but she was smiling a little shyly. What was one kiss, anyway? Besides, he really was totally hot. The kind of guy she'd have loved to date or hang out with if she was really honest.

"So, how about it? One kiss." He was

looking down at her, a slight challenge in his smile.

Well, Gina did like a bit of a challenge. So she was going to kiss him, but then she had to leave. She'd done too many reckless things that night and didn't want to add rebound sex to the list....

Who ever had written or said that a kiss was just a kiss had never kissed a man like Brandon.

Gina was able to realize her mistake the moment she placed her mouth against his. She had her arms linked behind his head, and he'd pulled her close and into him as their lips had met. And in the next second, she felt like she'd been hit by a bolt.

She could taste a trace of wine, mingled with the hot, fresh taste of sexy male. She was wedged against him, and her breasts started to tingle in almost instant response to being crushed against his hard-packed chest. Ooh boy, she thought to herself in awe, as his tongue slashed deep into her mouth and switched on some long-forgotten light deep inside her. She jumbled her own-seeking tongue to his and heard them both groan. She hadn't known it would feel so good to kiss him, or that his lips would feel so firm yet inviting against hers. She tugged at him, sucked on him, and felt a shudder reverberate through his frame and then hers. Damn, this felt good. She hadn't enjoyed a kiss so much in a long time.

She could feel his hands smoothing over her lower curves, and when he reached round to cup her ass cheeks in her jeans, she didn't protest. But then he hauled her closer and brought her into contact with an unmistakable hardness poking like a steel rod against her belly. She gasped in blistering, instant lust.

I shouldn't have drunk that last glass, she told herself, twisting her arms even tighter around his neck as she feasted moistly on his kiss. She told herself it was the wine making her so bold, giving her the daringness to trace her tongue over the outline of his lips and before shoving it deep into his mouth again. His hands were gripping tightly just underneath her breasts, and she almost wanted to sob out loud at the sudden wish that he would simply grab her mounds in his large hands and just squeeze....

"Stay," he said on a rasp, breaking the kiss for a moment.

"I can't," she sighed, even as her mouth clung to his, their lips making smacking noises as they pulled at each other sensuously.

"What if he comes around when you're asleep? You can spend the night here and then tomorrow, change the locks to the house," he told her sensibly, placing his hands on her shoulders and putting her at arm's length. He gazed down at her with eyes so dark the grey was almost black. "I wasn't so happy to drive off from that bar earlier tonight. I'd been in there and had seen him drooling all over that waitress. What I'd really wished to do was punch him in the face for not appreciating having a woman like you. I'd never hurt you, Gina."

His voice was soft and almost hypnotic, his hand lifting to comb through her dark hair. "You're so fucking sexy: your smile, your smell...it drives me crazy. I just want to make love to you, show you how it feels for a man to touch your body like it was the most precious thing in the world."

Gina was trembling with the need his words invoked deep within her. She looked up into his eyes and was lost. Even if her lips had wanted to say no, there was no way her body was going to let her get away with it. A coil had started to form deep within her pussy, making her outer lips swell in her crotch till she felt like ripping off her jeans and just getting naked. And then thinking of being naked in front of Brandon made the coil tighten even more.

"You know...," she murmured, slipping her arms around his neck again, "Usually, a guy takes me out for a movie or some dinner before he gets to the part where he wants me to jump into bed with him." Her eyes were dancing—teasing, tempting him.

He growled deep in his throat, reaching beneath her knees and then whipping her easily into his arms. "Well then, so I owe you a movie and some dinner then," was his humorous reply, before he locked their lips in a moist, searing kiss.

Brandon's master bedroom was nicely done, in deep, masculine hues and tones. He had a huge four poster which seemed to be the main attraction, judging by its size and how it was strategically placed in the center of the room. He'd dimmed the lights to a more romantic, calming setting, and yet there was that blaze in his eyes that glowed so brightly, it was almost like being under a spotlight.

Gina turned into his waiting arms, a twinkle in her own eyes as well. "Well...it looks like I'm going to be the first notch on that giant bedpost of yours. I guess I should be honored."

His gaze sobered, and he cupped her face so he could look deeply into her eyes. "I'm not that kind of guy, Gina. And I don't want to keep bringing him up, but I'm not Hank, either. Yes, I want to fuck your brains out. But I also have utmost respect for you. And it's going to stay that way even if you decide tomorrow that a one-night stand is all you want." His lips curved in a very lethal, sexy smile as he sank his fingers in her hair, "However...I'm hoping you're going to want a repeat performance..." And then, tugging on her dark locks, he pulled her head back so that he could run his lips over her arched neck.

Gina hummed, loving his roughness and the way her scalp tingled as he pulled on her hair. She felt him press hot, hungry kisses over her bare neck and shoulder blades, and wished she could just rip her clothes off so he could kiss her all over. She needed those heated lips trailing on every inch of her skin, nibbling, biting, sucking. Her breath was ragged as she felt his free hand reach into her blouse and simply pull one full, rounded breast free. His fingers were firmly caressing as he cupped her, squeezing her so hard she groaned out his name.

She clutched at his broad shoulders when she felt his head dip low so he could place his lips over her exposed, erect nipple. And then she almost melted into a puddle from just having him grab her in his mouth like a starved being. He suckled her tit hard, making her frantic with lust as he also fondled the swollen flesh in his strong fingers. Her knees weren't going to support her much longer if he kept wrenching on her nipple that way, twisting and rolling it in his masterful mouth.

"Oh, baby," she purred, sinking her fingers into his hair and just losing herself in the bliss he was making her feel. She was grateful when he swept her into his arms again, this time laying her across the bed. Next, he took his time to undress her, peeling off each item of clothing like he was unwrapping a special box of chocolates. And it seemed like he was looking forward to enjoying every single bite....

Now. it was her turn to undress him. Gina's hands were far more hurried as she unbuttoned his shirt and pushed it off his shoulders. His body was like carved marble, all hardness and firmness, yet so warm and virile. She'd never been so turned on by a man's body before. had never seen anything so beautiful. And indeed, the word fit his body perfectly. His muscles were rippling beneath his golden tanned skin. his chest was so broad and wide that she trembled to lay her fingers against its beating solidity. Her hands slid lovingly over his six-pack torso and she couldn't help the moan of delight that tore through her. Just touching him made her wet, and coupled with the way he was still tormenting her breasts, it was a wonder she hadn't exploded into a million pieces yet.

But she knew there was still more of him to explore—and she didn't want to wait. Driven by her incredible, untamed lust for him, she worked on the fastening of his jeans till she had his fly open. He helpfully lifted his hips so she could pull them down till he simply kicked them aside. The next things to go were his boxers, and then she had all of him to feast her eyes on.

Gina gazed at him unabashedly, drinking in the size of his cock which reared and throbbed beneath her gaze. She couldn't describe to herself how the sight of him, so big, the length reaching straight up past his navel, made her feel faint with need. His cap was thick, chiseled, and his thick shaft ridged with angry-looking veins. She loved his balls and how they hung low, making her want to take them in her mouth and suck on them.

"You have such a sexy body," she told him in lustful admiration, as she shoved him on his back. "I just want to lick you all over and find out if you taste as delicious as you look."

"Hell Gina, you're killing me," he groaned,

but he lay back obediently as she snaked her body all over him, teasing him with the lush swells of her breasts which she brushed over his skin. He was shuddering with pleasure and the exertion of holding back from grabbing her. First, she stole a few wet kisses from his lips, then she slithered her way down to his nipples, kissing them both in turns. And then she drew one into her mouth, making him gasp. Smiling to herself, she sucked on him as teasingly as he had done to her earlier. She was going to make him suffer—by pleasure, of course. She was going to punish him with as many caresses and kisses as she could bestow on his gorgeous, sexy body.

After sucking on his nipples, she dipped her tongue into his navel, and licked him there too. He seemed to like that as well, judging from the way he writhed beneath her. But the perfect torment was when she finally cupped his dick in her hands and stroked on him, looking up into his tortured face with a wicked smile. It was that same smile she wrapped around his cock.

He bucked into her at the first touch of her mouth on him. She covered his cap with butterfly licks, savoring the taste of his musky precum. Sucking on him got her so freaking hot she was like a tigress, bobbing her head on him and almost gagging herself when too much of him was shoved down her throat. She paid equal attention to his balls, sucking on them too and making them tighten into hard sacs of pleasure. His hands cupped her head gently as she worked his meaty inches up into a hot, pulsing pole that seemed even bigger and harder than ever. Just imagining him finally penetrating her with that beautiful monster was enough to make her thighs quiver with ecstasy.

Soon, he was pulling her away, his breath coming out in short and heavy gasps. He drew her up so he could kiss her lips roughly, hungrily. And then he instructed her to sit on his face. "I want to eat you, baby," he said hoarsely, his eyes boring into hers. "It's all I've thought of this past two weeks. Seeing you every morning and wondering what lay beneath your skirt. I've hardly had any sleep since I moved in with you so close by. Just dreaming of you with your pussy jammed to my mouth was enough to get me busting my balls every time."

His erotic words did unbelievable things to her already-fevered imagination; she felt her whole body shivering as she readily straddled his face, positioning herself so she could hold on to the iron bedposts for support. Nothing in the world had prepared her for the sensation of grinding her cunt all over Brandon's lips and nose as he ate her, lapping his tongue into her slit and nibbling on her swollen outer lips.

She felt dazed with bliss, her head thrown back as she cupped her breasts and stroked her nipples, while her pussy dripped gallons just by having his mouth and nose rubbing into her secret core. She felt his large hands grab her ass and squeeze roughly, even as he went on tonguing her mercilessly.

It was no use trying to fight it; she could

feel the fountain building up deep within her, ready to erupt. He was nibbling on her clit now, making tears of pleasure seep into the corner of her eyes. Her hands were gripping the iron bars of the bedpost tightly while she ground her hips even harder on his face. She could hear his muffled moans of pleasure, and it added its tune to her own cries. In the next second, she was cumming, her pussy gushing on his face.

Gina's thighs quivered convulsively as he lapped up every drop from her slit, his fingers biting into her ass with the force of his passionate lust. Her mind went blank for at least ten seconds as her climax rode on almost endlessly.

At last, she was able to lower herself to the side, her eyes wide and dazed as she tried to catch her breath. Soon, she was blinking herself back to consciousness to find him gazing down at her with a tender smile. "You okay?"

She was still dazzled from the powerful release she'd just experienced, but she found the strength to draw him to closer. "Baby, I don't want to be okay," she told him, her voice thick with desire. "Not when it means the party's over. And something tells me I don't want the party to be over either...."

They made love all through the night, reaching for each other again and again. It was like they were insatiable. Gina had never known she could be capable of having such a frenzied sex drive, as she let him take her countless times. She'd stopped trying to count how many times she'd cum, and now, only focused on getting as much loving as she could squeeze into the hours they had to share before morning.

A lot of pleasure could be squeezed into one night, as Brandon was happy to show her. After her first, tempestuous climax, she readily invited his cock into her, spreading her legs wide as he settled between them and thrust himself inside to the hilt. She was already so wet, hot and ready. He groaned as she wrapped her walls greedily around his shaft and made him feel right at home. With every thrust, he rocked deeper and deeper into her sweet, velvety bowl. She clung to him and raked her fingers down his back as her whole body shuddered with pleasure, giving him the motivation to hold back and keep going till there was nothing left.

He fucked her long and hard that first time, gritting his teeth as he fought against the rising urge to explode deep inside her tight, moist enclosure. He stretched the dance as long as he could, maintaining a steady, piston-like pace that built a rhythm her body seemed to love and understand. It was that same steady rhythm which brought her to her second, equally powerful climax, and she cried out in amazed delight. He felt her bucking wildly beneath him, felt her inner muscles seize him all the more tightly, and before he could stop it, he too, was pushed off the brink.

Cumming deep inside her had been as

paradisiac as he'd always known it would be. It had felt...like a taste of heaven. He told her so as he settled next to her once the storm had raged past. She clung to him, and giggled, and said he was such a sweet talker. And she told him that now she truly believed he was a writer.

Then they shared a long, warm shower, soaping each other tenderly as they smoothed over the sweet aches from their first coupling. The steam, the slipperiness, and the enticing image of wet, naked skin, was enough to rake up the flames again. Their lips molded together moistly as their bodies clashed a second time. Brandon lodged her against the wall, easily lifting the weight of her legs up to wrap around his waist, as he shoved his thick, upright cock into her. They both groaned, the sound echoing against the tiles with the falling shower acting as a perfect backdrop. Gina had her arms locked around his shoulders for support as her pussy was pounded into a mush of pleasure by his rampaging shaft. They kissed with constant hunger, letting go of time and space as they drove themselves into another wall of rapture. They crashed and burned, cumming together in the same perfectly synchronized moment.

Afterwards, he carried the trembling Gina back to bed with him. And the next time, he was lying on his back as he let her straddle his hips, while bringing her pussy slowly, painstakingly, unto his waiting cock.

Their loving was more leisurely this time. She danced her hips upon him, moaning with erotic bliss as his cock shafted her deepest walls with precision. She lifted herself up on her knees, making him withdraw almost to the tip, before she sat down on his cock again, swallowing him whole and causing him to grind his jaw in deep, painful delight.

He cupped her breasts as they swayed temptingly before him, he fondled and squeezed them; he teased her nipples. There was nothing his hands couldn't do; they seemed built just to give a woman pleasure— just as his cock seemed designed to do the same to her pussy. The sensations of having his cock slide in and out of her in a now achingly familiar beat were almost too much to bear. She propped herself on his ripped pecs as she started to bounce even faster, slamming her ass unto his flanks as she quickened the ride. He couldn't stand it; he gripped her tits and then he bust, simply snapped what ever was left of his self control. He was roaring like a tiger as he pumped his cum into her, slamming himself upwards and spurting all he had up her sweet, honeyed cunt. His loss of control had been so beautiful to watch, and Gina gladly succumbed to her own release, her belly and thighs shuddering as she too, tripped over the edge and came.

There should have been nothing left, but there was.

Just before dawn broke, Gina stirred and felt Brandon's solid frame spooned behind her. She snuggled back into him, humming with delight as she felt his cock stiffen into hot, hard steel against her ass. He cupped and stroked her breasts, with just enough roughness to communicate his urgency and to build up her own. Without delay, she'd raised her thigh so that his shaft could slide past her bottom and into her waiting pussy.

Holding on tight to her, he rocked his hips against her ass, ramming her with his cock so deep Gina was sure her belly was jiggling inside her. His hand reached over her belly and down to thumb her hard little clit, intensifying the pleasure all the more. They were so perfectly tuned to each other now that even their bodies could speak the same language. This was the most sedate of all the fucks they'd had since the night began—and yet it was the most potent. On and on, they rocked against each other, welded together like they'd been conjoined. It was only a matter of time, and soon, they crested the wave in that same perfect sync, the impact so massive it had them both shuddering and clinging to one another like two castaways in a storm.

Gina was turning the final page of the bound sheets of paper lying on the kitchen table before her. She sighed deeply with a happy smile, looking up to find that Brandon had turned from the cooker to raise a questioning brow.

"Well?" he asked lightly. "What do you think?"

"I loved it," she gushed, jumping from the stool to go and hug him by the waist.

"Hey! No distracting the chef," he growled,

but allowed her to grab a quick kiss before he shooed her away.

"This will definitely be your bestseller," she told him firmly, pinching a piece of vege from the chopping board. "I haven't read anything so riveting in a long time. It was really good, Brandon."

He sent her a lop-sided smile. "I know you wouldn't believe this, but it was mostly thanks to you I got to finish it. The book was only halfway done when I moved in. But then the first morning of my stay, this hot lady walks out of her door and past my window. Next thing, the creative juices got flowing, and in two weeks, it was all done. And that was the night we met."

"The night you rescued me," she added with a twinkling eye. It was now a week since then. Things between her and Hank had been long over, while with Brandon, they seemed to be just starting. Every morning was like a new beginning for them. When they fucked, it always felt like the first time. Even now, she shivered to think how the night would end once they finished the elaborate meal he'd insisted on preparing.

"And of course I believe you," she continued, sending him a warm gaze. "I believe you mean everything you tell me, Brandon. And trust me, you had a monumental effect on my life, too. You made me seize the moment, retake my life from the vagueness it had become. You showed up, and you made me realize everything that was missing: spontaneity, excitement...pleasure." This time, she went to leisurely wrap her arms around his neck and planted a slow, heated kiss on his lips. And this time, he didn't complain but kissed her right back.

Soon, he was serving out the dishes, and as they settled in the living room, he switched on the T.V. "Now...for that dinner—and movie I owe you..." He had a huge grin on his face as he inserted a new-release blockbuster DVD.

Gina took her seat with her plate of food, shaking her head. "I should have known you were a cheapie," she teased, forking a morsel into her mouth. And then she moaned with pleasure, closing her eyes briefly. "For goodness' sake, is there nothing you can't do? Heck, you cook even better than me. And that's saying a lot."

"Thanks. I hope you like the movie I picked just as well," he replied with a smile as he took his place beside her. She quickly gave him a hug.

"This is such a nice touch, making dinner and then renting the movie. I think it's far more romantic than taking me out for a fancy dinner or to the movies."

"I like a woman who shows appreciation," he declared, grinning. "And I'm going to have to remind myself to show her some appreciation right back when we hit the bedroom later. Since this is officially a date, we might as well round it off with the traditional date-night fuck."

"Hmm...a man who knows and follows procedure, what woman in her right mind could argue with that?" Gina asked with a teasing grin of her own, even as her pussy twitched in anticipation for the close of night which lay ahead....

She kept expecting it to change; that soon he would touch her and the magic, the thrill would be gone. It had been one week of constant, mind-blowing sex, and part of her was trying to believe it was too good to last.

Well, she'd been wrong, so wrong. That night, when the nights were low, and they fell into his huge, inviting four-poster, it got even better than ever. All he had to do was kiss her and she became battery-charged. That night was really wild; he tried on some mild bondage by blindfolding her with a sleep mask and then lashing her to the bedposts with two of his ties. It was freaky at first but then when he started to glide that ice cube all over her body she started to get into the game!

He'd put it in his mouth to get it all slippery, and then he got it in his fingers sort of rolled round and round her hot spots. He set her nipples on fire with running the cube around them. She was writhing against her bonds, shocked at how delicious it felt to only focus with her sense of feel. And though she couldn't see him with her eyes, she could hear him—hear his deep, hard breathing as he trailed the melting cube down her quivering belly and then to scrape it all over the swollen outer lips of her pussy.

"Brandon...please," she moaned, trembling all over with need. The torment of never knowing what next he had in mind, whether he was going to keep going with the ice cubes or whether he'd push her knees apart and mount her...Just not knowing was killing her! And when he started tracing his way right back up again with that wicked little cube of ice, she was already on the brink. She was straining out for him, seeking his lips, his touch. But he held back, caressing her with only his voice as he proceeded to tell her, in a whisper to her ear, exactly what he was going to do to her next.

She shuddered uncontrollably as she felt his fingers undo her restraints. But then he was flipping her over on her stomach while he took her wrists and bound her once again, this time with her arms stretched behind her. Gina couldn't help moaning with hot, restless lust, the sounds muffled by the pillow into which her face was buried. And when she felt his hands on her hips, propping them in the air, she could do nothing but shiver all the more.

He had her ass cheeks in his hands now, and he parted them, giving him more access as he bent his lips to tongue her exposed pussy. Gina almost sobbed, her bottom quivering in the air as she could do nothing but bear his moist, fevered onslaught. He ate her pussy, got her dripping faster and more plentifully than ever. She felt helpless with desire, unable to do anything but stay in place and let him punish her with more and more pleasure. He slipped his fingers deep inside her, shoving in and out in a steady fucking motion that made her feel ready to combust.

It was almost too much to bear, but then she knew there was more. And "more" was his cock, hard and reassuring, lining up close to her now sodden pussy. Gina could feel the tip stroking her slick surface, driving her almost insane with want. She pleaded, begged, for him to fuck her, to ram his cock deep inside her from the back. For her audacity she got a sharp, sudden smack on her left bottom.

"Oh!" she cried at the sting, and then prayed that he'd do it again. He did. He spanked her, just a little bit harder this time, and she almost climaxed. The hot, biting sensation was causing her pussy to twitch madly in response and the pain and pleasure seemed almost connected. She blinked behind her eye mask and felt like she was falling into a dark, swirling mist of lust.

"Brandon...," she moaned, unable to bear it much longer. Her whole body was ablaze, engulfed. And only when he was finally buried deep inside her could she let out the scream she'd been holding back all the while. He slammed into her unexpectedly, driving in his thick mast of a cock and sending the pleasure ripping her through the middle.

There was no use trying to hold back: she felt herself explode on impact. By his third thrust she'd climaxed in a heady, body-shaking rush, her whole consciousness centered on Brandon's cock and how it filled her, owned her. He didn't stop his ramming, increasing his tempo as he plunged in and out of her pulsating cunt. She was barely down from her powerful high before she heard him start to grunt and heave with each thrust, before he finally surrendered and blasted his cum into her.

There were no words. Nothing could describe how monumentally wild it had felt, and when he untied her, took off her blindfold, all she could do was fall into his arms and escape into an exhausted, satisfaction-drugged sleep.

12 DO MY WILL

Prologue

Calling Brianna a spoiled brat wouldn't be totally fair—but she usually got what she wanted. After all, she was young, beautiful and rich. But she was only twenty and had never really known what it was to know real passion, to be possessed completely by a real man who could make her feel truly alive.

Ramond was one handyman who was too cocky for his own good. Brianna wasn't sure what annoyed her more: his insolence and being constantly ignored by him—or the fact that it only made her want his muscle-bound body even more. And then when she finds out his secret and blackmails him into doing her will, she understands for the first time the true meaning of pleasure.

It might seem crazy, but one thing Brianna knew was that she was going to get Ramond in her bed, now.

The whole episode had begun more than a month ago. Ramond was the guy her mom had hired to handle their swimming pool repairs among other things around the place. He was the big, brawny type, not usually the kind of guy Brianna was into. He had muscles bulging out of everywhere, a very intimidating stature for a more petite and small-boned Brianna. Ever since her mother had begun renovating their townhouse, Brianna had seen a lot of workmen come and go. But for some reason, Ramond really stood out.

He was very good looking, with deep caramel skin and curly dark hair which stuck close to his nicely shaped head. She figured he was of Latino descent and had a very slight accent, but she couldn't place if it was Mexican, Puerto Rican or Cuban. All she knew is that whenever she came across him, she felt something thrill up and down her spine. She told herself it was discomfiture due to the fact that he wore only the barest minimum of clothes and she wasn't used to seeing guys so scantily clad.

She was just twenty-one and had lived a mostly sheltered life. Her father had died when she was very young. As a successful businessman, he'd left a thriving company that her mother had had to take on, as well as a hefty inheritance for Brianna. This made her mother very protective of her, and she screened many of Brianna's boyfriends, hardly allowing her to even date or stay away from home. She was almost done with college, and she could still say she'd never known what real love or true passion was.

In the past few months, her mother had started to take on more work and was always travelling around the globe on business for the company. And when she was in town, she left for work very early and came home late at night. This caused Brianna to be left alone most of the time. And since she didn't really have many friends, thanks to her mother's strictness, Brianna found herself basically left with nothing much to do during the holidays except go shopping or stay at home and sunbathe by the pool.

The renovations were still going on in full force, and she didn't mind that sometimes her mother left instructions for her to supervise the men and make sure they were working. That day, however, it was just Ramond who showed up to finish the side paving next to the pool. Today, as she stood in front of the picture window which had a full view of the swimming pool area, she noticed that he was dressed as scantily as ever. All he had on were a pair of combat shorts, his broad shoulders, muscled chest and six-pack abs rippling in the gold of the sun as he went about his task. She bit on her lip as she took a few minutes to watch him and asked herself why she noticed him so much. He had that body, of course, and he could be around his mid-twenties, close to her age. But that didn't explain why she followed him with her eyes when he was around.

She kept telling herself she didn't even like him. He was the cocky type, the kind who knew they looked good and weren't reluctant to show off. That "sexy and I know it" persona set her teeth on edge. One other thing that irked her, she had to confess, was that he barely have her any attention and generally acted like she didn't even exist.

At twenty, Brianna knew she'd turned out quite well; though she was on the small side and weighed less than a hundred pounds, she had a generously curved body: C-cup breasts, a nice ass, and shapely hips. She did much to sample these whenever she could, especially when any of the workmen were around. It felt somewhat gratifying to catch them ogling her as she walked past in her bikini top and shorts, or in her tight jeans and revealing tops. She heard them whisper among themselves and knew they were speculating what it would be like to fuck her. They wouldn't try anything though, because they were too afraid of her mother, and besides, Brianna gave them no encouragement and even ignored them mostly.

However, to be ignored right back by Ramond was not pleasing in the least. Brianna didn't even know what she was looking for. Well, apart from trouble, that was. But she sensed deep down that there was something out there that she had no clue about concerning men. She knew that they loved a great body, especially when it was paraded around them everyday. And yet, she was still in the dark about what it entailed to have a real man do things to her.

Brianna wasn't a virgin; she'd had a boyfriend or two, but neither of them had been much older than she was, and certainly not that experienced. Their clumsy, eager lovemaking had been satisfying without being thrilling. Definitely, nothing worth repeating too frequently. Now, she was happily single and enjoying her freedom, as it were, now that her mother was a busy business executive.

That afternoon passed like any other. Ramond worked outside, and she stayed indoors and came out only once to sunbathe for an hour or two. As usual, he barely spared her a few words of greeting or even a glance. Brianna tried not to bristle too much at this and sat across in a lounger in her tiny black bikini. Once, it was late afternoon, she went to the kitchen where the cook, Marcella, was working on dinner. Marcella was a plump, pretty woman, almost thirty with a cheerful face and a cloud of blonde hair she kept tightly in a bun. She'd lost her husband two years ago and now had a room on the grounds of the house. This meant that she was also consigned to doing some housekeeping when required.

Brianna told her that she'd be going out for a movie with a friend and that she shouldn't bother with anything for her, that she'd be back late. Afterwards, Brianna dressed and left in the silver Range Rover on her way to pick up one of her few close pals, Veronica. Brianna was just fifteen minutes from the house when she realized she hadn't even taken her purse with all her credit cards and even her license.

"For goodness' sake!" she swore, as she took the next turning on the road. If she didn't hurry up, she'd make them late for the start of the movie. Speeding as fast as she dared, she stopped in front of the house, not parking inside the driveway because she'd soon be going back out again. Hurriedly, she let herself into the house. As she was about to bound up the stairs to her room, she couldn't help but overhear some hushed voices in the kitchen. She was surprised because she was sure Marcella had been alone in the kitchen when she'd left. Was she on the phone, or did she have a friend over?

Brianna knew her mother strictly prohibited this, and frowning, she tiptoed to the doorway of the kitchen. Pressing herself against the wall, she peeked in and saw that, indeed, Marcella was not alone.

"Hmm, something smells good," Ramond said, coming to stand behind Marcella who was turning a pot on the cooker. The woman squirmed as he wrapped his arms around her and nuzzled his face in her neck.

"Behave, Ramond! I need to get this stew ready before Mrs. Stark comes back."

"So is the girl brat gone out now?" he asked, making Marcella shriek suddenly as he dropped his hands on her ample tits and squeezed through her apron and blouse.

Brianna bristled from where she stood watching them undetected, her eyes blazing in shock and anger.

"Oh! Yes, Miss Brianna is out to the movies and probably wouldn't be back till late, but..."

"So in short, we have plenty of time, hmmm, baby?" He punctuated his words by fondling her tits amorously and nibbling the bare skin of her shoulder. The older woman moaned softly and leaned against him for a moment, before snapping her head up again.

"No Ramond, be serious. Mrs. Stark said she'll be home for dinner and that could be any moment now."

"Come on, we can at least have five minutes or so..."

"Five minutes!" the woman said in a mock-offended tone, though she was switching off the cooker and turning into his arms.

"I'll make it count, I promise," he growled, his hands rocking up her skirt and cupping her ass as he half-lifted her sizeable frame easily. Brianna's eyes widened as the normally sedate Marcella began to kiss Ramond passionately, wrapping her arms around his broad, naked shoulders. His bare muscles were bulging as he supported the woman on his slightly bent thighs as their lips ground hotly into each other. Suddenly, things started to pick up pace as they broke the kiss and fumbled with the apron and the buttons of her blouse. Soon Marcella's breasts were freed; her bra simply pulled up so that the full mounds hung proud and free. She had enormous nipples which were placed right in the middle of her tits and looked pretty nice for her age and size. With a grunt, Ramond bent his head to suckle her roughly, shifting from one to the other in hungry haste.

Marcella's soft moans were filling the kitchen, and she arched her back, giving him easier access to her titties which he cupped in his hand as he feasted on them. In the meantime, Marcella was deftly working on the zipper of his shorts, and seconds later, his cock popped out into her hands.

Brianna had to clamp a hand over her mouth to stifle the gasp that passed through her lips. Her eyes were fastened on what had to be the biggest dick she'd ever seen. She hadn't been acquainted with that many, but for a curious twenty-one year old, she'd come across a few porn movies and even the largest dudes hadn't sported anything like this. It hung downwards, the skin a shade darker than the rest of him, though the cap was slightly pink and very chiseled. It was massive, thick and long and had to reach halfway down his thigh. She didn't have a measuring tape in her head, but that was a terrible lot of inches he was carrying around. Even Marcella's large working hands seemed dwarfed taking hold of that cock, which she fondled lovingly.

"Can I suck it, please?" the woman moaned. Shocked to her marrow, Brianna had to watch as her thirty-something-year-old housekeeper and cook went to her knees in front of the younger man's monster of a cock and started to give him a very earnest and slobbery blowjob. He grasped the back of her head, caressing her blonde hair as she sucked on him greedily, coating him in squelching saliva.

Brianna stared in curiosity, amazement, and desire. All three emotions clashed along with jealousy which hit her unexpectedly. She never had a cock in her mouth, and certainly not one that seemed ready to choke Marcella as she gamely tried to stuff her face with it.

"That's it, baby," he purred, throwing his head back and closing his eyes. Marcella was gagging from attempting to swallow up too much of his meat at a go. She pulled back and instead focused on bathing his cap with her flickering tongue.

"I think it's all good and wet now," Marcella said after a few minutes of furious sucking, as Ramond drew her up for a kiss.

"Let's see if the same goes for your pussy, hmm?" he said huskily. He'd jammed his hand up her skirt, pushed her panties to the side, and then skewered her with his fingers. "Hmm, nice and wet," he noted in approval

"Oh!" Marcella cried out in delight. "That feels good, Ramond. Fuck me with those thick long fingers."

He obliged her for the next minute or so, and soon she was shuddering like a leaf. But they must have realized they'd taken too much time on foreplay. Suddenly, he withdrew his fingers. And it seemed Marcella knew just what to do; without being told, she turned to lean over the kitchen table, using her own hand to spread her ass cheeks. She was positioned with her ass facing Brianna, who starred open-mouthed at the picture of Marcella's thick pale bottom held apart with her fingers. Her pussy lips were very big and well developed, and they were shiny with moisture. Still, Ramond was busy coating his cock with more saliva as he licked his hand then rubbed it over his cap.

"Whooo-wee! Can't wait to fuck that sweet white ass," he said with thick-throated lust. He was fisting that beast of a cock, and even in his large hand, it still looked able to rip Marcella's pussy in half. Brianna almost groaned out loud when her vision was blocked by Ramond who came up behind Marcella and thrust himself into her. Now all she had was a view of his muscular shoulder, back and butt as he began to fuck Marcella in fast, deep strokes.

"Ah! Ah! Ah!" Marcella cried with every thrust, and the kitchen table seemed to shake with their animalistic coupling. Suddenly, a thought occurred to the watching Brianna, who quickly withdrew her iPhone from her bag as quietly as she could. Putting on the camera, she trained it on the humping partners. Ramond had now taken hold of Marcella's legs and held them up on either side of his hips, in a kind of scissors position.

Marcella kept herself stationed to the table with her hands gripping the sides, and Brianna tried as much as possible to get bits of Marcella's body into the frame as much as she could. In a way it was a good thing their backs were to her, this made Brianna able to move out from behind the wall and get a better shot.

Ramond had picked up a punishing pace now as he buried himself deeper into Marcella's cunt. From the woman's louder screams, Brianna could only imagine the mixture of discomfort and pleasure the woman was feeling taking in that cock at such a fast, heedless speed.

"I'm cumming, baby," he announced suddenly, and she quickly moved. He slipped out of her and stood to the side, while Marcella instantly came forward to squat in front of him and start sucking and fisting his giant cock. With her free hand, she rubbed furiously at her clit.

Perfect, Brianna thought, as now she had them both in profile, though she had to hide more carefully so that she wouldn't be noticed from the open doorway. But the two lovers were not in the position to be aware of much else but themselves. She was able to video them as Marcella jacked and sucked Ramond off till he groaned loudly and starting cumming in her mouth. His hips were jerking powerfully, and he kept her head in place so that she swallowed every rope of cum he produced. In the next second, Marcella too started to tremble, her own cries of pleasure muffled by the cock still in her mouth as she frigged herself to a climax.

With a grunt, Ramond withdrew from her mouth, and a few drops of thick white sperm still dripped from his slit to the tip of Marcella's nose. They both chuckled as she promptly swiped it off and licked it from her finger.

"Now you can get on with cooking, hmm, baby. Thanks for satisfying my cock; it had been starved for much too long," he said as he hunched, folding his still very large and erect member back into his shorts.

"Not my fault, honey. You know Miss Brianna hardly goes out, and we can't do anything while she's around." Marcella was doing up her clothes as she spoke.

"That's true. I wish the rich snotty chick would make more friends already and get to leave the house more often."

"Be that as it may, Ramond, we're taking a very big risk doing this at all..."

Brianna was dumbstruck at the way they seemed to go straight back to normal, conversing as Marcella washed her hands and went back to work on dinner. How could they act so calmly after what Brianna had just seen them do? But she decided it was too dangerous to linger and hear what more they'd have to say.

Treading silently, glad she had sneakers on and not heels, she went up to her room to get her purse which was in another bag from which she'd forgotten to transfer it. She was hoping she could leave unnoticed, which, thankfully, was how it went. She sped through the front door and down the driveway to the front of the gate where the Jeep was parked. Minutes later, she was speeding off.

Brianna became confused about a whole lot of things after that afternoon when she witnessed Ramond banging the cook and housekeeper, plump and pretty Marcella. She was losing a lot of sleep in the next few days that passed. Anytime she closed her eyes, all she could see were images of them doing it to each other, with Ramond's smooth olive skin contrasting with the soft white of Marcella's as he'd been banging her while hoisting her feet in the air.

Brianna was confused because she knew she should be disgusted. She was! She'd never known people could act like such...such animals. And yet, that was what had made it feel so exciting. That was what made her belly twist in knots every time she thought of them going at it and fucking like a dog and bitch in heat. She could still remember the grossly massive size of Ramond's cock, remember the way it had hung low and menacingly. It confused her how wet her pussy got when she thought of this. She tried very, very hard to get it out of her mind, but the more she blocked it, the more it came up again. It was driving her insane. And even if she wanted to forget the whole episode, traumatic as it was, there was still that video she'd recorded on her iPhone. One night, she'd secretly watched it and had the greatest urge to touch herself. It was so dirty and wrong!

Brianna's mother seemed to notice the change in her and asked her several times over if something was wrong. And each time, Brianna felt tempted to blurt out the truth. It would get both Marcella and Ramond fired on the spot, she knew. So why was she holding back? She'd always loathed Ramond for his cocky way of ignoring her. And of course, the things he'd said behind her back hadn't helped to endear her further to him. But Marcella, she really liked the woman and felt reluctant to get her in trouble.

She figured Marcella was a woman with

needs and so that was why she gave in to a brute like Ramond. And yet, every time Brianna saw Marcella or had to be around her after that day, there was that image burned at the back of Brianna's eyelids of Marcella spreading her ass cheeks with her fingers so that Ramond could penetrate her glistening wet pussy....

"Are you okay, Miss Brianna?" Marcella asked with concern, watching Brianna's face as the young girl stood beside her in the kitchen.

Brianna had to shake off the disturbing and very stirring images, and simply mumbled and ducked her head into the fridge. It was hard trying to act normal around Marcella, but Brianna knew she had to try. For now, she just couldn't figure out what to do. Part of her wanted to face Marcella and blurt out authoritatively, "I saw you fucking Ramond right in this kitchen three days ago. I want it to stop. I never want you to take his beastly cock in your mouth or in your pussy ever again!"

But instead, she swiveled blindly with a can of soda in her hand and left the kitchen like it was on fire.

She could hardly face Ramond either. Every time he came into view or they were about to bump into each other, she ducked into the first room she could find. She was positively avoiding him now, sure he'd look into her eyes and immediately see that she knew. She was still smarting in many ways by what he'd said about her, but that didn't even bother her as much as the scary vision she had whenever she saw him. Visions of him looking like just one gigantic, walking cock in shorts. It was unnerving.

Then one afternoon, things came to a head, so to speak.

They were officially the only ones on the whole grounds. Brianna's mother had left town on business and wouldn't be back for two days. Marcella was on her day off. None of the other construction guys doing the renovation had come in that day, only Ramond who'd been working in the garden all morning.

Brianna had stayed in her room throughout the day, but then had needed a cold drink and that was when she came down the stairs to get one from the kitchen. It was as she returning to go back upstairs that she glanced outside and saw a figure swimming energetically in the Olympic-sized pool.

Realizing it was Ramond, she felt her teeth grit together. Suddenly, she dumped the can of soda on the nearby table and stalked out of the French windows to the edge of the pool.

"What the fuck do you think you're doing?" she cried out in fury, fists on hips. "Get the hell out of that pool!"

He seemed to ignore her, finishing his lap. And then, he took his time coming out, pushing his dark hair back from his face as he walked up and out the pool steps right in front of her.

For a few moments, all she could do was gape at his muscle-bound, gleaming body as he emerged, water streaming from him. His broad shoulders, his hairless, massive chest, and his tapering, six-pack torso was almost obscenely bare, and this time instead of shorts he was wearing trunks. Very small black trunks which seemed like they had a difficult time keeping his thickly wedged cock in place. It was practically bulging as obscenely as his body—and he wasn't even erect yet.

Her head swam for a few moments, before she looked into his eyes and saw they were mocking, irreverent.

"You should wash out that mouth with soap, Miss Brianna," he said calmly, standing in front of her in an insolent stance. "Or I may have to dunk you in the pool and do it for you."

"How...how dare you threaten me?" she gasped, reaching the end of her tether. She felt something snapped inside her and for a second something went dark in her head. She blinked, facing him with eyes blazing. "You do know you're prohibited from using the pool?"

He shrugged his hard-packed shoulders. "It was so hot. I couldn't help it. Besides, I wasn't sure anyone would notice or care."

"Oh, I care," she said vengefully. "And I'm sick of your crap. You've been a pain in the ass for a long time and I think it's up to me to show you who's boss around here."

He tipped his head at her with a quizzical smile. "Your mother's the boss, little woman. Not you. I don't have to take orders from you."

"Is that so?" she gritted, fishing her phone from her pocket. It took a second for her to get the required video playing, and she held it up to his frowning face for a few moments. Loud moans and grunts filled the air, and she saw his eyes widen suddenly as he watched the images on the screen.

"You see that? You know what I can do with that?" she said with a cold, pleased smile as she saw Ramond look worried for the first time ever. "You may not care about your own self, but think of Marcella. I show this to my mother, she's gone. No references, nothing. You'd have ruined her fucking life. And she's worked for us more than three years."

"Look, miss...."

"No, you look," she bit out, ignoring his now subdued tone, "I'm going up to my room. I'm giving you five minutes to think about what I said. And then I want you to come up and show me you understand who's in charge here. You, or me. If you don't, then in five and a half minutes, I'm sending this video to my mom. You can bet that not only will she get you fired, she'll also get you locked up and the key thrown away. Think wisely, Ramond." She spat his name out mockingly, and turned sharply on her heel.

Five minutes later, her bedroom door opened. Next thing, Ramond appeared.

Brianna smiled thinly, lying back in her bed propped up on her elbows. He had a look on his face that told her he knew exactly what he was in for. Feeling her heart begin to pound, she crossed and uncrossed her jean-clad legs.

"So, Ramond. What's your decision? Who's the boss around here?" she asked coolly.

"You are," he said, tone and face without expression as he stood there in his wet trunks. Then he began to say, "Look, Miss Brianna, I...."

"Did I give you permission to speak?" she cut through, edging towards the end of the bed and sitting up slightly. Watching him squirm in front of her was so gratifying. He'd lost much of his cockiness and she felt turned on by the fact that she had him in her power now. And she could make him do whatever she wanted.

"Now," she went on in a lighter tone. "I know for a fact what you happen to be packing in that tool box of yours. Now I want you to take it out."

"What?" he asked in confusion.

"Your cock," she said coldly. "Take it out."

"But..."

"Do it!"

Slowly, his teeth obviously grinding in his jaw, he stuck a hand in his trunk and held out his cock. Brianna smiled in satisfaction. She'd sat up earlier to get a better view, and now she licked her lips in appreciation.

"That's nice. Now, I want you to stroke it. Make it hard, very hard. I want to see how big that monster can grow."

She smiled to herself when this time, he did not argue. He began to fist his pole of meat, his eyes never leaving her face. Her eyes were tied greedily to the thick, long dick he was pumping, and she watched as the pink head grew larger, just as the shaft grew longer, fatter. He seemed to have no problem getting hard with her watching.

"I'm impressed, Ramond. It looks even bigger and harder than it did three days ago when you fucked Marcella so hard in the kitchen. Bigger than when she put it in her mouth and blew you till you blasted yourself down her throat." She smiled wickedly at his obvious discomfort, and crooked her finger at him. "Take off those trunks. And come here."

He obeyed, kicking off the wet material and then walking up to where she sat on the edge of the bed. His ten inch cock swung from side to side as he moved, and she couldn't help biting on her lip in hot, fevered delight. Now he was standing just a breath away, and she reached out to grasp the thick, long plank of meat that reared in front of her. She closed her hands around it and sighed at how it felt: pulsing, hard, fleshy. And so huge now that it was this close up, that she felt her pussy clench in fear at the thought of this monster tearing into her.

Brianna looked up into Ramond's face with a sweet smile, and had to use both her hands just to get a good hold on the pole-straight shaft. She was licking her lips and watching his every expression, saw how tortured, even angry he looked. She liked to see him angry like that; he hated being in her power. It felt so much fun that way.

Still keeping her eye on him, she warned him softly, "I don't want you to touch me. Just keep your hands to the side and don't move." He nodded curtly at her instructions, and still smiling, she fisted his cock in both hands. She continued pumping on the meat and loving how it felt within her fingers, like something alive, even threatening. It was just like a separate entity on its own, designed and built for both pleasure and maybe, pain. She shuddered at the thought of how it would definitely hurt when the time came for him to fuck her.

Slowly, keeping her eye on him, she leaned forward to lick at the large, smooth cap, her tongue rolling over the slit. She watched him grimace as if in pain, and her lips curled in delight to see him suffer so much. She laid her lips around him and sucked, focusing on just the tip and twirling it with her tongue on the inside. He groaned beneath his breath.

Gripping him firmly, she stretched her mouth lower on his shaft, and felt her lips stretch almost painfully. His girth was almost frightful, but the lust burning in her core didn't let her consider the ache her mouth was feeling for the unusual way it was expanded on his hot meat. She'd only sucked dick once, and it had been so small she'd been able to take the whole length in her mouth. It had been her boyfriend and it had taken him less than two minutes to cum. She'd had to run to spit out the sperm in disgust, but she could still remember the power she'd experienced, and how good it had felt to make her lover lose control and explode like that.

She wondered how long Ramond was going to hold. She pulled back and spat on his cock to moisten it, while her hands rubbed the saliva all over the shaft to get it all wet. She was mostly improvising, but she seemed to be doing okay from the way his hips were jerking. Fisting him in a firm grip, she bent her head to the side so she could pop one of his big, swinging balls in her mouth. She inhaled his delicious musty smell and felt her pussy begin to melt even more. He groaned, seemed to want to lift his hands to her head, but then also appeared to remember her orders and his hands fell to his sides again.

Brianna was pleased that he knew who was boss now. She took his cock in her mouth again, and tried harder to take more of him past her lips. Back and forth she moved, running her mouth up and down on the thickly veined shaft while her free hand fondled his balls. Moans were spilling from his mouth now, deep and throaty. It made her wetter knowing that she was giving him pleasure despite himself. His dick seemed to stiffen even harder, stretch even longer inside her mouth. She too moaned, and never wanted to stop.

But she was curious to try so much more. After sucking on him eagerly for five more minutes and making him shudder with ecstasy, she pulled back, and started to undress. She threw off her shirt and then her bra, keeping her eyes on him. He watched her every move, not speaking. But his dark, hooded eyes seemed lit up with lust, his cock bobbing at the sight of her now exposed tits. They were firm, pointed and big as oranges. She leaned back on her elbows and commanded him to take off her jeans. He obeyed, unbuttoning and then unzipping the thick denim before pulling it down her legs.

"The panties, too," she instructed, and felt her skin heat up at the touch of his fingers hooking into her panties. He drew them off her slender hips and then her ankles, flinging them to the side. She scooted back into the middle of the bed.

"I'm going to let you fuck me, Ramond," she announced matter-of-factly. "And you're going to do it hard and rough like you did with Marcella. But first you're going to have to suck my tits and lick my pussy till I'm wet enough and able to take that beastly cock of yours in my cunt."

She could see his expression was not so much tinged with anger now. He was still annoyed that he wasn't in charge, maybe. But he didn't seem to mind so much that he was being ordered around. So long as he was going to have some young, fresh, hot pussy, Brianna guessed.

He advanced unto the bed, taking his place beside her and then reaching a large hand to cover her breast. Brianna laid back with a moan, her body trembling at the feel of those warm, rough fingers stroking her small breasts. She could hear him breathing hard, and she arched her back, waiting impatiently for him to suck her tits.

Moments later, she felt the warmth of his mouth cover her nipple, and she shivered. With his free hand, he rubbed his way down her concave belly to her pussy. He lay his fingertips flat on her folds and went on rubbing, stroking, patting till she was a shuddering mess beneath him. He was able to grab a whole tit, nipple and all, into his mouth, and he sucked roughly and with deep hunger.

Brianna writhed beneath him, dazed by the pleasure of being touched and pleasured by a real man. He knew just what part of her cunt needed to be stroked and just the right pressure to make her wail in sweet bliss. He knew just how to stick his thick long forefinger into her pussy and thrust, applying the right speed and depth to make her see stars at the back of her eyelids.

And when he made it two fingers, she almost passed out. He finger-fucked her thoroughly, making the juices flow out of her like a waterfall. His mouth was still latched to her breasts, where he teased one nipple mercilessly, before switching to the other. In the meantime his thumb was flicking her clit, making it so hard that it throbbed in delight. Brianna had never known such pleasure, didn't even know what to expect till it suddenly hit her from nowhere.

It was a spiral and it carried her round and round in a hot, blissful vortex that had her screaming out loud in sudden, unexpected release. Her whole frame jerked and shuddered from the force of it, the sensations from her breasts and pussy falling into each other as they tried to gain dominance. She went limp upon the mattress, her body still vibrating internally like someone had forgot to turn of the switch.

She glanced sideways to find Ramond watching her with a small, tight smile. "You liked that, huh?"

"Maybe I did," she said, getting back into character. Next she parted her knees and drew them up. "Now I want you to lick me. Lick my cum, the way Marcella licked yours."

Brianna felt pleased that he obeyed without a word, lowering his head to where the juices were spilling from her still quivering pussy.

She hummed as he expertly licked her clean, focusing on her moist slit and then down between her globes to where the wetness had dripped to her crack. He lapped at her with obvious pleasure, his throat thick with moans. She saw that he was touching himself, fisting his cock as he feasted on her pussy. She liked watching him touch himself, liked to see him try to tame his own monster that was attached to his own body.

As he ministered to her pussy, Brianna felt her arousal start to rise again into dangerous proportions. She was reminded how many sleepless nights she'd had thinking of being fucked deep by his huge, menacing dick. She felt that her recent climax had relaxed her and whetted her body—and appetite—enough to handle his man meat.

When she was ready, she instructed him to climb on top of her and penetrate. "Miss Brianna," he began a little reluctantly, his teeth gritted as he braced his top weight on his arms. He was positioned between her legs, the tip of his cock mere inches from her waiting cunt, "You're very small, and I don't want to hurt you...."

"You won't hurt me," she said firmly. "And if it gets too painful I'll tell you to stop."

She looked up at him and he seemed to shrug, before taking his cock in his hand and guiding it to her slit. The next moment he pushed strongly, and he was in.

Brianna couldn't help the scream she sent piercing through the air. Ramond had been right; it did hurt. Like mad. And he didn't break her in gently. No, he pumped right into her from the start, shoving himself at least half way in and making her pussy walls screech in protest.

She gasped, gripping on his shoulder as the most indescribable and most incredible pain she'd ever experienced resonated from her pussy to the rest of her body. She pounded on his chest in a bid to ease off the focus of discomfort spreading through her cunt and belly. He mistook her actions for a command to stop, and he paused. With a yelp she told him to keep going. She told him to fuck her as deep as he could.

They both groaned when he thrust into her again, and then again. His hips were clenching and flexing as he pounded his cock inside her, making her grow accustomed to the width as the pain gave way in turn to pleasure. It still hurt when he pushed in and out, but there was so much pleasure echoing just behind that Brianna never, ever wanted it to stop. She was moaning, sighing as his cock touched deep inside her walls and made her come alive. She writhed and danced beneath him, gulping him in with her pussy which grabbed greedily on his plunging shaft. He could never go completely in, but even with half of his cock he was ripping her apart. Brianna could have sworn her vagina was ripped in two—but no, it was just her imagination. He was grinding into her and groaning out her name, losing control as he began to pump into her with greater force.

She almost wanted to faint with all the tumult of pleasure she was made to experience all at once. That monster cock of his sawing into her was able to do things no other cock she'd fucked ever could. He hit all her spots, switched on all her buttons, and made her scream. It was like being pulled apart by a massive flag staff, but the pleasure always overtook the pain.

But then suddenly he withdrew, and she gasped as her pussy made a "pop" sound when his cap pulled out. She was staring at him. "What the hell do you think you're doing? Fuck me, damn it!"

"Oh, I'll fuck you," he replied softly, deeply. She felt him take hold of her waist and in the next moment, he was flipping her over on her belly. "I'm going to fuck you like I should have long ago, when you kept strutting your tight little ass around in front of me. I wanted you so much it drove me insane." As he spoke, he pushed her head down into the mattress, his other hand drawing her knees apart and arching her ass into the air. Brianna's words of anger and protest were muffled by her face being shoved deeper into the mattress.

"And now you want my cock," he growled, bending his lips to her ear and smiling at her furious expression. He was so strong that Brianna couldn't move beneath his grip which kept her head down and her ass in the air. She glared at him, even as she felt a hot tide of anticipation expand around her belly down to her pussy.

"Well I'm going make sure you get it, sweetheart," he continued tightly. "I'll fuck you with my big fat cock till you'll gush all over it and still ask for more. Fuck your tight little pussy so hard you won't be able to walk straight for a week."

"Ramond...," she half-moaned, half-warned. But he wasn't listening, coating his fingers with spit before rubbing it into her raised and exposed cunt. She was shuddering with blissful trepidation of how terrible it was going to feel having him fuck her from the back. She felt so vulnerable in this position, and yet so turned on she was ready to cum in a second. She knew she'd lost control of the situation by now, and felt it was time to just let go and enjoy the ride he was about to give her.

"That's it, say my name," he rumbled, fisting her long hair and tugging her head back till she cried out. "Say my name and tell me how much you love my cock, my big fat cock, ramming into your pussy." As he spoke, he entered her with a smooth plunge. The impact of that monster meat knifing into Brianna was enough to make her howl in pleasure-pain. The torment was fierce, powerful, and she didn't want it to stop. Didn't want him to stop bumping his hips against her pert ass and burying his punishing cock deep inside her again and again. The force of his thrusts sent her jumping forward on the bed, till he held her still by gripping her hips. Now he had all the more power, and could control how deep and ferocious he was going to fuck her.

"Say it, Brianna!" he rapped out suddenly, and she had to blink and focus before she could decipher what he meant.

"Ramond," she gasped. "Oh my gosh, Ramond. I love your big fat cock—I love it ramming into my pussy. Ram it into me!" Her voice grew louder with each word, and she felt her hips shoving back against him of their own accord. He had so much cock up her she was sure she could feel it in her breast bone. Dazed with the ache and sweetness of it, she quickly reached for her pussy and stroked herself, sobbing as the pain eased just enough to be bearable. The exquisiteness of the whole encounter was one she knew she wouldn't soon forget, if ever.

Ramond was bending over her back, humping and grunting and licking at her ear. They were savage and shameless in their lust, and now no one was in control, nothing but the pleasure mattered now. He was groaning, pumping and slamming against her and making her scream his name over and over. Brianna rubbed faster on her clit and felt the fullness inside her cunt begin to throb and tighten. She was lost, shook, broken. Sobs of ecstasy poured from her parted lips as she tried not to black out from the pleasure. All she could think of was how her pussy loved so much cock ripping into her and scraping the very depths of her vagina. It was a matter of seconds later that she arched herself backwards almost in half and then came in an eruption of screams.

Ramond anchored himself on her breasts, gripping them tight and arching himself against her as he too, climaxed. These last few thrusts went the deepest of all as he lost all control and tore his way in to rest balls-deep within her cunt, making her scream loudly. Thrust after thrust he fucked the last ounce of lust out of his cock which soon exploded into her vibrating walls. She was shuddering beneath him, a mere bundle of shivers and sighs as finally, they slumped unto the mattress.

"You were never going to show your mother that video, were you?" Ramond asked, stroking her hair as he looked down at her. It was at least a half hour after their ravenous fucking, and now she lay next to him, barely able to move. Her pussy felt deliciously frazzled, yet already anticipating its next encounter with that long, meaty dick lying across Ramond's lap. Sighing, Brianna reached for it to stroke him possessively.

"Oh, you bet I was," she told him, looking up at him with those flashing eyes he knew meant trouble. He sighed inwardly, but didn't reply.

"And I still can," she added with a wicked grin, rubbing her fist up and down his burgeoning staff. "But if you keep making my pussy happy and giving this hot monster cock only to me, then you—or Marcella, will have nothing to worry about...."

13 THE ACCIDENTAL HOOKUP

There was one thing Chelsea could say about Liam: he was persistent. If there was one guy in the office who never seemed to give up, it was him. He just couldn't believe she wasn't interested. He, like the several other guys she worked with in her new job as copywriter at the advertising firm, still thought she was up for grabs.

After all, she was the new chick. And not that she was vain, but she knew she looked hot – great shape, fantastic auburn hair that was all hers, and a brain to actually be good at what she did. She really liked working there; the opportunities as well as the pay were great, but she really was getting fed up being stalked by the many male coworkers who seemed to have only sex on their brains.

Okay, being single should have made her more interested in at least going out with one of them. But she wasn't. They were mostly good-looking and certainly had the other girls in the office drooling. So why wasn't she falling over for any one of them?

If only Liam would just slacken off and stick with being just a friend, she'd be happy. She liked him; he was one of the few guys at work she did like. He was witty, was handsome without being cocky, and was also great at his job. She found him useful in helping her ease into the new workplace. They hung out for lunch or some drinks after work, but that was all. She put her foot down on actual dates, romance, or even – especially not even – sex.

Chelsea knew it was the "thing" now: people fucked around and had a fling with two or three guys in the office with no strings attached. Everyone seemed into it right then but Chelsea wasn't going to take that route. She wasn't into fairy tales, but she at least expected a bit of "zing" before she'd be lifting her skirts for anyone. Alas, it looked like Liam hadn't got the memo.

He'd taken to pursuing her with a vengeance, buying her flowers and gifts, bringing her expensive takeaway when she was too busy to go out for a bite, and generally just choking her with adoration. Chelsea desperately needed an out.

That week, there was going to be an office party – the head honchos wanted to celebrate their latest mega-million acquisition. It was going to be Chelsea's first party as an employee there, and she was looking forward to it. Liam insisted on trying to take her, but she knew she'd be making a big mistake if she let him escort her to the party. That would be as good as telling everyone that they were dating or that they had something going on. It was stupid, but that was just the way things were construed in this fish tank of an office. So she couldn't do it.

So how the heck was she going to convince him she couldn't accompany him to the office "do"?

"I've told you, Liam, it's not happening," she said patiently as she walked down the corridor on her floor. He was right beside her, hands in his pockets and that relentless gleam in his eye.

"So if you aren't going with me, who are you going with?" he pressed. "Showing up alone would be like feeding yourself to the sharks. Trust me, I've been to most of these parties and you definitely don't want to be dateless."

"I'm not dateless," she said quickly, turning to him as an idea suddenly formed in her head. "I do have a date to the party. That's why I can't go with you. Sorry." She smiled apologetically and wondered why she hadn't thought of this before. But Liam wasn't buying it.

"You have a date? Since when?" he asked doubtfully. "Is it someone here at the office? Chelsea, you don't have to make this up, you know...."

Chelsea was really getting fed up – and desperate. And when just then her helpless gaze fell on the figure approaching, she suddenly had a brilliant idea.

"Of course I'm not making it up," she

declared, raising her voice and then beaming happily at the man who'd just turned the corner. "Hello, Matt!"

The man named Matt looked up in surprise when she hailed him cheerfully. His dark blue eyes showed mock amazement too that she seemed to know him by name. But of course she knew him; he was one of the hunkiest guys at the office and probably the only one who hadn't even tried to force his attention on her.

Chelsea glided over to him quickly and then fell into his arms in a tight embrace, gritting into his ear, "Do me a favor and play along."

And then she drew back with a deep sigh and a smile. "Well! I was wondering when you'd come by to see me. Ready to take me to the party tonight? Because I've been looking forward to it ever since you asked me."

"Wait, you're going with Matt?" Liam cut in with even more disbelief than ever and looking far from pleased.

"Oh, sure. He asked me last week," Chelsea said lightly, her eyes wide and innocent. And then she turned to Matt with a wide, warm smile, asking pointedly, "Isn't that right, Matt?"

She kept her fingers crossed behind her back, not sure he'd go with it. But to her surprise, he did. His tone was smooth as he replied easily, "That's right. Was actually surprised she even agreed." He smiled casually at the scowling Liam.

"But do you guys even know each other?" Liam said, his voice filled with suspicion. "I mean Chelsea has been here for three months and not once have I seen you two even sharing a greeting."

Chelsea had to think fast. But no...she wasn't even thinking. She definitely did not think it through when, without a word, she turned to Matt, wrapped a hand around his neck, and kissed him.

She felt him go rigid in shock, but she only deepened the kiss, slashing through his parted lips with plenty of tongue. For a second she was worried he was going to fling her off, but suddenly, he was crushing her to him, eating into her with a ferociousness that stole her breath. Her whole body seemed to click into overdrive as his masculine, fresh hot taste filled her senses. They dueled passionately with their lips for a full minute, sharing serious openmouthed action that would have been more fitting to a porn movie than in the middle of an office corridor.

Moments later, she was drawing away, but not without a couple of moist, hard tugs on his lips. She stared up at him with hooded eyes, disorientated to see the hard, hot lust blazing in his gaze.

Breaking the spell, she quickly turned to the gaping Liam. "Does that look like we don't know each other?" she asked, her voice somewhat breathless.

Liam seemed unable to reply, and he simply gave them a disgusted grunt before striding off in a huff.

Phew, she thought. She just may have gotten rid of him for good. But then she turned to Matt, who still stood there in the corridor, reflectively rubbing his handkerchief over his mouth. She cringed a little when she saw her fiery red lipstick stains on them.

"Look, uh, Matt, sorry about all that drama. It was Liam. He's been bugging me for months and I just had to think fast." She smiled tentatively, though her heart still pounded from experiencing what had been a surprisingly juicy kiss. "Thanks. A lot. For um... playing along that is." And thanks for the hottest kiss I've had in almost a year, she didn't add.

She nodded and made to walk away, only to be surprised by a hand enclosing her wrist and causing her to turn back in surprise. "Is that it?" he asked casually, one thick dark brow lifted sardonically.

Confused, Chelsea tugged her hand out of his grip, looking up at him quizzically. "Look, Matt, I'm sure we're both very busy, so...."

"Hey, lady, I'm the one who was minding my own business before I got grabbed on my way to a very important meeting – which I am now horrendously late for. And I'm the one who got jumped with a kiss – a very hot delicious kiss, I might add – but I hope that's not all I'm going to get for my trouble," he drawled, eyes raking over her.

Chelsea gasped in suppressed outrage, hands on her hips. "I can't believe this. Liam was right – you haven't even spoken a complete sentence to me since I got here, and now, just because you did me a small favor...."

"Small favor?" he echoed, eyebrows lifting even higher. "Lady, I just saved you from Liam's notoriously evil clutches. However, if you want me to go look for him and tell him it was all just a ruse...."

Chelsea was trying hard to control her temper. But as she looked up into his eyes, she saw he wasn't bluffing. She bit down an angry sigh. "What do you want?"

Chelsea could not believe how angry she was. It was bad enough that she'd got herself entangled into letting Matt take her to the party – now she had yet another ordeal to look forward to.

Well, served her right for thinking up that dumb stunt and kissing Matt like that – not to talk of pretending that they were an item. But she'd thought it would be so harmless that she could get away with it. After all, he'd shown zero interest in her as a woman since she'd arrived. He was in a whole different department and they never had to cross paths professionally. And on a personal level, he'd chosen to stand back while the other "wolves" had tried to make their play. She'd been curious about him though. He appeared to be single and was quite handsome if one liked those "silent hunk" types. Once or twice she'd found his indifference somewhat pricking. But then she had hated herself for being so perverse. So one guy didn't fall all over her, and she was complaining? Get over yourself, a voice in her head had told her.

And now this. One mindless kiss later, she was stuck with a date for the party. And then afterwards....

She shivered despite herself as she remembered Matt's conditions. Part of her wanted to tell him to go to hell. She didn't have to do anything. And she could go alone to the party anyway and damn what Liam or what he thought.

But somehow, she decided she just didn't need the aggravation. Matt could well go to Liam and tell the truth, and she'd look pretty dumb plus she could risk Liam continuing his pursuit with a vengeance. Anything, she vowed, would be better than that.

So that evening, she was dressed and ready when Matt arrived at her door. She opened to his knock, saw him standing there, and caught her breath.

It was hard not to stand and just stare at him looking hot like that. Dark hair stylishly swept, tall, hard-packed body encased in a sharply cut blazer with an open-necked shirt, which perfectly matched his eyes.... She'd always known he was good-looking, but tonight he was drop-dead gorgeous. He cleaned up nice – very nice. Looking up into his handsome face and at those full-bottomed lips of his, she was reminded of their steamy kiss in the corridor in front of the gaping Liam.

His eyes were ranging their way over her, and she felt his gaze almost like it was a laser beam being trained on her body. Chelsea squirmed in her little black dress – her very little black dress. It had cost the earth and had also been hanging in her wardrobe for months – one of those impulse buys that one made without ever dreaming there'd be the chance to wear it. It clung to her slim, curvy body jealously and left her long, shapely legs bare. They were smooth and sleek for the night, with her feet shod in very sexy black pumps.

She'd done her hair up, in a fashionable braid, and she had diamond studs in her hair. Her makeup was just simple, yet elegant. She thought she looked okay. But judging by the sudden blaze of admiration she saw in Matt's expressive blue eyes, she figured maybe "okay" was a too-modest word.

"Ready for the show?" he asked softly, and then she remembered everything – remembered why he was even here. Thanks to her dumb feat just hours ago, Matt was her date to the office party, where they were going to try to be convincing as a couple so that pesky Liam would stay off her back. And then, she was supposed to return his "favor" and help him out of an equally uncomfortable situation....

She nodded mutely, wrapping her shawl around her and going out with him to where his car was parked.

It was very hard to surprise a man like Matt. He felt he'd seen it all, done it all. But that afternoon, he'd been knocked for six by the woman named Chelsea.

He knew her, of course. Had known exactly when she'd started working for the firm. He'd watched as his randy colleagues had fallen over themselves to be the first to get her into bed. He'd chuckled to himself and stayed back, knowing she would never be "got." He'd wanted her as badly as the rest of them – which red-blooded man wouldn't? She didn't know it, but the way she looked, even in her most formal and severe suits, was like a red flag to any full-grown male. A perfect hourglass figure, big hair, and a cool, unattainable aura that had the opposite effect: instead of scaring men away, it magnetized them.

He'd always wanted her. Even when he ignored her and acted like she was just any other girl who worked in the same office. She only had to walk past and his cock stood at attention. She had a unique, sense-tripping exotic perfume that once he entered an office or a room, he would know she'd been there. It was faint, yet unmistakable.

Matt had stayed clear of the "madding" crowd, not out of sense of tactic in order to make her notice him but due to something more serious. He'd just survived a very messy breakup of his engagement. His fiancé of almost a year – who had been his girlfriend for two years prior – just still couldn't understand it was over. She'd been caught cheating, but she still didn't get that he was done. They were through.

It had been by chance that he found out she was fucking her boss – some big-shot celeb lawyer. Heather, his girlfriend, had been his PA for the last six months. He'd been happy for her getting such a high-profile job – until he'd realized that the job entailed servicing the boss' cock with her mouth and pussy whenever the guy needed it.

Matt had walked in on them going at it when he'd unexpectedly shown up at her office, about to take her to lunch. She hadn't been at her desk and something had made him curious enough to go up to the door of her boss, which was next to her desk. The sounds he'd heard coming from the inside had been hard to ignore. He'd shoved open the door that they'd forgotten to lock and had caught Heather with her head lost behind the man's desk.

Her boss was seated in his chair with Heather's unmistakable curly blonde head bobbing on his crotch. Matt had taken a wild guess and figured she'd been having her own lunch already – stuffing her face with dick, no less.

She'd looked up and seen him there, and her face had gone white. Needless to say, the wedding was off.

That was two months ago. And she was still begging and asking to be taken back, reasoning that she'd been made to do it by her controlling boss and that it was Matt whom she loved. Yeah, right. Like he wanted to believe any of that crap. She'd finally confessed that she'd been sleeping with her boss almost from the day she got the job and that she wouldn't even have gotten it if she hadn't agreed to let him have his way.

"Well, good for you, hon," he'd told her calmly. "Don't let it be said I stood in the way of your career progression."

But now, after weeks of more intensified

begging, calling off his phone, countless text messages, and even voice mail on his phone, he was fed up to the teeth.

Chelsea's surprise stunt in the corridor had given him an idea. It had also had him going hard as a pole when he realized that she was one hell of a kisser – and just as beddable as he'd imagined. Yep, she was hot enough to melt an avalanche, but that didn't mean she'd be such an easy lay. She'd proved very hard to get already despite her many admirers. So what made Matt think he had a chance?

That was what he was going to find out tonight....

Everyone seemed surprised to see her with Matt that evening at the party. Well, so was she! When she'd kissed him in the corridor, she hadn't exactly foreseen the consequences.

She hadn't imagined firstly that kissing him would feel so damned good, secondly that he would actually take her seriously about being her date for the party, and thirdly that she'd end up thinking about him in ways that she shouldn't. Had never even dreamed she would.

Now she was hanging on his arm and smiling, acting as if they were a couple. For the night anyway. As he took two glasses of wine from a passing waiter and handed one to her, she heard him murmur to her, "Looks like half of the guys in the room hate me now."

Despite herself, she smiled. It was probably

true, especially when it seemed to them that Matt had managed to "get" the most-sought-after chick in the office – and no one had ever even seen him trying.

"Well," she purred, taking a sip from her wine, "I also can't help noticing that half of the women in the room also seem to be giving me dirty looks. Seems you're quite a catch yourself, Matt. I'm sure you've made a few conquests with some of them."

He glanced her way with a wry smile. "On the contrary, no. I was engaged for the past year so trust me, messing about with female colleagues was never an option."

Hmmm, that made sense, Chelsca thought, some of her resentment suddenly fading. So that's why he'd never come after her; he was engaged. And he sounded like it was actually in past tense, too. She turned to him curiously. "You were engaged?"

He sighed heavily. "Long story. Not worth the telling. But that's the main reason I'm going to need your help. Good of you to agree to lend a hand, Chelsea."

She felt her lips curve testily. "Not like I had a choice, did I? Especially when you threatened me with that turd, Liam."

"Who's coming our way right now," Matt announced, taking her drink and placing it on a nearby table next to his. Next, he grabbed her wrist. "Let's dance."

"Wha...," she began but did see Liam over Matt's shoulder, bearing down on them. Suddenly she couldn't help but feel glad Matt was whisking her off to the dance floor.

As she allowed him to pull her into his

arms for the slow number, she tried not to focus on how big and solid he was. She could barely reach his chin, and she was tall herself. She placed her hand on his broad shoulder for support and marveled at the play of muscles she could feel rippling beneath her fingers. His arm wrapped around her narrow waist, bringing her closer than ever. His musky cologne teased her nostrils and seemed to ignite a sudden awareness deep inside her. She had to shake off the immediate thought of what it might feel like to be fucked by him. Now where had that come from?

But she couldn't help wondering, now could she? What with being in such a close, intimate proximity to him – and not to talk of that incredibly spicy kiss they'd shared. No doubt there was a lot of potential there. Was I willing to pursue it? she mused.

Well, for one thing, it was against her sworn principle of never getting involved with anyone at work. Sexually or emotionally. Those guidelines had helped her through her last job, which she had left with her dignity intact. But then...Matt seemed like a sensible, discreet kind of guy. The kind you could have a fling with and just know he'd see to it that your wishes were respected. If you wanted it to end, it was your call, and he'd stand by it.

I can't believe I'm actually even considering going to bed with this guy, she fumed suddenly at herself. Was she that much of a horny slut? Fine, she'd been celibate for far too long, but that had been her choice. And besides, she'd been too occupied with settling into her new job to take a lover or anything.

Well, maybe it's not out of place to finally get some "me" time, she told herself with a secret, wicked smile....

"Just why don't you like him anyway?" Matt asked, breaking into her amorous thoughts, swinging her round on the crowded dance floor. "Liam, I mean. He's not that bad for a guy. A bit overzealous, maybe, but then no one can blame him once they've set eyes on you."

"Hmm," she murmured at his teasing words, though she looked up at him to reply seriously, "It's a simple matter of chemistry, Matt. And I don't feel any for him."

"OK. Makes sense," he drawled. "So...do you feel any for me?" At her outraged breath, he continued mildly, "I'm only asking because I could have sworn I felt some sparks flying when we kissed. Definitely felt something, though. And I've been told I'm not bad with the smooches."

"Oh really?" she said, tone cool as she glanced up at him. "I never would have figured you to be the cocky type, Matt."

He shrugged. "Not cocky, just stating facts. You can doubt me, but then that would be like a challenge. And I won't balk at the chance to prove myself. Just say the word, and it's on."

"Seriously, Matt," she huffed, shaking her head in annoyance as she looked away. No way was she going to even consider it. Another kiss with Matt? It was far too risky, she decided.

"Never would have figured you to be a scaredy cat," he returned in a mocking tone, throwing her words back at her. Her green eyes flashed up at him angrily.

"Trust me, Matt, you're not as irresistible as you might think you are," she said haughtily. "And I can bet that even if I do kiss you again, you'll be the one at my mercy. I'll make you want me so bad you'd be practically begging for it."

"Now that's a challenge no self-respecting man can resist," he murmured against her ear, his lips so close his breath tickled the tiny hairs there. "Name the time and place, baby."

"Oh, forget it," she snapped, shocked at the way her heart pounded almost painfully in her chest. What the heck had come over her? First she'd jumped him with a kiss, and now she was "daring" him sexually. It was so unlike her. She was sensible, a full-grown woman who knew how to control her own darkest emotions. She would not allow Matt to make her sink to such a debased level.

"Chicken," he teased, as he swung her one more time on the floor. "Come on! I think he's gone off in a huff again. Can't seem to find him anywhere." He was talking about Liam, and Chelsea looked around and saw to her relief that he was nowhere to be seen.

Thankful for that reprieve, she was finally able to relax and enjoy the party. There were plenty of wine and food, and the music really pumped up the crowd and everyone was finding it easy to let go and have fun. Even the top execs seemed to have let their hair down and were having fun with the rest of the staff. Chelsea was really glad she'd decided to attend and even Matt proved to be a charming and stimulating companion.

Soon it was time to leave, and as she went to grab her coat and join Matt outside, she was waylaid by Liam, who made her jump when he finally appeared. "And where are you guys sneaking off to?" he asked, tight-lipped.

Chelsea wrapped her coat tightly about her in a self-protective gesture. Okay, seriously, Liam was really starting to creep her out. "Look, we aren't 'sneaking' anywhere. Matt and I are going to some nightclub downtown to hang out with a few of his friends."

"So now what, you guys are really serious? You're an item?" Liam growled accusingly. "I can't believe you could treat me like this, Chelsea. You know how I feel about you...."

"Oh, for goodness's sake, Liam," Chelsea began to protest impatiently, when just then, Matt appeared. She gratefully turned to him and found his face thunderous as he regarded the equally irritated Liam.

"Look, buddy, the girl's not interested. Maybe you should move on, okay? It's not like it's the end of the world," he said, his eyes dark and almost threatening. He looked ready to punch Liam in the face if the other guy persisted or even argued.

Liam didn't seem ready to risk a physical altercation. "You know what? Forget it. I don't even know why I bother."

"Yeah, neither do I," Chelsea threw at his retreating back and was giggling as she strode out with the grinning Matt. "Gosh, he looked pretty scared, like you were going to floor him or something."

"Well, he certainly needs knocking down a peg or two, that's for sure," Matt teased, opening the car door for her. "So...shall we do this?" he asked with a quirked brow.

Chelsea shrugged. "You've held up your end of the bargain. I guess it's only fair I'll do the same." And then with a slight smile, she got into the car.

"Are you certain she'll be here tonight?" Chelsea asked doubtfully, as she glanced around the swanky, packed nightclub. Beside her, Matt was ordering them drinks at the bar. He handed her a long, chilled glass and then let his eyes scan the music-filled surroundings.

"I got it on good information that she will be," he said assuredly. "We still basically have the same circle of friends, and they all still hang out here – even her. I've bumped into her several times before after we broke up. This is the first time she'll get to see me with another woman."

"So, you want to get rid of her for good, right?"

His eyes turned and held hers soberly. "Just like you, I hate it when people just can't let go. Besides, Heather is insanely jealous. If she thinks I'm now dating such a hot and sexy chick like you, she'll go ballistic. It's a drastic and maybe far-fetched idea, but something tells me this is one way to make her finally get the message."

"Just what happened between the two of you anyway?" she asked curiously, not wanting to show how her heart had tripped to hear him describe her as "hot and sexy."

When he didn't answer, she added, "Look, if I'm going to be instrumental to the breakup being final, at least tell me what it's about. Maybe you two can end up working things out."

"Not a chance in hell," he growled, then told her with an angry sigh, "I found out she was sleeping with her boss. I actually caught her red-handed doing a 'Monica Lewinsky' on him at the office. It wasn't an image I relish having whenever I think of my ex."

Chelsea had a hand over her mouth. "Ugh. Sorry," she said, grimacing slightly. "I can't believe you found her giving her boss a blowjob. That's really messed up."

"Yeah, it is. I think I've found out that romance and fidelity aren't all they're trumped up to be. I stayed faithful with her for the whole year we were engaged and even when we were just dating."

"I can understand," she murmured. And then her eyes suddenly widened as they fixed on something beyond Matt's shoulder. "Uh, Matt, don't look back now, but there's a pretty blonde striding very quickly over here."

"Should be her," he muttered, downing his drink casually. "Let's hope this ends quickly and without getting too ugly."

Chelsea couldn't help being curious as she watched Heather break off from her group of friends and make her way to Matt's side. She was cover-model material, that was for sure, and had just the glossy good looks that would make her fit into her role as a PA to some hotshot lawyer. She had sleek blond hair parted in the middle and falling to her narrow, tanned shoulders. Her dress was a strapless electric-blue number which set off her brown eyes perfectly. She gasped in pleasure when she faced Matt.

"I just knew it was you. I'm always looking out, hoping you'll show up. It's great to see you tonight," she said gaily, trying to embrace him, but he stiffed her and instead put his arm around the silent Chelsea.

"Heather, this is Chelsea," he said, his tone light. "We're dating."

Heather's pretty smile faltered at those words, and she swept her eyes from Chelsea to Matt, who had a careless smile on his face.

"Dating? But..."

"We met at work," he went on in the same easygoing tone. "And I can barely stand to keep my hands off her." As he spoke, he wrapped a possessive arm around Chelsea's shoulders and bent his head to plant a kiss on her exposed neck. Chelsea couldn't help but shiver slightly at the sensuous warmth of his lips on her skin. And then of course there was the venomous look on Heather's face as she took in the gesture.

"You can't be serious about her," Heather spluttered, sending Chelsea a furious glare. "I mean, I thought...Matt, I was so sure we could work it –"

"Heather, you were fucking your boss. What

could we possibly have to work out?" Matt said bluntly, eyes devoid of emotion.

She seemed to grow really red, and she drew in a ragged breath. "Look, I know it was unforgivable of me. But I told you, Matt, I've changed. I quit that job and I...."

Matt was shaking his head. "For Pete's sake, Heather, move on. I have," he said impatiently. "Come on, Chelsea. Let's get out of here."

"Matt, wait!"

He paused, turning slightly and looking down at the elegant hand Heather had gripped on his forearm. Her voice was low as she said, "I...I could come over tonight. We can talk things out. I'll do whatever it takes to make you see how much I want this. And I can make you want it, too... just like you used to." Her green eyes held his meaningfully.

Chelsea couldn't help overhearing and thinking how really desperate this chick was. She wasn't surprised when Matt let out a disgusted grunt and shook off Heather's hand.

"You know, you surprise me every time. Just...give up, okay? And besides, Chelsea – my girlfriend," he added pointedly, "will be with me at my place tonight. So you can scuttle your little seduction plan. Goodbye, Heather."

After those finalistic words, he placed his hand behind Chelsea and led her out of the crowded club without a backward glance.

Chelsea couldn't help but glance at Matt's rigid profile as he drove them through the deserted streets. "Do you think it'll work?" she asked softly, breaking the silence. "I mean, that she's got the message?"

Matt grunted, looking away for a moment. "Trust me. Heather has a serious problem handling competition. She's never really seen me with anyone so she always figured she still had a chance. But after tonight she may have a rethink and just get on with her life."

"How about you? Have you got on?" she asked, sounding more than a little curious. "You say it's been a few months since it's happened and you obviously haven't started seeing anyone. Maybe... you need a bit of closure too."

"Or maybe I'm still too battle-scarred to jump in once more," he growled, turning into the road leading to her house. "It's too hard to trust again and certainly too hard to fall in love. Especially not after Heather's cock-up – excuse the pun," he added drily as he stopped in front of her apartment building.

Chelsea undid her seat belt and then turned to face him in the dim confines of the car. "Maybe you're simply overthinking stuff," she said softly. "At least take some baby steps...stick one toe at a time into the pool...and then perhaps you'll find your way back on the saddle." With every word, she was drawing nearer, closing the gap between them. Soon, she had her face mere inches from his, and he didn't pull away. With just her lips, she touched him, fitting her mouth over his in a soft, tasting kiss.

Moments later, she broke it off, eyelashes fluttering open to meet his darkened gaze. "What are you doing?" he asked in a voice husky with raw need. "If this is your idea of trying to baby-step me, then...dammit, it's working."

With a growl, he swiftly unhooked his seat belt and crushed her to him, molding his firm lips to hers, claiming her roughly till her mouth turned all the more pliant and soft beneath his.

Taking hold of her face, he finally drew them apart with reluctance, his eyes piercing into hers. "Since that first time we kissed in that corridor, my life has been flipped upside down. I've never wanted anyone this bad in a long time, Chelsea. So I guess you were right about the power of your kiss. Right now, I'm totally at your mercy." He was grinning wolfishly. "And I'm not too proud to beg if I have to."

Her smile was equally wicked, as she gathered her shawl about her. "Mmm...maybe you wouldn't have to beg after all, mister. Let's call this a tie, shall we? Because I want you like crazy, too. Right now. No holds barred." She grabbed her purse, her eyes twinkling as she got down from the car. Bending to look at him through the passenger window, she added softly, "Don't keep me waiting."

Matt was guessing he'd created some kind of world record with how quickly he got the car safely parked before virtually sprinting up the walkway to her front door, which was unlocked. Shutting it behind him securely, he looked around her nicely furnished apartment, his heart thudding with excitement.

"In here," her voice sang from somewhere on his right, and he homed in, turning to walk down a corridor that led to an open doorway, obviously her bedroom.

He pushed the door all the way open and stood there with his mouth hanging slightly open to find her waiting totally naked in her bed. She had a bowl of strawberries by the bed, and she sensuously picked one and bit into it slowly, eyes closing briefly in pleasure as she chewed.

Matt could feel his cock literally clawing for release behind his trouser front at the sight of her delectably nude body. She was spread over the sheets like some golden platter of breasts, thighs, and pussy. She was propped up on her elbows, one knee bent in the air and the other leg slightly at an angle, giving him a perfect view of her pussy with the tiny landing strip of hair trailing to her swollen, inviting clit. He stared tearing off his clothes.

She smiled encouragingly, looking pleased at his enthusiasm. This time Matt was definite that he'd broken some kind of record for undressing, as he got naked in five seconds, tops. Her eyes were ranging over him in appreciation, and once her gaze landed on his cock, he heard her draw in a sharp breath, her eyes lingering as she bit on her lip and grimaced with lust.

"Mmm, and it's not even my birthday," she murmured softly as if to herself. Her obvious desire and physical admiration for him was enough to make him even harder, and he felt his shaft thicken and throb beneath her fixed gaze. Damn, she was sexy.

"Chelsea," he heard himself grit out with the force of his ache, as he made his way to join her on the sheets. His hand reached out slowly to touch her, his fingertips barely brushing the gentle jut of her shoulder blades, then down to her thrust-out nipples, which were very light pink and very large and pebbly. He swallowed harshly with the need to grab them both in his mouth, to cup her lovely, firm tits in his hands, and fondle them passionately while he suckled her.

He looked up into her deeply inviting eyes, at the way her lips were parted softly, enticingly. He could see the white edge of her teeth sinking into her full bottom lip, and he wanted to grab those in his and kiss her senselessly. He definitely wanted a lot of things: he wanted all of her and he hoped he had the whole night to do it.

"It's been...months," he told her huskily, as if in warning. "I've literally kept myself celibate for so long...."

"So have I," she told him, placing a hand against his chest, which started to pound beneath her soft palm. She trailed that palm down to his sucked-in torso, which rippled beneath her seeking touch. He let out a deep groan.

"It's been a while for me, too," she told him clearly, looking up into his eyes at the exact moment her hand grasped his rearing cock. "And you can bet that I'm hungry...."

They were both hungry and ferocious in their passion for each other. They tumbled over and over on the sheets, hands squeezing, fondling, stroking. Their lips merged again and again in hot, frenzied kisses that were more like tongue fests. He tugged on her lips, she pulled on his, and they swapped tongues in moist, heated licks.

Sliding his large hands down to her breasts, he cupped them and then squeezed with just the right roughness to make her gasp in surprise and deep, hard lust. Breaking their slippery kiss, he bent to nip his teeth into her neck, and Chelsea threw her head back, losing herself in passion's swirling, blinding mist.

He massaged her right breast strongly and then the left, watching and feeling them swell in his waiting palms. Her nipples were rock-hard now, and he took one in his fingers and pinched; Chelsea moaned as a red-hot bolt of lightning shot straight between her thighs. Her pussy quivered and dripped as he rolled her aching nipples in his fingers, punishing both at the same time now.

He was staring into her face, and she met his smoldering gaze with her eyes half-lidded, lost. And then he told her, softly but clearly, how good he was going to fuck her. How he was about to lay his tongue to every inch of her body till she was a hot, wet mess of pussy just waiting to be pounded. He was going to fondle, suck, and tease her breasts till she screamed for mercy, and then he was going to lick on her pussy, beat on her clit, and nibble on her cunt lips till all she could think of was how the torture would end with his cock buried deep within her.

"Oh my God," Chelsea gasped, fingers digging into the sheets as his words washed over her like a wave of pleasure. Already, her body was responding to his wicked promises; her breasts felt heavier, weighed down with lust, while her pussy equally pulsed and shed gallons of moisture that seemed ready to soak the bed beneath her.

He kept each and every one of those promises: in the hours that followed, Chelsea felt herself punished with so much pleasure she could have easily blacked out at least ten times. She'd never had a more skillful, more tender lover. Matt took time, effort, and pleasure in tormenting her; he rubbed on her breasts with those big, strong hands of his and made them sensitive to his every touch. He baited her nipples with his twisting fingers, and then he tortured them some more by using his mouth, pulling strongly on them till she shuddered with ecstasy. He rolled them over and over using his tongue expertly. Chelsea sunk her fingers in his hair and tugged on the silky locks, unable to keep herself from moaning out his name.

He seemed reluctant to release her breasts, but then when he dipped one hand to the juncture of her thighs and found her pussy virtually flowing, he allowed himself get sidetracked. Shifting lower, he pushed her knees further apart and gazed down at her pretty, pink-lipped pussy, all drenched and soppy. He inhaled deeply and felt his senses reel with the hot sweetness of her musk. He bent to lap at her sodden lips, and she jerked into his face, his name spilling from her lips in a gasp.

Matt loved that she kept calling out his name like that; it made him feel he was imprinting himself on her subconscious. That the next time any man ever touched her, or ate her pussy, she'd think of him, think of how he'd owned it, owned the scene of wild sex they were playing out. She was writhing helplessly beneath him and he held her in place with his hands. And then with just his lips and tongue, he feasted on her pussy, paintbrushing her clit and lathering her slit with hungry force. She half surged from the bed suddenly; she came, surprising even him. He hadn't seen it coming at all – but that deterred him none. He went on lapping, locking her down and making sure he got all that juice she gushed out. Damn, it tasted good and made his dick pump almost painfully with blood. He was ready to shaft that pussy so bad....

But no, he still chose to hold back. She was limp now, lying there like a battered rag doll as her climax ebbed and flowed out of her. He lifted himself up to lay by her side and saw that her eyes were dreamy, lost. Smiling, she reached out to grasp his cock, but he took hold of her wrist, stopping her. He wanted it to be all about her for now; he wanted to show her his mastery, his potency. And he couldn't do that if she touched him or pleasured him. What with the way he was dizzy with lust for her, he may not last a second that way. No, he was going to draw out her pleasure, then his.

"Matt," she said in confusion, her gaze quizzical as it held his. But he only shook his head, his hands gripping both her wrists and lashing them above her head.

"There's more," was all he said, and he saw her eyes widen and gleam in surprise and expectation. He rolled on top of her, covering her with his hard, chiseled weight. She gasped with delight at the sensation of his solidness half-crushing her, enveloping her in his dark male essence. She was mesmerized, dazed by his feel and smell. He snaked over her, sliding his length against her soft frame till every inch of her could tell the story of every inch of him. His broad, hairless chest, his hard nipples, his six-pack torso, his marvelously rigid cock. Their legs entwined, locked in a dance that was yet to begin – and yet which had never even stopped. It felt like they'd been dancing forever.

Chelsea had never felt so aware of a man's body and had never known such proximate pleasure in feeling a man's skin and flesh against hers. It thrilled her and built her desire up to even more frightful proportions than before. She wanted him – needed him to fuck her and claim her with his cock till everything in her universe tilted and swayed.

He released her wrists, and she sighed in relief, thinking that the time had come. But no, it hadn't. Gently, he turned her on her belly and made her lay still as he started to run his lips down the length of her smooth back. She shivered, her breasts aching as they were crushed beneath her. She shuddered all over at the feathery touch of his tongue dipping into the line of her back. She could feel his hands caressing her bottom, squeezing the firm cheeks and them parting them, exposing her. Her pussy started to run like a tap again, drenching her thighs.

She stiffened with surprised delight when she felt his tongue on her now open ass crack. He rimmed her, keeping her ass separated as he bent again and again to eat her secret place. She was moaning into the pillow where her face was buried, and she was ready to dissolve into a pool of pleasure at the way he lashed her butt hole. Every few moments, he dipped lower to her fluttery pussy lips, but then he was back to anal-fucking her with his tongue, digging into her tight sphincter as far as it would go. Chelsea felt she could pass out any second.

"Matt...please," she begged, unable to stand the pressure. She'd go mental if he didn't fuck her soon; she needed something hot and hard and thick to fill up that void he'd created deep in her core. Her body shivered convulsively as if she were on a narcotic dependency. And that narcotic was him – his touch, his tongue, his dick (which he still kept away from her). He didn't even let her touch or feel it; she just wanted to reassure herself that it could be hers when she wanted it. But no, he wasn't giving her even that little mercy.

At last, he lifted his head but replaced his tongue with his fingers, which probed her wet rear orifice. He began to finger-fuck her, first gently and then more roughly as her muscles relaxed around his thick, long finger. Chelsea was groaning deeply, bucking back into his finger and wishing it was his cock buried so deep within her. As if he read her mind, he leaned forward, whispered in her ear. He asked her if she'd let him fuck her pussy, then her ass! Then, he asked her if she could take his girth in that tight back hole of hers....

"Yes," she sobbed, her arm stretching behind her to try once more to grasp him, touch him. But he kept himself just far enough out of her reach to make tears of longing seep into her eyes. "Oh Matt yes, anything."

He smiled, stroking back her hair with tender fingers. Her face was flushed, made all the more lovely by her obvious desire, her wanton lusts.

"Okay," he said softly at last. "I guess maybe I will do as you've asked...maybe I will fuck your pussy and then your ass. You've certainly been a good girl and you certainly deserve some cock now."

Chelsea lifted hopeful eyes and found he was now kneeling close to her head, his shaft held out just close to her lips. Sighing with pleasure, she readily wrapped her fingers round the thick, hot pole and stuck out her tongue. Her first taste of his cock almost sent her into orgasmic shivers; it was all she could do to hold back the surge of heat that tore through her core. She held on tightly to the solid base as she rolled the tip of her tongue over his tapering cap. Hungrily, she sucked on the slit and swallowed the delicious precum, savoring the taste as well as the sounds of his deep, encouraging moans.

"Yes...oh yes," he growled, fingers cupping her hair and wrapping it up away from her lovely face as he watched her wrap her sweet lips around his cock. She was thorough in her task, edging further and further up his length as she stuffed his meat more deeply down her throat. His hips jerked and then thrust involuntarily as the warm wetness of her mouth sucked him like a suction pump.

He could feel her tongue bathing him, even as her lips bobbed up and down his shaft, and she showed him just how much she had waited and longed for this moment, for the chance to tease and torment him as he had done her.

"I can't – take it," he gritted out suddenly, pulling her head back with a gentle tug on the thick strands of her hair he held in his hands. He groaned as his cock popped from her lips, the ache in his loins almost reaching the point of no return. She stared up at him with gleaming eyes, and he smiled.

"Looks like I'm not so tough now, am I?" he said with a self-teasing, cheeky grin. "One more minute of that and I'd have exploded." He bent to kiss her lips hungrily, easily pulling her down beneath him. She knew what he wanted because she wanted it as well. Their lips were locked even as their bodies positioned to merge and forge as one. She parted her thighs willingly as he settled between them, his hands gripping either one of her knees and pushing them back, way back so that he could plow into her with increased depth and ease.

"Whoa," Matt breathed as he jammed into

and felt her quivering pussy enclose him like a velvet trap. Her gasp of shocked pleasure echoed in his ears, as she dug her fingers on both sides of his ass, cupping, guiding. She wouldn't have let him take things slow even if he'd wanted to. She rocked herself up against him, even as her hands on his ass pushed him closer and deeper. He let out a beastly growl and snapped, working up a machine-like rhythm that had her sighing continuously in delight.

How long he shafted into her he couldn't tell; he just kept going, urged on by her pants of pleasure and her writhing, giving body. He was lost, drowned in her. The power of her pussy overtook him and for the moment his whole essence was centered on being claimed by his passion for her. Now he was the one being owned; now even as he rammed into her again and again, he felt like he was the one being pierced, ripped in half by the bliss she made his cock feel.

And yet, drawing upon almost superhuman strength, he pulled from her once again and heard her cry out loud in protest. He merely chuckled, kissed her on the lips, and whispered endearments in her ear. All the while, he was working his finger into her ass, and then another. She sighed, understood, and wrapped her arms around him. When he stuck two fingers into the tight, squeezing muscle, she gasped, but she told him she wanted more... much more.

He lubed her up with plentiful saliva and stroked her patiently and expertly till she was positively turned to mush. Once again, he placed himself between her open legs, which he pushed back one more time, till her feet were almost parallel with her face. And then, with infinite care and slowness, he probed at her rear hole with his cap. The tip nudged in, inch by inch, and she spread around him, breathing hard and fast. With every bit more of him she took inside her, she felt closer to imploding. She felt the unmistakable sensation of being filled, of her body being invaded by something fabulously built to bring both pleasure and a sweet pain. She welcomed it all, moaning in delight because she'd never felt anything so good.

He fucked her ass more leisurely than her pussy, sliding in slowly and then out again. He had only half of his cock in but he knew that in time, before the night would end, he'd be able to slam balls deep into her tight, hot hole and then explode his cum into her rear walls....

Chelsea literally couldn't move. She was sure she'd passed out because she couldn't remember what had happened after she'd climaxed. After she'd felt the earth shift on its axis as Matt had plunged so deep into her, she'd felt the sensation vibrate through her rib cage. Now that was what was called being fucked inside out. She shuddered for a full minute, triggering his own release as he groaned, gripped her hips, and thumped her butt hole full of his cum.

Her body couldn't move, but at least her eyes could. She opened them, and she could see Matt lying right beside her, his face mere inches from hers.

He looked almost relieved she was awake, and he grinned wickedly. "You got me worried for a moment there. I guess maybe I got too carried away, huh? I feel like I've maimed you or something." Behind the humor though, there was a slight frown of worry. "You okay, baby?"

She blinked and discovered that she could move. She shifted up on her elbows so she could gaze down at his gorgeous face and kiss his Roman-like nose. "I'm not going to be okay for a long time, honey," she told him dreamily, as she felt her body ache deliciously in memory of the last few hours. "And I think I like it. I've been too 'okay' for my own good, sticking to routine, finding solace in normality.... I'm done with that."

"And I'm done with being scared," he replied, cupping the back of her head tenderly. "I could have sworn I could never be with another woman the way I was with Heather. But now that I've baby-stepped my way out into the world again...." He humorously reminded her of her earlier words, and she rolled her eyes.

"At least we get to have mind-blowing sex with each other whenever we like, huh?" she teased, slipping her hand between them and finding his cock. Mmm, it was reassuringly thickening even beneath her fingers.

"Done," he said gruffly, taking her by the waist and pulling her atop him as their lips merged once more in a kiss.